A SIMPLE CONFESSION

Tony grinned a quick grin, lightening the moment. "You won my mother almost instantly. She likes you, you know. She told me I'm to treat you properly or she'd have words to say to me!"

Libby blushed. "But, Tony, what did I do? I don't recall anything special at all."

He smiled and, acting without thinking, touched her cheek with one gentle finger. "Libby, you don't *have* to do anything special. You simply *are* special."

Libby felt her heart quicken. She stared at her husband. "Do you truly believe that?"

"Of course."

Tony was more than a trifle astounded to discover that he *did*. . . .

Books by Jeanne Savery

THE WIDOW AND THE RAKE

A REFORMED RAKE

A CHRISTMAS TREASURE

A LADY'S DECEPTION

CUPID'S CHALLENGE

LADY STEPHANIE

A TIMELESS LOVE

A LADY'S LESSON

LORD GALVESTON AND THE GHOST

A LADY'S PROPOSAL

THE WIDOWED MISS MORDAUNT

A LOVE FOR LYDIA

TAMING LORD RENWICK

LADY SERENA'S SURRENDER

THE CHRISTMAS GIFT

THE PERFECT HUSBAND

Published by Zebra Books

THE PERFECT HUSBAND

Jeanne Savery

ZEBRA BOOKS
KENSINGTON PUBLISHING CORP.
http://www.zebrabooks.com

One

Lady Lillian Temple very carefully closed the door to her and Elizabeth's room. She breathed a sigh of relief that Beth had not heard her, had not awakened. Beth would not approve. Not that Lady Lillian approved of what she meant to do. It was merely that she could think of no other solution to her desperate problem.

A half-sad, half-angry word, which should not have crossed Lady Lillian's lips, was a breath of air into the dark hall. *My father,* she thought bitterly, *is a fool. The worst sort of fool.* But unfilial thoughts of her father faded. Her situation *was* desperate, her plan despicable, but, for Willie's sake, she would do it. Determination filled her. Her mouth firmed, her chin rose and . . . !

A door opened somewhere down the hall. The sibilant sounds of a whispering male voice assaulted Lady Lillian's ears. Somewhere between where she stood and her goal, a man had entered the hall.

Half in panic, half in relief, Lady Lillian slipped back into her room.

"Libby?" asked a sleepy voice from the bed.

"Shh. Go back to sleep."

The friend with whom Lady Lillian shared the room, Miss Elizabeth Browne, rose up on one elbow. "Can you not sleep, Libby?"

Lady Lillian sighed. "I wish you had not roused, Beth."

"But I did. Is something wrong?" Elizabeth yawned as she swung around, and, in another moment, Lady Lillian heard the rustle of her friend's shift as Elizabeth moved toward the faint red glow of the well-banked fire. Beth stuck a spill into the embers and lit the candle sitting on the mantel. The flickering light did odd things to her face as it was carried to the lamp on the table by the bed. She lit it as well, and now her complexion glowed in the soft light.

Lady Lillian's lips compressed. She did not wish to confide in Beth. Her situation was far too horrible, and the solution at which she had arrived was not one she wished to share. "I wish you'd go back to sleep, Beth."

"Something is bothering you," objected her friend. "I've known that ever since you read that letter from your father. Libby, you know you can tell me anything."

"Anything?" Lady Lillian grimaced. "I doubt you will want to hear this!"

"Libby!"

Lady Lillian sighed, pushed her shoulders away from the door against which she had been leaning, and strolled toward the bed. She stared across it to where Elizabeth stood.

"Your father. Was it very bad news?" asked Elizabeth gently.

"Yes."

Elizabeth hesitated. "Is he ill?"

"Ill?" Lady Lillian's laugh was both sharp and unhappy. "That might be a blessing! Oh, no," she continued hurriedly, "I do not mean that! Truly I do not." She sighed, sat down on the side of the bed and, her shoulders drooping, admitted, "He has grown desperate. The old trouble, Beth."

"His, hmm, investments?"

"His speculations! Do not fear to call them as they are! The last failed miserably as I predicted it would."

"Libby," asked her friend, a frown forming to mar her smooth brow, "how do you know so much about such things?"

Lady Lillian straightened, her expression lightening. "It is fascinating, Beth, the study of finance. I began by reading the journals Father would leave lying all around the house. He never picks anything up, you know. Then—" She felt heat rise up her neck and feared she blushed rosily. "—I began looking at his papers. He leaves them all over, too. The leaflets he'd bring home from the coffee houses he patronizes, for instance. And drafts of the letters he would write asking for more information that he'd attach to the responses he received. It is exceedingly interesting."

Elizabeth's expression revealed her thoughts on that.

Lady Lillian laughed. "You do not agree, of course." She sobered. "Please do not tell me I should not pry into his papers, Beth, because I know very well I should not. It was only when he began dropping hints, so that I was forced into the suspicion he was in financial difficulties, that I brought myself to pry. Beth, he has lost very nearly the whole of Willie's inheritance! Unfortunately the estate is not under entail. He has heavily mortgaged it and would sell it if he could get enough to pay them off and have money with which he could continue his speculations. Fortunately no one would be fool enough to pay him what he wants. Beth, I must do *something* before it is too late. It is so unfair that Willie should suffer because our father is an idiot!"

"I have heard all that before, have I not? What has happened to put you in a dither? In the past, you trotted along quite happily knowing things were not going well. Or so I thought. Surely nothing has changed so very much."

"Has it not?" Lady Lillian slumped again. "He has taken the money set aside for my dowry, my mother's little inheritance. He means to use it in his latest insane attempt to recoup. Beth, those funds are the very last on which he can get his hands. And that is what his letter was about."

Elizabeth was silent for a moment. "Can he do that?"

"It must be possible, must it not? Since he has done it? Further, he says I am to discourage any man's attentions—any man who might propose marriage, that is—until he has the funds to replace my dowry, you see?"

"But that is iniquitous!"

"More so than that he has lost Willie's patrimony?"

"That is not a good thing, of course, but a man may make his way in the world. You cannot."

Lady Lillian sighed. "Yes, I suppose that was in my mind as well."

Again Beth was silent for a long moment. "In your mind?" she asked.

"You will not stop until you know the whole."

"Of course I will not. Libby, I know you of old, and I cannot leave you in a muddle without doing what I can to help."

"Except, in this case, you are more likely to hinder." Lady Lillian continued before Elizabeth could respond to this muttered comment, "Beth, I mean to wed. Instantly. I will do what I must to bring that about."

"But your father . . . your dowry. . . ." Elizabeth blinked. "Has someone been wooing you and I not know it?"

Libby laughed sourly. "You know they have not. The poor gentleman will be surprised to discover he is affianced!"

Understanding widened Elizabeth's eyes. She gasped. "You would compromise yourself?"

Lady Lillian chuckled. There was a touch of hysteria in the sound. "Myself? Do you not mean the poor fool

I've decided I'll have to husband? The perfect husband," she finished and was uncertain, herself, whether she jested or was serious.

"You cannot do it."

"I can. I will."

"Libby, please. You must not!"

"And I do not, then the instant it is known my father is a pauper, I will be forced to disappear. I will be buried in the musty dusty Harrowgate house of Great-aunt Thrimble where I will spend my days brushing her spaniels and reading aloud nothing but improving works and running errands and feeling the sting of her cane against the backs of my legs when I do not move quickly enough to please her."

"No," said Elizabeth, revolted by the thought of such a future. "It will never happen. You will live with me. And you *will* marry." Elizabeth bit her lip. "Perhaps not the sort of man you *should* wed, but a man who will love you and care for you and keep you in all the pretties you desire."

"No." Lady Lillian spoke softly. "Beth, I could not." She looked into the far corner of the room. "I am very sorry for your brother, Beth," she said quietly. "Sorry that he was so foolish as to fall in love with me, but I would be a terrible wife for him. You know I would."

Elizabeth sighed. "Well, you will live with me. Always. I will never turn you away."

Lady Lillian cast her friend a fond look. "I know you would not. And I love you for your generosity and your loyalty. But it will not do."

"Neither will your plan."

"Will it not? Very likely not," said Libby, speaking in a weary tone. Then she forced a quickly flashing grin. "Certainly it will not if I continue to lose my nerve before I ever move two steps from our door." She yawned. "Let us go to sleep, Beth. It will not do if we look hagged tomorrow. A peaked complexion is no way to forward our chances in the marriage stakes!"

Anthony, Lord Wendover, Tony to his friends, strolled after the other men gracing Lady Weatherbee's house party. The men had returned from a ride, breakfasted, and were headed for Lord Weatherbee's private study.

Again.

Tony sighed. He was not at all interested in the politics that appeared to have caught even his friend Lord Princeton in coils too thick to escape. He slowed his pace still more and then paused, raising his quizzing glass. The painting was by that new artist, Constable. He could not see what was so wonderful about the rather messy brushwork, but recalled another by the same man that was owned by his friend Lord Merwin. He had been encouraged to view that one from a little distance and been surprised at the difference a yard or two made. Unfortunately, even when he put his back to the opposite wall, he hadn't the perspective needed to see this one properly. The hallway was too narrow.

"Coming, Tony?" called Princeton.

"Hmm?" Tony turned, swinging his glass by its ribbon. "Coming?" He made an impulsive decision. "I think not. Frankly, Jack, I have learned far more about the war and international agreements, both secret and open, than I ever wished to know. You, of course, have an interest in it," he added quickly. Tony forced himself not to glance at the crutch Jack, an ex-cavalry officer, was forced to use since a festering wound in his thigh nearly did for him. "Besides, they need you to keep them from going off half-cocked in some odd direction which will help no one, especially Wellington."

"I doubt I do much to keep them on the straight and narrow. They don't *want* to hear what I've got to say."

Jack grimaced and then smiled the crooked grin that was so much a part of his monkey features. "I think I'll keep you company instead."

A round or two of billiards perhaps? thought Tony. He shook his head. "You go on, Jack. They may not *wish* to hear your words, but they *need* to hear them."

Tony had very nearly given in to the temptation to take Princeton away from the political discussion. He refrained simply because it was untrue that no one listened. Several of Weatherbee's guests had commented on the usefulness of Jack's knowledge, and he had overheard one politician berating another for stubbornly holding to an opinion Jack had proved indefensible.

Tony had a suspicion it was ridiculous for politicians to take any sort of role in the war effort. War, Tony felt, should be left to the Military, to the men who understood war. Wellington, for instance, appeared to have a notion of what he was doing. So why did they not let the man get on with it in his own way?

Hearing giggles, Tony put the problem from his mind. He turned, raising his glass. "Ah ha!" He pointed the glass toward the young female guests. "Lady Lillian and Miss Browne, you have changed since breakfast! That lilac, Lady Lillian, looks very well with your hair. As I suspect you know since your style is always right up to the knocker!" He studied Miss Browne as well and nodded approval. "That yellow suits your coloring just as nicely," he told her. "How very lovely you both look this bright and sunny morning."

"And you, my lord, are fine as fivepence!" responded Lady Lillian promptly. Tony frowned, and her ladyship covered her mouth, stifling laughter. "Or do I mean tuppence?"

Tony grinned. His opinion of her sartorial expertise had not been in error. She merely teased him for being seen in the old but comfortable coat he would dare wear nowhere but in the country and a vest striped in tan and green about which he had serious doubts. Certainly the common everyday biscuit-colored inexpressibles covering his lower limbs did not call for compliments! Except for his exceedingly well polished boots and a cravat tied in a neat if complex style of his own, he did not feel he deserved praise, so he was glad to realize Lady Lillian was bamming him in that delightfully teasing way she had.

"What have you ladies in mind to do today?" he asked.

"But what *is* there to do? You gentlemen secrete yourselves away where we ladies are not allowed to join you. Pity us, my lord. We simply pine away!" She adjusted her posture to one of the classic poses, this one a drooping figure representing ennui.

Tony chuckled appreciatively. "If you promise not to tell, I will reveal a deep dark secret."

Lady Lillian and Miss Browne looked at each other. "We'll be nibbled to death by ducks before we reveal a word!" promised her ladyship solemnly. But little glints danced in her eyes.

Tony dropped his voice to a whisper. "I, too, find their discussions a dead bore, so, instead of improving myself by joining the meeting, I mean to take a drive. Would you care to chance that we find a single shop worthy of your notice in a nearby village?"

"We'll chance it," said Lady Lillian, brightening, already backing away toward the front hall. "Do hurry, Beth. We must instantly change into gowns appropriate to such a treat." She smiled. "You will see, my lord. By the time your carriage is at the door, we will be there as well." She turned, picked up her skirts just a trifle, and darted down the hall.

Miss Elizabeth Browne thanked Tony for his offer in a far more conventional manner and then, at a more restrained and ladylike pace, followed her friend.

Wendover strolled after them in his usual languid fashion but only so far as the entry hall where he requested a footman be sent to the stables with orders that his coachman was to bring his carriage around in half an hour. He then, equally without haste, inquired into the various possibilities for their outing.

If not *quite* so quickly as Lady Lillian predicted, the trio was on its way far sooner than Wendover had thought possible. He knew how long a lady's toilet took, and Lady Lillian was not, he had noticed, one to stint the process which, he thought, showed a proper appreciation of the importance of fashion. Although she must have hurried herself more than a little on this occasion, there was no evidence of it.

"We can go west to Lambourn Woodlands along the road which runs beside the Thames," he told Lady Lillian and Miss Browne while his coachman tooled the coach down the Weatherbees' drive. "Or we may go east to Shefford Woodlands, or inland to either Eastbury or East Garston. Those are the nearest villages. Farther away is the larger village of Lambourn, and, of course, Reading is worthy of a visit—assuming you require the advantages of a town." His tone sounded apologetic as he finished. "That last is, perhaps, a trifle far for today."

The two women conferred. Lady Lillian thought Lambourn the most likely to have a few good shops. Miss Browne, however, was in favor of Eastbury, where, she said, speaking hesitantly, there was a church with a few remaining Norman relics. Lady Lillian made a comical face but, knowing her friend's deep interest in such things, gracefully acquiesced.

"Thank you. I would like it of all things," said Miss Browne softly, and then cast Tony an apologetic glance, "assuming Lord Wendover does not object?"

Tony, sitting with his back to the horses, smiled sweetly. "Of course I've no objections. I feel certain we have time for both a tour of the church and of any shops that are available. Perhaps Lady Lillian—" He broke off, his brows arching, as her ladyship shook her head vigorously. "You disagree?" he finished, forgetting what he had begun to say.

"Oh, not that there will be time for shopping, my lord, but that you call me Lillian. I do wish people would not."

"How do you prefer to be styled?"

"Libby."

The shy tone in which she spoke surprised Tony, who had not thought her at all shy.

"It is a nursery name, I know," she continued, "but I much prefer it."

"Not Lily?"

Her rosebud mouth formed a moue in that charming way it had. "I have never been Lily. Not to anyone."

"Perhaps," teased Tony, "I will call you so. I do so like to be different."

Her ladyship cast him a glance pregnant with surprise. "I had thought you entirely conventional, my lord," she said when he quirked a brow in query.

He chuckled. "Perhaps, Lady Lily, it is that you do not know me very well?"

Her ladyship's unpredictable practical side surfaced. "Well, no, of course not, my lord. How could I? We have danced at balls, something I have enjoyed very much, and we've exchanged a few words at one or two soirees; but one cannot talk properly during a set, and one has no time at a soiree for more than commonplaces. I drew my opinion from the fact you are always so point device and always seem to know exactly what one should say at any given time, in even the most difficult of situations. Polite in the extreme to everyone, and—" She shrugged slightly. "—of course, you are a pattern card for a Tulip."

Wendover smiled, nodding agreement with her comments. "I thank you for the compliments, my dear, but you must know that those things come easily when one has been in the Ton so long as I have been. It is when I am alone or with friends that I allow myself the freedom to be different." Since he did not wish to explain the ways in which he made his small rebellions to the strict standards of the Ton, he changed the subject, asking if either had found the Weatherbees' secret room.

The Weatherbees' *cottage orne,* newly constructed in the Gothic style, was not overly large, but it was a fascinating structure with odd corners and turrets and cupolas as well as the secret room of which his lordship spoke. Neither young woman had found it, although Miss Browne admitted she had tried.

"Would you like a hint?" asked his lordship.

"You know where it is?"

"Yes. I have visited the Weatherbees on several occasions. The room is well hidden, but one can locate it if one tries. *Would* you like me to help you?"

"Oh, no." Miss Browne blushed for an abruptness that was nearly rude. "At least not yet," she continued. "We've still a bit more than a week before our visit ends. Perhaps if I have not found it as the time draws near for us to leave, I may ask you for a clue?"

"Of course. Anytime." His lordship turned to Lady Lillian. "You have no interest in such things, Lady Lily?"

"Oh, yes," she said with as much enthusiasm as she could manage. "I just have had other things on my mind and have not thought about it." Since she had no desire to explain *what* occupied her to the exclusion of all else, she glanced out the window and was glad to see they approached the village. "I believe that is the church, is it not?"

Tony leaned so that he could peer forward out the open window. "You are correct. Yes, that must be your church, Miss Browne."

He opened the trap and ordered his driver to stop at

the lych-gate to the churchyard. Once the footman put down the steps, Tony helped Miss Browne and then Lady Lillian from the carriage. As he held her hand, he looked into her ladyship's eyes and was surprised to find them beautiful. They were large and sparkling, surrounded by lashes that were quite dark when compared to her oaten-colored hair. The center of the irises were an unusual brown, almost that of good sherry, but that was surrounded by a bluish ring.

"What strangely beautiful eyes you have," he murmured, his hand tightening around hers.

Libby focused on him, her color rising. "Thank you," she said, pleased by his admiration. "I am told they are exactly like my grandmother's on my mother's side. Lady Settle, you know." Her lovely eyes widened slightly. "It is said hers were much admired by her king."

Beth made a strangled sound, and Lord Wendover's expression chilled slightly.

Opening her widely opened eyes still further, her ladyship looked from one to the other. "What have I said?"

Perhaps, thought Tony, *she does not understand what is meant when it is said of some woman that she has enjoyed the notice of a king.* Deciding to give Lady Lillian the benefit of the doubt, his features softened, and he smiled again.

"It is nothing," he said. "Merely a thought that crossed my mind. Shall we enter the churchyard?" He offered his arm first to one young lady and then to the other.

Two

Tony hummed softly as he strolled down the hall to Lord Merwin's room. He had enjoyed his afternoon with the two young ladies. The church was something of a disappointment, the Norman bits hidden beyond their finding, but he had found it rather humorous that in the dusty village shop, Lady Lillian had managed to find several things to buy that for reasons beyond even her inventiveness, had been deemed absolutely essential. The seat beside him on the homeward journey had been filled with her bundles so that he was forced to sit immediately across from her, their knees bumping whenever one or the other moved without careful aforethought.

As the remainder of the afternoon drifted by Tony discovered that whenever he was not thinking of anything in particular Lady Lillian popped into his mind's eye. She was not exactly a beauty. Except for those eyes, of course. There was something rather *taking* in the unusual expressiveness of her features. Too, he found her witty, but—the humming stopped abruptly—she was also more than a little brittle. Brittle in a fashion curious in so young a lady, who should not have the worldly knowledge that usually led to that particular trait in a woman.

Tony scolded himself. He was doing it again. He wished the young lady would cease to invade his thoughts every time he turned around. It was exceedingly uncomfortable!

At that point Merwin's door loomed before him, and Tony knocked softly. If his friend was occupied with political work, he would ignore the sound, but if he was not, then perhaps they could have a comfortable coze before it was time to go down to dinner.

And perhaps he would get Lady Lillian out of his mind!

The door opened, and Merwin grinned at him. "Just in time, Tony. I am celebrating!"

"Celebrating? What?" Tony strolled into the large, airy corner room. "You know, Alex," he added before Merwin could answer, "I envy you this bedroom. I am sharing with old Farthington. We are in a poky little room, which should not house a valet, and worst of all—" His eyes rolled. "—the gentleman snores. I do not get a wink of sleep."

Merwin chuckled. He brought Tony a glass full nearly to the brim, the wine colored the deep red of a garnet. "Poor Tony. We cannot have your lovely complexion ruined by lack of sleep. You must use this room. At least—" Merwin's slashing eyebrows formed a faint vee shape. "—I know no reason why you should not. I am to be gone for no more than a few days, but even that—" A quick flashing grin appeared. "—will restore the roses to your cheeks!"

Tony felt the heat of a flush putting those roses where he did not want them. "Give over your funning, Alex," he ordered. Then the meaning of Merwin's little speech sneaked in under his embarrassment. "You mean it?" he asked.

"Why not? I am to leave my traps, taking only what clothing I'll need, so you'll not have so much space in the armoire as a man of your stripe finds necessary, but you need not move everything since I'll be gone only three or four days."

"When do you leave?"

"As soon as my man has us ready to depart. The temperature is mild and there is a good moon, so we should have no trouble making it into London."

A knock sounded, and Jack Princeton entered. "Ready to go down?"

"Come have a glass with us," countered Merwin. "I am celebrating that I have finished all my work early and may actually enjoy a few minutes' peace and quiet before I depart." He raised his glass. "I can pretend I am a normal man. A man who does not slave away deep into the wee hours of every night for the betterment of England!" he finished in dramatic fashion.

Jack grinned his characteristic one-sided monkey grin. "Give over, Alex. You almost had poor Tony there sputtering wine all over his pristine neck cloth."

"Ah! That would never do."

The two teased Tony a bit longer about his point-device manner of dressing until, seeing that their friend was becoming a trifle heated by it, Jack asked if the politicians had actually managed to come to an agreement.

Merwin sobered instantly. "They did. I leave for London within the hour carrying orders for three or four people and strong recommendations for another handful. Assuming, of course, that I can locate everyone with whom I must deal, none of it will take long. If I cannot . . ." He shrugged and looked through his wine at the fire.

"But you will return?" asked Princeton.

"Oh, yes. I am determined to enjoy the remaining days of the party once this work is done! It was Christmas at Renwick's Tiger's Lair when I was last able to relax. That is, I did once *you* ceased acting the idiot! You, Jack, will recall that the first half of the holiday was spent in a fashion far from that I'd planned!"

It was Princeton's turn to endure some teasing, but he was too happy in the marriage resulting from his "idiocy" to care and actually added one or two detrimental adjectives of his own to those the others offered. "I was an ass, was I not?" He grinned that lop-sided grin. "I truly behaved like the jackass my lovely bride insists I am not. I must apologize for putting all of you to such trouble!"

"All ended happily," soothed Tony. "Lady Princeton appears more than content, I'd say, and that is the important thing, is it not?"

"She makes me feel a whole man," said Jack softly. "She does not mind that I limp or that the scarring left my leg an ugly thing to look on."

"A limp or even the loss of a limb does not make a man less than he was, Jack," said Merwin. "It is what it does to the inside of a man's head that causes problems."

"As it did me. My valet who has only one hand learned to deal with the world. And Renwick! His blindness did not make him bitter, as it might have done. I was a fool to try to hide myself away from life. If I have not, allow me to thank you both for all you did to help me. With all my heart."

Merwin's straight brows dipped into a vee shape, and he looked a trifle uncomfortable. Tony swung his quizzing glass with a trifle more fervor than was his habit, his neck and ears touched with pink. They looked at each other, recalling what a worrying time they had endured when Jack, his wound not fully healed, disappeared and they could not find him.

But that was over.

"As the bard says, *All's well that ends well,* and you must admit, Jack, it ended very well indeed."

"Oh, indeed." Jack's eyes sparkled. "It could not be bettered. My Trixie is a jewel and I a very lucky man." He lifted his glass. "To my bride," he said and drank off the last of his wine.

The others followed suit, and, the bell ringing, they took themselves down to the large front hall where the company met before going into dinner. Merwin, a word to this person and then that, left the house quietly and,

with a well-filled hamper containing his dinner to keep
him company, began his journey to London.

Elizabeth, waiting at the top of the stairs for Libby,
idly watched him go, her mind too occupied with the
hours spent with Lord Wendover to think anything of
Merwin's leaving the party. Then, suddenly, Elizabeth remembered something she had not done, and with an almost silent "botheration" she returned to her room.

Lady Princeton paused. Ahead of her, her hands clutching the balcony railing, was Lady Lillian. The young
lady's head was bent, and her eyes were glued to a group
of politicians standing below who argued fiercely. There
was an intensity to the girl's features, her ears cocked to
overhear what was said, and it startled Patricia a great
deal since Lady Libby, as the girl insisted she be called,
had appeared no more than the usual skitter-witted young
female one found at any house party. Obviously more
went on under that well-cropped head than one might
have expected.

A door opened down the hall, and Lady Lillian swung
around, expectation fading beneath a distinct trace of guilt
as she saw Lady Princeton. The guilt marring her features
was instantly erased.

"Good evening, Lady Libby," said Patricia, wondering
if she had correctly interpreted what she had seen.

"Lady Princeton! I didn't hear you . . . Ah!" A touch
of color warmed Libby's cheeks. "Good evening to you,
too." Libby looked beyond Lady Patricia. "There you are,
Beth. Finally. As you see, I have waited for you. Beth,"
she added, a twinkle in her eye, "was reading." It was not
a complete lie. Beth had been reading up until the dressing
bell ran. Libby dropped her voice to a confiding tone. "She
insisted she must finish the chapter." Still no lie. Beth had
finished. "Is it not terrible that I have a bluestocking for

a friend? So distressing!" She adopted a pose denoting ruefulness.

"Libby Temple!" exclaimed Miss Browne, the humor of Libby's jesting fighting for supremacy with her irritation that her friend stretched the truth to suit herself. "That book is yours, as you very well know! Don't you accuse *me* of being blue!"

Lady Princeton chuckled. "A case of the kettle and the pot?" she asked. "Do I dare ask what tome is in dispute?"

"Merely a silly novel," said Lady Lillian, interrupting her friend, who, obviously, was about to say something quite different.

Lady Princeton was curious as to exactly what book Lady Libby had brought to the house party. She suspected it might be one of those fast French novels that circulated among young women, but, sensibly, decided it was not her business. She merely nodded, suggested they all go down together and, when they had done so, discovered her husband awaiting her at the bottom, his crutch firmly under his arm and his free hand extended.

Lady Princeton forgot the girls, her features glowing with her love for her husband. "Jack," was all she said, sliding her hand into his.

Libby, hearing the emotion in the one word, felt an odd lump in her throat. There was a depth of satisfaction in Lady Princeton's tone, which was not lost on Lady Lillian. In fact, the love revealed was such as to tighten bands around Libby's heart and send a rush of regret through her that she would never have the opportunity to experience the obviously wonderful warmth of a love shared as Lord and Lady Princeton did. Envy was added to regret. For a moment, as she watched the newlyweds stroll off arm in arm, Libby continued to feel the heavy mixture of envy and regret.

And then she took herself firmly in hand. The curt message from her father left her no choice. Delaying even another night might leave it too late. *She had to act!* Tonight would be the night, and she would not allow panic to deter her as it had the last time. She would succeed.

Beth pinched her arm, and Libby looked around. "What is it?"

"Hmm? Tonight . . ."

"You mustn't," Beth whispered.

"Must I not?" Libby looked around to check that no one was listening. "Are you a witch that you know what I am thinking?"

"You are plotting, that is what you are doing."

"And if I am?"

"Libby, you know you cannot do this!"

"You mustn't concern yourself so, Beth. We are at a party in a wonderfully Gothic house with any number of young men who would not be put off by the fact your father was born a Cit. Remember? You are supposed to be looking about you for a husband."

"But you know I can never relax and think of myself when I know you are plotting something gooseish."

"You know nothing of the sort!"

Beth brightened. "Then, you have decided against—" It was Beth's turn to check for eavesdroppers. "—your notion of . . . of consolidating your position?" she finished more discreetly than she might have done.

"I'm still thinking about it," admitted Libby, deliberately misleading.

"Oh, well. If you are merely thinking!" Beth smiled shyly at a young man who came up to her just then, asking that she partner him for the first set at the impromptu dance Lady Weatherbee promised the party for that evening's entertainment.

Libby moved away, tactfully leaving Beth with the obviously smitten lordling, the second son of an earl. She pretended to study a painting and edged nearer to a trio of older gentlemen, those to whom she had listened earlier. They were discussing a fourth who had invested heavily in an absurd project and deserved to have lost all for being so silly. Libby wondered, rather bitterly, if the investor about whom they spoke was her father. The men went on to speak of a newly conceived project, speculating on whether it might not be quite a sound prospect.

"If it comes to anything, I believe I will buy shares in it," said one. "The designing engineer has done good work in the past. Even his worst endeavor wasn't exactly a failure."

"Is that so? Remember to inform me if it comes to anything. I, too, could do with a good investment!"

"Could not we all," laughed the third.

They changed the subject to talk of the war, which seemed to dominate far too much conversation for Libby's taste. She moved on, smiling at Lady Weatherbee, nodding to Lady Princeton, and, when asked if she knew a new arrival, said, "No, I do not believe we have been introduced."

Beth joined Libby just then and was included in the introduction. "Not the Miss Wroth who . . ." Beth reddened. "Oh, I beg your pardon. I apologize for mentioning something you must wish to forget!"

Miss Wroth chuckled. "When I set out for Constantinople with my father I hadn't a notion I would become so notorious," she said in a delightfully husky voice. "Both my father and my brother attempted to persuade me to stay with my grandmother, but I wanted adventure."

"I believe you found it," said Lady Princeton, her eyes smiling.

"More, perhaps, that it found me," said Miss Wroth. "I discovered something," she added.

"Yes?" asked Libby, hanging on the woman's every word.

"Adventure," said Miss Wroth in a confiding tone, "is exceedingly uncomfortable!"

"Well, I think it marvelous how you managed to hold your father to that mast until you washed up on that island and how you didn't know your brother was only a little way farther along the coast. Not for more than a week while you nursed your father back to health!"

"And," said another young woman, "to be rescued by no other than Lord Byron's friend!" She lowered her voice. "Did you meet the poet?"

"No."

Was there just a hint of wistfulness to that no? wondered Libby.

"Our rescuer's boat came up with a British frigate returning to Naples, and my brother hailed it. We returned to England immediately in order to prove my father and brother still lived. My cousin, who had just begun to acquire a taste for standing in my father's shoes, is not pleased."

"But how romantic to be washed up on a desert island," said the woman who had wondered about Byron.

"Romantic? Not at all. Luckily it rained unusually often or we'd have had no water. Food was a problem"—she grimaced—"and we'd only the clothes we'd worn when our ship went down in that storm. It was all exceedingly uncomfortable, and romantic is the *last* thing in the world I would call the situation."

Patricia, who believed the young should not be encouraged to dramatize a situation, was pleased that Miss Wroth's tone did not allow one to believe anything other than the truth. Adventure was, as the woman said, exceedingly uncomfortable!

"When did you discover your brother?" asked Libby.

"He discovered us. He was looking for better shelter than that where he'd been stranded."

"He broke his arm, did he not?"

"Yes, and had no one to set it properly. He will never have the strength he once had, and he is a trifle bitter"— she smiled, her visage lightening—"except, of course, when he is thanking God that we, none of us, died!"

Dinner was announced. Libby found herself partnered by Lord Wendover. She wished it were his friend Lord Merwin, but, since it was not to be, she put aside her chagrin and did her best to entertain him. They soon discovered they had several acquaintances in common and that they were both to continue on from the Weatherbees' to the same house party before going up to London for the Season.

"I will, as usual, live with my grandmother, Lady Settle," said Libby in response to Tony's question. "Grandmother hasn't the strength to entertain as she would like, but she has many friends who are kind to me and take me around with them, escorting me to parties and the like."

"I am not certain if my parents mean to come up this Season, but if they do, my mother will take you up. Neither of them truly enjoys the Season, and they rarely come for more than a month. Some years they do not come at all."

Libby turned slightly in her chair to stare at him. "Not enjoy the Season?"

Tony smiled and lowered his voice, leaning toward her slightly. "You see, they are so very much in love they find other people a nuisance. Even me, if I stay around for too long at a time. Someday I hope to have their sort of marriage."

"Like John, Lord Princeton, and his lady wife?"

"John? He would laugh to hear you call him that. He insists on Jack. He says John is the godfather for whom he was named, and he has no wish to be mistaken for the old curmudgeon!"

"Jack. I will remember."

Tony sobered. "But you are correct, Lady Lily, when you say that they are in love with each other. My friends have been particularly lucky in that respect. First Jason—Lord Renwick, you know—wed his Eustacia, and then Ian married Lady Serena."

"That would be Ian McMurrey?"

"Hmm. We thought that marriage might be a disaster, but it came right in the end."

"Do I hear a story?"

"A rather long one, I fear. Perhaps someday we will have time for what we have come to call Lady Serena's surrender!"

"How intriguing. I will look forward to it!"

The covers were removed for the next course, and they turned, as was proper, to their other dinner partners. Libby sighed. Her other partner was an older man interested in nothing but politics and his food. He had no conversation and was no distraction to thoughts of the night to come. Lord Wendover's conversation had taken her mind from her problems, but now they loomed up to choke her. Libby found she could eat no more than a bite of the lovely turbot a footman deftly transferred from his platter to her plate.

She put her hand into her lap and touched the embroidered reticule laid there. Her fingers searched for the letter from her father, which, tightly folded, she had put into it . . .

. . . except it was *not* there. Frantically, but surreptitiously, she slid her fingers over and around the reticule. No, it was not there. Where could it be? Had she left it on the dressing table? Libby wished she could think up an excuse for returning to her room. Then a still more horrendous thought entered her head: Had she, perhaps, pulled it out when she extracted her handkerchief earlier that evening? Was it lying around somewhere, waiting to be found?

Panic rose to choke her. If the note were found, if news of her father's financial situation were to become common knowledge, she would be lost! Anger filled her, smothering the

panic. *Why must Father be such a fool? Why did he do it?*
It wasn't fair. Not to her and, still less, to her brother.

And what had he in mind now? What did he mean to
do with her dowry? He would lose it, too, of that she
was certain. And when he did? What then? When everything was gone would he sit in his study, drinking himself
to death . . . ? Oh, no, there would be no study. No estate. So perhaps he would take the kinder, quicker route
of a bullet to his head? Would he find the courage to
tell Willie he had become a ruined man while still no
more than a boy? And if he did not? Would he, instead,
leave Willie to discover the truth through the harsh news
of his father's death and the cruel words of a solicitor?

Libby cast a quick look at her dinner partner, but the
man was still ignoring her and had not noticed her preoccupation. She looked at her plate, but her appetite was
gone. She prayed her father hadn't the courage to kill
himself and that she had it, the courage, to put her plan
into action. With any luck at all, her brother might even
have a commission before the news of Lord Eaton's financial disaster became general and reached the avid ears
of the Ton! Or would it be her foolish loss that allowed
word to spread?

Where, she wondered, *is that letter?*

Three

An evening of pleasure had never passed more slowly. Libby smiled until her teeth ached and then smiled some more. She danced whenever asked, which was frequently, but there was no satisfaction in a pastime that was usually a favorite. When she did not dance, she sat with Beth.

"Libby, can you not sit still?" asked Beth, speaking sternly but in an undertone.

"I am sitting perfectly still," objected Libby softly. And she was. It was her fidgeting with her reticule that bothered her friend.

Beth put her hand gently over Libby's. "It is the letter, is it not?"

"I should have put it in my dressing case," said Libby, forgetting that Beth was unaware she had lost it.

Lord Wendover approached in his usual languid manner. He raised his quizzing glass, and when his magnified eye stared her way Libby raised one eyebrow. He dropped the glass and smiled. "You do that well," he said. "I don't believe Brummell could do better!"

"Ah! A compliment, indeed!"

"May I have this dance?" he asked politely.

They joined the line forming for the lancers. It was not Libby's favorite dance. The waltz was by far the best, but forgetting that scandalous pastime, allowed by only a very few hostesses and then only within a select group, she preferred the less rambunctious dances. Still, she was graceful and agile, and, as the lancers progressed, she was surprised to discover how well her steps fit with Lord Wendover's. Especially when the musicians mischievously increased the tempo and the set ended in something very near a romp.

Both Libby and Lord Wendover were breathing heavily when the last bow and curtsey were exchanged. "Very well done, Lady Lily," said Wendover, once again complimenting her. "I know of no one who could have kept to the measure right to the end! After such exercise I find myself thirsty. Will you join me for a lemonade or perhaps a negus?"

Libby nodded and accepted his arm. When she strolled beside him in silence he asked if she was tired. "A trifle," she admitted. "I am unused to sleeping with anyone, and even when it is a friend as beloved as Beth, I find that sharing is an irritant."

"Does she snore?" asked Wendover with mock seriousness.

Libby, surprised by the sly question, trilled a delightful laugh. "My lord! Of course she does not!"

"Ah, then you must consider yourself lucky, indeed. I have been sharing with Lord Farthington. He makes so much noise it is impossible to sleep a wink."

"Poor Lord Wendover," she said and patted his arm. "How terrible for you."

"I would be flattered," he said, eying her a trifle ruefully, "if I thought you truly meant that."

Again she laughed. "It is true I meant to tease you a trifle. You see, my lord, you are looking very well for someone who has not had a decent night's sleep since arriving here well over a week ago."

"Thank you for those kind words. Now I will reveal the secret of my continued health and good looks." He laughed. "No, do not raise that eyebrow at me, my lady! I swear yours should be as famous as the Beau's! My secret is nothing more than that I have taken to indulging myself in a nap each day. You see? There is always a solution if one takes the time to consider all sides of a question."

"Always, my lord?"

There was an edge to Lady Lillian's voice that startled Wendover, and he cast a quick appraising look at the chit on his arm. Did her mouth droop slightly? Was there a touch of strain about her eyes? "Are you in difficulties, my lady?" he asked after a moment in which he hesitated over the question of whether he really wished to become involved.

"Difficulties?" Libby blinked. "Of course not, my lord." She laughed.

But it was not the delightful tinkling laugh that had rather captivated him earlier. It was far more shrill, far less spontaneous. Wendover frowned. "I think there *is* a problem. If you were to ask around, you would discover I am a safe confidant."

"Ah no, my lord. I assure you! And here we are. Will you fetch me a glass of wine punch please?" She seated herself at one of the small tables placed around the room for the guests' convenience, a few slender chairs at each.

Relieved Lady Lillian had not taken him up on his offer, and wondering why he had made it, Wendover obediently moved to the serving table where he accepted two glasses of punch from the footman. But then he considered the odd feelings swirling around inside himself and was startled to discover they were a result of the fact he had been rebuffed! Why it should bother him was a question. Surely he hadn't *wished* to become embroiled in Lady Lillian's problems, whatever they might be, so why this sense of rejection? This feeling she had found him an inadequate knight, unable to fight her particular dragon?

His conclusion she had a problem was reinforced when

he returned to the table and discovered his delightful dance partner had metamorphosed into a perfect example of a tonnishly featherheaded young lady, chattering about trifles and giggling rather too much over outdated gossip. He, of course, upheld his part in the ridiculous spate of conversation, but it was not to his taste. As time passed he formed the suspicion that likewise, it was not to hers! Again, the question passed through his mind as to what had upset her—but his curiosity was not so great that it mitigated the relief he felt once he had returned her to her place beside Miss Browne.

The instant Lord Wendover passed beyond hearing, Lady Lillian, exhausted by her performance in the dining room, whispered to Beth that she was going up to bed.

"So early?" asked Beth. "Libby, are you quite certain there is nothing wrong?"

"Nothing more than usual," responded Libby, her tone more tired than tart.

Beth touched her friend's arm. "Should I come up with you?"

"No, of course not. Besides, is this not your next partner approaching?" Libby escaped before Beth could respond.

Libby prowled the room allotted the girls. She picked up a bibelot here, rearranged items on the dressing table there, peered through a slit she made with two fingers pushed between the drawn curtains, and then began her perambulations all over again. She had changed into her night shift and covered it with the most delightfully frothy robe in her wardrobe. The soft material swished softly about her ankles as she meandered from place to place within the room.

Every thought of the lost letter added an increment of panic. She had searched for it immediately upon returning

to her room and not found it. If news of her father's
imminent financial failure became common gossip, it
would be too late. She would be shunned, all hope lost.
And poor Willie. Some kindhearted soul would find him
a clerking position somewhere. Perhaps with the East India Company. He would survive, but not in the position
to which he was born. She must help him . . . and she
must do it tonight!

"But can I?" she asked herself for the umpteenth time.
Her failure of the night before had eroded her courage
more than she cared to admit.

I must, she answered herself. *I must think of Willie.*
Instantly a further, more selfish, thought added itself to
that: *Think of Great-aunt Thrimble!* The self-interest of
that last had her scolding herself. *Willie. It is for Willie
I must do this terrible thing.* She swallowed, a vision of
a tumbling pile of spaniels, all in need of brushing, filling
her mind.

"If only they did not smell, perhaps I could bear it,"
she muttered. *But Willie.* "No," she muttered, "I cannot
bear for Willie to suffer for our father's folly." She firmed
her chin and turned to look at the door. *Tonight. I will
do it tonight.*

"Ah! But Lord Merwin will be so very angry!"

The words erupted in a subdued wail. Her chin quivered dangerously, and once again, she lifted it a notch,
firming it. It was not unjust that his lordship be angry
with her, and she would solve that problem when it arose.
Then it occurred to her that perhaps her father's letter
had dropped off the dressing table and been tidied away
by the maid. Perhaps there was no rush and she could
delay. . . .

She searched for it. Again she failed to find it.

Tonight. It has to be tonight. She stared at herself in
the dressing table mirror. *There ought,* she thought, *to be*

some change when one becomes a cheat. Something in one's countenance anyone could see.

But there was not. Her image changed to one of utter sadness as further thoughts rampaged through her head.

If only I could convince myself I am making this sacrifice solely for my brother! Despair was added to the guilt she felt. *If only I were unaware that I am a selfish beast and frightened of being poor and doing this awful thing as much for myself as I do it for Willie.*

But the decision to act promptly had been forced upon her by the loss of her father's letter, and Libby began plotting in earnest. First and foremost, she must not fall asleep. On the other hand, she must fool Beth into *thinking* she was asleep. Libby removed her robe and laid it over the chair by the door. She would take it into the hall when she left and slip into it there.

When she left.

How late would the men remain below once the dancing ended and the women returned to their rooms? Once this week she had roused to the sound of large feet creeping by their door, making the sort of noise large feet made while attempting to be quiet—and she had noticed that the draped window glowed rose, showing that the sun had risen! Could she remain awake so long?

She could not. In fact, exhausted by her anguished thoughts, she drifted into sleep pretty much instantly and woke only when Beth returned and moved around the room, preparing for bed. The soothing sound of a brush pulled through long hair very nearly put Libby back to sleep, but then she recalled her plan. Again she quailed at what she would do. It was a terrible thing. But—she saw her father's words in her mind's eye—what choice had she?

Still—what if she failed? What if Lord Merwin woke as she joined him in his bed? Or if he woke too early and discovered her there while there was still time to thrust her from his room with no one the wiser? There were so many ways in which her plan might fail. Thinking of all one hundred and one complications made it impossible for her to go back to sleep.

Which was just as well, of course.

Clouds had drifted in, and it was very dark when Libby finally slid from the bed and tiptoed toward the door. She gathered up her robe and slippers and then pressed her ear to the door panel. Silence surrounded her. A dark velvet silence which both reassured and frightened her half to death. How it could do both she didn't try to understand. Understanding something so mysterious would take far too much effort and more time than she dared indulge.

In fact, if she did not carry on with her plan right this instant, it was all too likely she would lose every ounce of courage she had managed to retain. She would go directly back to her own pillow and, very likely, indulge in a flood of tears that she had failed.

Libby bit the edge of her lip as she slowly and carefully opened the door a crack. Again she listened. Again silence blanketed her, soothed her, frightened her. Taking a deep breath, she slid through a narrow opening and, just as carefully, closed the door.

She placed her slippers on the floor and put her cold toes into them and then slipped her arms into the sleeves of her robe. She tied the ties and looked toward the end of the hall where, dimly, she could discern the faintest of lighter black.

The window, she told herself. *It is the window at the end of the hall.*

Her eyes never left that faint square as she tiptoed toward it. It was her goal. Not the corner room. Not the door into that room. The window. If she thought only of the window, perhaps she would not falter. Perhaps she would manage to reach it, manage to control her beating heart, manage to find the courage for the next . . .

No, she would not think of the next step. Only the window.

Except—then she reached it. The next step was upon her. She turned and faced the deep, dark blackness of the hall. Somewhere way down toward the far end she heard the click of a latch. A door opening! Libby whisked herself behind the drapery, her heart pressing so hard against her throat she thought she was dying.

". . . and so you see, my lord," she heard a deep whispering voice say, "it is imperative that—"

"Yes, yes," interrupted another male voice, which was merely impatient and not at all softened. "We are agreed. We have all said so. Assuming all is as we predict. You need say no more."

"But my lord . . ." the whisperer began.

"No, no," was the instant testy response. "No more tonight. In fact, not another word until we hear from London. When we've that report in hand we will make a final decision. Now good night," said the cross voice.

The other man sighed and steps returned the way they had come, and very soon, Libby heard a door click shut. Then another. Very slowly she lowered herself to the window seat behind her. Her legs were trembling so badly she feared she might never rise again. But then the fear of discovery, here in the hall where she should not be, and which would do her future no good whatsoever, had her peering between the curtains, straining her ears, and deciding that she must try. Now.

Right now.

After scolding herself only a bit longer, she moved to Lord Merwin's door, opened it softly, and slipped inside. And then her legs, in fact her whole body, once again began to tremble.

I have achieved this much, she told herself, *and I can do what still needs doing. I can!*

Surprisingly, the room was a trifle lighter than the hall.

She stood quietly until she realized why: the windows were undraped! She shivered slightly—but not like the earlier trembling which was fear induced—as a faint chill breeze wafted across the room and touched her sweat-filmed skin. Her eyes widened. *Lord Merwin sleeps with the night air blowing in?* For half a moment every lecture she had ever suffered concerning the dangers of night air filled her head, driving out far more important fears concerning her next move.

I am behaving in a most nonsensical way, she chided herself. *Willie and I long ago decided it was all nonsense that the night air was bad for one for the simple reason that if so, there would be no entertainments lasting beyond sundown, did we not? Now, do it. Just walk across the room and do it!*

If she had thought herself slow removing herself from Beth's side, Libby discovered she moved barely an inch at a time when inserting herself into Merwin's bed. She had breathed a special sigh when she had managed to discern a lump on the far side of the bed, the sleeping man turned toward the window. It had meant she had room into which she could tuck herself.

When, finally, she lay there, her head on the pillow and the covers drawn up to her chin, she *almost* dared to breathe freely once again. But there was still the possibility Merwin would wake before the maid, arriving with Merwin's morning chocolate, caught them together. There was *still* the possibility of failure.

The irritation of nerves she had experienced in gaining her present position had been tiring. In the midst of, once again, outlining all the many ways in which everything could yet go wrong, she yawned. And, without wishing it, she drifted into a doze, deep sleep impossible. . . .

She continued to sleep in that half-hearted fashion until the sound of a rather shrill male voice just outside the door had her eyes popping wide open.

"Here you say? A room to himself, you say? Why that lucky dog! But I'll roust him out!"

And the door was flung wide.

"Aha! What have we here?" A masculine giggle followed the words. *"Now* I see why the sly dog wished privacy! Wendover, you rake! You dog you, *what* are you up to?"

Crude laughter followed the man's words, and Libby's eyes scrunched shut as she squirmed farther down into the covers. The bed moved, and she felt the man beside her roll over, push himself up onto one arm. She heard exceedingly soft swearing. So soft the words barely reached her ears. She opened one eye and closed it quickly. *Wendover?*

"A woman?" Libby heard. "There is a woman with Wendover?" It was another voice, a feminine voice, a sneer coating the avid tones with venom. "Let me by, Sir Herman," she insisted. "I bet you a guinea it is that sly Browne chit. Not the thing at all. I haven't had the courage to ask why she was invited. A guinea, I say. Oh, do move and let me see!"

The insult to Elizabeth filled Libby's very soul with outrage and pushed aside every smidgeon of embarrassment. How dare someone be so nasty about her friend? How dare she accuse Beth of such despicable behavior!

"Who will take my guinea?" screeched the woman.

Libby pushed aside the covers, her ire roused to the point she no longer cared who saw her or knew of her behavior. She would not have anyone speaking of Beth in such a way. "I will," she said, pushing by Sir Herman and facing Lady Belltower's glittering eyes. "I will take your guinea, my lady. And I have won it, too. You may pay up later this morning. Right now I mean to return to my room in order to change for the day."

Libby curtseyed in such a way it was an insult and then pushed through the small crowd rapidly forming outside what was *supposed* to have been Merwin's bedroom door. She was halfway to her room when the consequences of the fact that it was *not* Merwin in the bed finally registered.

Wendover! *She had compromised Wendover!* Oh, dear Lord in heaven! She had compromised the wrong man!

Libby felt a tear run down her cheek, down under the high neck of her robe. She had failed. After all her scheming and for none of the reasons she had dreamt up, *she had failed!*

Tears streaming down her face, Libby opened her door and ran into her room, throwing herself onto her side of the bed and sobbed wildly. *The wrong man.* How had it happened? Where was Merwin? Why was he not in his bed? Why was Wendover, of all men, there instead?

Libby swore in a surprisingly fluent manner, ignoring Beth's every attempt to soothe her and to discover what had overset her to such a degree.

"Wendover! I didn't think you had it in you," laughed Sir Herman in the vilest of tones.

"Wendover! How dare you?" shrilled Lady Belltower.

Tony, who had realized instantly that his life was to undergo a serious and unwelcome change, swore silently. He reached for his robe and managed to put it on without seriously flouting convention. He wished with all his heart he dared order everyone from his room. He turned, and his eyes met Jack Princeton's as, brought there by the uproar, his friend pushed his way into the room.

"Ah, Jack," said Tony, pretending a languid ruefulness he did not feel. "I fear the secret is out. And in the worst of all possible ways." His eyes narrowed slightly.

"Is it? That is too bad," said Princeton into the silence.

Princeton, arriving late, hadn't a clue as to what had happened, but Tony knew his friend would back him up. He breathed slightly more easily. "Yes. The very worst."

"Now what will you do?" asked Princeton, obviously feeling his way.

"Lady Lillian and I must wed at once instead of waiting as we'd meant to do. It is really too bad, since I have yet to speak to her father! I would think it not so difficult a notion that one might have at least a modicum of privacy in one's own room, but I suppose I am wrong," he drawled with only a touch of sourness. He retrieved his quizzing glass and raised it to sweep a look around the room. "I haven't a notion where all these people came from," he added querulously.

Princeton kept his lips firmly pressed together and shook his head. He sighed. "Morning visitors before one is dressed. Such a nuisance," he said as languidly as Tony might have managed. He, too, cast a disparaging look around the room.

Wendover's unwanted "guests" wilted under his insouciance and slipped one after another from the room. Once he and Princeton were alone and the door shut, Wendover's expression changed to one mixing anger and chagrin. "I will kill her!"

"What happened, Tony?"

"Damned if I know. Sir Herman opened the door, waking me. There she was. Right there in the bed beside me. I thought for a moment she was going to dissolve into hysterics, but Lady Belltower was nasty about Lady Lillian's friend. Miss Browne, you know? Lily reacted with magnificence, defending Miss Browne with royal fervor before stalking from the room, dignity intact. Still," he added, admiration fading into irritation, "I will kill her!"

"Oldest trick in the book, Tony," said Jack with sympathy. "You'll have to wed the chit."

"You think I don't know that? Haven't I already said I would? But, Tony, I don't want to wed her. She's a featherheaded little minx. I'll never have a moment's peace! And—" His whole body seemed the epitome of sadness.

"—what of love? Ain't I always sworn I'd only marry for love? Like m'mother and m'father? I wanted a marriage like that, Jack. You know how I've always said it was the only sort of marriage I'd ever have! You know I . . . But—" He broke off and drew in a deep breath. "—no use thinking of that now. Must do the proper thing. Will you toddle off to London to buy the license for me, Jack? Or—" Wendover's brows flew up. "—no! That won't be necessary, will it? We've a bishop right here among us, and I can do the trick myself." He sighed.

"Is Lady Lillian of age? Will she need a guardian's signature?"

"What is the age for a female? Do you know?"

Princeton shook his head. "Bishop Hurd will know."

Tony nodded, his morose expression not lightening. "Leg shackled. And in such a way! Ian will not be happy."

"Ian? He won't?"

"Hmm. He made a prophecy that we Six would end, one and all, with happy marriages."

"Three of us have done so, despite rock-strewn and abyss-wrought beginnings. You cannot know that you will not."

"Swore I'd only marry for love," insisted Tony stubbornly. "I'll kill the wench!"

"You don't mean it, Tony. Not literally. So you'd better stop saying it. A man can get himself into serious trouble that way."

"*Am* in serious trouble," said Wendover, half angry and half amused. Anger won. "And it is all her fault."

"Yes, it is her fault, but you have decided to do the necessary, so, my old friend—" Princeton caught and held Tony's gaze. "—it behooves you to *do* what I did *not* do when I was in trouble!"

Wendover frowned.

"I ran away, remember? Oh, it was a different sort of trouble, and I was running from myself; but it was only when I faced up to it and fought it that I found happiness. I'm no soothsayer, like our friend Ian, but I predict you will come to think this marriage no bad thing."

Wendover sighed. "I doubt it. And even if I do, it won't be for love, and I did want love. Like my parents, you know," he finished wistfully.

Jack had no answer other than trite platitudes and this was no time for those. "Tony, I'd better inform Patricia. Your fiancée—"

Tony winced. "My fiancée," he muttered.

"—is very likely in need of a feminine shoulder and, very likely, of feminine advice. I will tell her you are arranging for a license and that as soon as possible the wedding will take place. Lady Lillian may wish to make some sort of preparations."

Tony swung his glass at the end of its ribbon. Then, exasperated, he swung it in a complete circle, something he never did. "My *fiancée!*" Disgust wrapped the word. He very nearly spat it out. "You better go, Jack. I will be fit for neither man nor beast for some time to come!"

A discreet knock at the door and Wendover's valet entered, carrying a tray. He was followed by footmen carrying the bath and several cans of hot water. "My lord," said Abley. He bowed slightly, a frown marring his brow. "I have brought a light breakfast, my lord, and the bath. As you see."

"Already heard the news, have you?" asked Tony when everyone but Princeton and Abley had departed.

"Yes, my lord. Congratulations, my lord," said a morose Abley. The valet then gave Princeton a look that said as plainly as if words had been spoken that he was not wanted.

Princeton, not a stupid man, took the hint, and he, too, left the room.

Although she gave a soft knock to Lady Lillian's door, Lady Princeton did not wait for permission to enter, but immediately opened it and walked in. She closed it softly behind her and then leaned against it, surveying the room.

Miss Browne cast her a look that appealed for help.

Libby, beating the bed with one clenched fist, sobbed into the pillow.

Lady Princeton, shaking her head and sighing one long sigh, moved to Beth's side. "Has she been like this since she returned?"

"Yes. What happened? I do not understand what has happened!"

"Had you no notion what she planned?"

Beth glanced away, hanging her head. "She told me, but I didn't believe her. She even laughed and said it was all a hum, so I forgot about it. Except— " Beth frowned and turned back to meet Lady Princeton's concerned gaze. "—she *couldn't* have done it. Lord Merwin is not here."

"Lord Merwin?" asked Lady Princeton just as Libby lifted her head and, suddenly silent, turned over and sat up.

"He left yesterday just before dinner. I saw him go."

Again Libby pounded the bed beside her. "Elizabeth Catherine Browne, do you mean you knew Lord Merwin was gone and you did not tell me? How could you? How dare you keep such necessary information from me?"

"I forgot about him," retorted Beth. "We'd no opportunity to talk even if I had thought it important."

"But if I'd only *known!*"

Lady Princeton did her best to control her giggles. "You didn't mean to compromise Lord Wendover? You meant to force Lord Merwin into parson's mousetrap?" Her ladyship covered her mouth with both hands, her eyes dancing. "Oh, dear, what a comedy of errors."

"My lady, this is not comedy!" said Beth softly, rather horrified by such cheerfulness.

"Comedy? But of course it is comedy," said Lady Lillian, lifting her head from the pillow. "Sheridan could write a whole new version of *School for Scandal,* could he not? I want to wed Lord Merwin. I do not wish to marry Lord Wendover. *His* is only a courtesy title. *He* hasn't control of his fortune! What good is Wendover to me?" Libby burst into tears again, but this time they were tears of anger. "I won't marry him," she said, her tone rather wild.

"What good . . . ?" Lady Princeton looked to Beth for explanation but found the young lady would not meet her eyes. "Lady Lillian," said her ladyship sternly, "in what way can Lord Merwin help you that Wendover cannot?"

Libby froze. Then she slumped. "Oh, why not tell you? The whole world will know soon enough. My father has brought an abbey to a nutmeg as they say. His creditors will very soon fall on him like ravening wolves. My brother—"

She went so pale Lady Princeton feared she was about to faint.

"—my poor brother! What sort of life will his be if he grows up with his father in debtor's prison? How will he live it down?" Libby stared at nothing at all. "All he wants in this world is a pair of colors and a chance to smite Napoleon! In a few months he'll be through school and old enough, and my father will be unable to find the necessary. He has been unable to scrape together so much ready money for nearly a year now."

"Then, you have forced the issue of your marriage because you wish to help your brother?"

Libby bit her lip. "If I am entirely honest, not entirely. It is for myself as well. I—" She turned huge eyes stark with incipient terror on Lady Princeton, giving credence to her next words. "—fear poverty beyond anything."

"She believes no one would ever want to marry her once it is known her father has lost everything," said Beth.

"It would be less likely, of course, although not impossible," said Lady Princeton. It was her turn to frown.

"Are you so very certain your father is in such deep waters? It is not something a father would usually discuss with his daughter."

"What is that saying? A fool and his money are soon parted? I know that in the past he has been a fool often and often. Since coming here I received a letter from him informing me he has taken my dowry for his latest investment. I've a very good notion what he means to invest it in, and it is just the sort of wild speculation that always tempts him. And it, like all the rest, will be still another failure. I would show you his letter, but it is lost. The realization it is missing gave me the courage to do what I did. It frightened me, wondering when the axe would fall. I keep wondering when the person who has it will reveal to everyone that I am a pauper's brat!"

Beth turned, eyes wide-opened toward her friend. "But, Libby, it is in your dressing case."

Libby stared.

"I saw it on your dressing table and thought it should not be left there since it troubled you so. I tucked it into your dressing case."

Libby's body collapsed on itself, and she stared at nothing at all. "I have been so worried. Why did I not think to ask you?"

"Why did I not think to tell you?" Beth sat on the bed, taking her friend's hand. "I am so sorry, Libby."

"That is all very well," said Lady Princeton, speaking just a trifle sternly, "and I am glad you have not lost your letter, but the important thing now is to face the other houseguests and show them you are happy that your wedding to Wendover has been pushed forward even if it is for this scandalous reason. You will do it for Tony's sake." When Libby shook her head, her ladyship added, "You *must* put a good face on it, Lady Lillian, or you will bring the scorn of the Ton not only onto yourself, but onto Tony's head as well, and *he* does not deserve it, is that not so?"

The two girls stared at her, Libby forlornly and Beth nodding vigorously.

"The thing to do is to put on your loveliest morning gown and, smiling, go down to breakfast. I believe Tony wishes to talk with you privately as soon as he has arranged with Bishop Hurd for the marriage license, so that the two of you may make plans. And, my dear, if you will take my advice?"

Libby nodded.

"You will explain to him exactly why you did what you did. And you will tell him that you will do your very best to make the Ton believe the two of you are happy together. And then you will, of course, do all you can to promote that belief."

Libby sighed. She nodded again. "If only . . ."

"If only it were Alex? Lord Merwin, I mean?" asked Patricia.

Libby nodded still again.

"Have you a *tendre* for him?" was the next blunt question.

Libby nodded still again.

"Then, I am sorry for you, but believe me, you would not have liked being married to my cousin. He is not the man for you."

Libby stared at Lady Princeton.

"Very likely you do not believe me, but I assure you, it is true."

Libby nodded, but with an expression on her face that indicated she did *not* believe it true at all.

Lady Princeton sighed. "Never mind. You must dress and join the others. I will tell my husband to tell Wendover that you will be down in half an hour. Is that sufficient time?"

"Better make it three-quarters of an hour," offered Beth.

"I have never known Libby to prepare for the day in less than that. In fact, most often, it takes well over an hour."

Lady Princeton smiled at Beth's expression, a mixture of awe and disgust that it should be so. "Hmm. Perhaps it is as well. They will be a match in that respect, at least. Wendover, too, is known for taking forever over his morning toilet. Perhaps so much as three-quarters of an hour will push him a trifle as well!"

Beth's eyes widened still farther at the news that Lord Wendover could take so long dressing. She had never found it necessary to use up the whole of half an hour, and her father would have had words to say to her if she ever did. She whispered that information to her ladyship as she saw the older woman out the door, and Lady Princeton exited on suppressed laughter.

Which was just as well. Lady Belltower lurked nearby and felt a great deal of surprise to see Lady Princeton so gay. She was disappointed to observe it. Surely her ladyship would not find such humor in the situation if it were truly the scandalous incident one naturally believed it to be. Her ladyship sighed. *Ah well,* she thought, *it is still the biggest surprise of the new year, and I've many friends who must, instantly, be apprised of the news!*

Four

Lady Lillian was far more a realist than she allowed anyone to know. Even Beth, her very dearest friend, never saw Libby's most serious side. So, as Beth brushed her hair for her, pulling the bristles through her cropped locks in a most soothing fashion, Libby did not have to strain her mental faculties in order to come to the obvious conclusion that there was no way out of the dilemma she had wrought for herself and that she must make the best of it she could.

Furthermore, she scolded herself, *Lady Princeton is correct. I must do what I can to make this as easy as possible for Lord Wendover. None of this is his fault. My behavior must be such that he is not made to suffer for it. The Ton will make his life difficult enough merely that I was caught in his bed.* She sighed.

"What will you do?" Beth caught Libby's gaze in the mirror.

"What I must do. And then, once the deed is done, whatever I can do to make Lord Wendover's life tolerable."

"I feel sorry for him. I'd feel sorry for any man tricked as you tricked him, but Lord Wendover is such a nice man. He didn't deserve your tricks, Libby."

Lady Lillian's lips compressed. It was one thing for her to scold herself, and very likely she deserved something more than a scolding from his lordship, but for *Beth* to scold her! It was too much! She said so.

And then, instantly contrite, she turned and hugged Beth. "I didn't mean it. I have been saying to myself everything you say to me. Don't be angry with me. I could not bear it."

"Then, when you go to Lord Wendover, you will apologize?"

"I will certainly do so. I mean to make this a good marriage. Or as good as such a marriage can be. I will do nothing that will add to his suffering."

"Thank you."

Libby blinked. "Why?"

Beth smiled a tight little smile. "I believe I was beginning to develop a *tendre* for Lord Wendover. I will, I think, continue to bear a tender place deep in my heart for him—"

Libby stiffened.

"—but now," continued Beth, oblivious to Libby's tension, "it will grow into no more than friendship for the husband of my best friend."

Libby bit her lip. *What emotion caused that odd feeling just before Beth explained?* She pushed aside the unanswerable question. But Beth had been falling in love with Lord Wendover, which laid still another burden on her conscience. Lord Wendover had shown no signs of a developing warmth for Beth, but he had seemed to enjoy her company, and it was not an impossible thought that the two might have fallen in love and married during the coming Season.

But not now.

Libby, by her action, had put paid to that possibility along with all others! She reaffirmed her vow that she would do everything asked of her. Even if Wendover banished her to some isolated country estate and forgot about her, she would not complain! *It is,* the bitter thought intruded, *no more than I deserve.*

But the notion she might be sent to Coventry, as the

saying was, might find herself ignored, had Libby sighing another lugubrious sigh. She stood up and, passively, allowed Beth to toss her gown over her head and button up the row of tiny buttons which closed the front of the bodice from only a little under her breasts to up under her chin. She did not even look in the mirror, as was her custom, to check if all was as perfect as imperfect human hands could make her. Instead, she went directly to the door, her feet dragging ever so slightly, and out into the hall. There she paused to reaffirm her vow. She lifted her chin and proceeded to the breakfast parlor.

Facing everyone at breakfast was exceedingly difficult, but with Beth at her side and Lady Princeton supporting her, she managed to finish most of her usual bread, butter, and coffee before rising to go to her meeting with Lord Wendover.

Somewhere between the breakfast room door and the library where they were to meet, Libby's determination to do the right thing faded in proportion to her mounting embarrassment at the thought of facing Lord Wendover. In her mind's eye she again saw Lord Wendover rolling over, pushing himself up onto one elbow, and staring down at her there where she lay next to him. There had been a vee of bare chest below his chin. Bare skin sprinkled with pale hairs only slightly darker than those on the top of his head. Was it normal for men to have hair *there?* She felt hot all over at the thought. Facing his lordship seemed more impossible than ever.

Reluctantly, Libby entered the Weatherbee library. Just inside the door she stopped and stared across the room. A man stood in the window embrasure. He looked like Lord Wendover—and then again, he did not. Was it he?

Lord Wendover was normally a happy man. He was, by nature, a lighthearted soul who danced through life with nary a problem and only the brightest of futures to which he looked forward. It never crossed his mind that that future might not unroll exactly as he blithely assumed it should do. Was he not the beloved son of loving and beloved parents? Did he not have fortune? Friends? Had not the fates favored him in every way? Then, why should they not continue to favor him?

Anthony Wendover had never before faced disaster. His life had never offered a period of chaos. And, a kind man, he never indulged in the sort of hurtful gossip so common among bored tonnish souls—but he was not so obtuse he did not know it existed, and he knew full well that he would, for the immediate future, be the center of the latest scandal. Tony did not like scandal or the Ton's obsession with it. He liked even less that he was involved in one.

He was not a happy man.

Tony turned and noticed Lady Lillian standing quietly by the door. "My lady," he said, bowing.

"I'm sorry," said Lady Lillian quickly.

"Are you?"

Her head came up. "You will never know how sorry."

"It is a trifle late, my lady, for apologies."

"If it were not too late," she retorted, "there would be no need for one!" And then she gasped. "No, I do not mean that. Please forgive me, my lord."

"I will think about it," he said in cool, crisp tones very unlike his usual languid manner.

Lady Lillian digested that. This was, she feared, going to be even more difficult than she had expected. "Lady Princeton tells me you mean to wed me. I will understand if you would prefer to throw me to the wolves. *Your* reputation will not be harmed," she finished with only a touch of bitterness unrepressed.

"Will it not?" It was Wendover's turn to be silent for a thoughtful moment.

Libby felt a chill run up her spine as she began to fear he would take her up on her offer.

He shook his head. "Perhaps my *reputation* would survive, but my *honor* would not. We will wed."

"You give me no choice?"

His brows arched, and he raised his quizzing glass to stare at her. "My dear Lady Lillian, do you truly *wish* a choice?"

Libby turned aside, biting her lip. She put her hand on the back of the chair that stood next to the door, steadying herself. "I was unaware Lord Merwin had left for London," she said in a strained whisper.

Wendover leaned forward ever so slightly in his effort to hear her. "I see," he said, after still another pause. "Do you love him?"

Libby glanced across the room, back to the design of the petit point chair seat. "Do I? Oh, yes, of course I do! How could I not?"

Wendover frowned slightly, catching a hint of something he could not define. "Why did you do it, my lady? What drove you to such desperate measures? Surely not that he paid you little or no attention. I cannot believe you would revenge yourself in such a way for so petty a reason as that."

Libby cast him a quick horrified look and bent her head to stare at her toes.

"Is it such a difficult question to answer?"

Libby glanced here and there as if seeking escape. She straightened her back and drew in a deep breath. The words came in a stiff, formal manner. "I must," she said, "inform you, my lord, that I am penniless. For the past several years my father has done his best to lose the whole of his fortune. In a letter I received a day or so ago, he revealed he has taken my dowry, a last source of funds, to put into his latest scheme."

The bitterness at which her earlier tone had hinted was

now revealed in full. "He will lose that, too, my lord. And the instant word of his folly becomes general, I will be forced to take up the position of poor relation to whatever distant relative is willing to house me." She looked up, staring blindly across the room. "The letter disappeared, my lord. I thought it stolen, that word would be all over the house before a day passed. I—" She turned away from his stern expression. "—panicked." She swung back. "Not for myself. Or—" Inherent honesty forced her to modify that. "—not *entirely* for myself. Willie. My brother. Poor Willie. I doubt my father can salvage so much as is needed to purchase his commission—when he leaves school later this spring, I mean. It is his only ambition in life. And, worst of all, I—" A look of utter sadness passed over her features, then faded. "—doubt our father would think to do so even if he could. If he can scrape together even another few pounds, it will be gambled away on still another idiotic investment scheme. It will *not* be put to use doing what might ease, in any way, my brother's loss of his patrimony."

"There is no entail?"

"No. Something Nanny once said makes me believe my mother had nearly convinced my father he should see to safeguarding his son and grandson in just that way, but then she died. I think something inside my father died as well and was buried in the grave with her. And the babe."

Wendover nodded. "I see."

"I know it does not excuse me. What I did . . . well, I can do no more than tell you how sorry I am."

"There *is* more you can do," said Wendover, a muscle turning over in his jaw.

Lady Lillian, recalling her promise to herself, frowned. "Anything," she said when he didn't proceed.

"You may agree to pretend that our marriage is exactly what you want, that we are happy and contented. In public,

I mean." The wisp of a sour smile, the faintest of sneers, curled Wendover's lip. "I believe, in private, we will neither wish to maintain that fiction, that we will find it a relief that we need not. Did you say something, my lady?"

The sneering tone, faint as it was, was so out of character for the man Libby thought she knew, she was shocked by it. *I did that,* she thought. *My despicable trick soured him.*

"My lady? Do you feel such a trifling thing is more than you can manage?"

"It is, as you say, very little to ask of me," she said quietly. "I will do my best to convince the Ton I am madly in love with you. I will sit in your pocket, dance only with you, and become broody when you go about your business and cannot be with me."

"Sarcasm ill becomes you, my lady."

Libby bit her lip. She had not meant it sarcastically. She had meant to lighten things a trifle, but, perhaps, it had come out with a touch of the bitterness that had settled into her heart as she first read her father's letter. Besides, Lord Wendover was not the only one to be disappointed by the outcome of her contemptible conduct. She was disappointed in herself!

"My lady?"

"You are correct, my lord."

"And that is the first thing, is it not?" He sighed. "You must cease my lording me, Lady Lillian. My name is Anthony. Tony to my friends."

"Anthony, then."

"Tony would be better if you could bring yourself to use it."

She cast him a surprised glance. "But I am not your friend!"

"Ah! But you must be perceived to be my friend, my lady."

"Only yesterday you called me Lady Lily," she responded, once again trying for a lighter note. "If I am to call you Tony, then you must also use the diminutive."

After a moment Tony nodded. "Very well. I will call you Libby as does your Miss Browne."

He is too angry to use the name he himself devised, thought Libby sadly.

"There are other things which must be discussed. The usual settlements of course, and pocket money for your daily needs and where I will set up accounts in your name and . . ."

"And that is another thing," said Libby, hurriedly, wishing to get through all necessary confessions as soon as possible. "I have great difficulty with money. I spend it."

"It is there to be spent, of course," said Tony politely.

"No, you do not understand. I see something. I like it. I buy it. I do not pause to think. I merely open my purse and buy it. And if I do not have the money, I will borrow from whomever I happen to be with. I am impelled to do so. I do not understand it, my lord. Tony," she amended when he looked about to object. "But you need to know that I cannot control my spending."

"You must."

"Must?"

"You must control it. I will promise to buy your brother his commission if that becomes necessary, but you, Libby, must not make it impossible for me to do so. You must not run into debt."

Libby bit her lip, her eyes huge and staring. "I do not know if I can resist," she said in a small voice. "You do not understand how it is with me."

"Will you promise to try?" asked Tony. "And that you will come to me if you are ever in debt? No matter how small a debt? Surely you can see how that would hurt not only me but you yourself as well."

The muscles around Libby's eyes felt strained. She

sensed a headache coming on. Could she promise? To try? She could *try*, of course, even knowing she would fail. Did such a promise have any validity? Whether it did or did not, she must agree.

"I promise to try," she said.

He nodded. "We will be wed as soon as it is legal to do so. The bishop will provide the license, and Lord Weatherbee has offered to introduce me to the local vicar. I believe, by law, we must wait a day or two or three, so if you wish to invite your father so he may be here to give you away and to witness your marriage, there is likely time to do so."

Libby felt prickles under her skin and again reached for the back of the chair. "He will be so angry."

"Angry?"

"His letter. His taking the moneys set aside for my dowry. He told me only because he wished to order me to form no attachments and prohibit me from forming an alliance until he replaced the funds and could face talks about settlements."

"I had forgotten that. So you will not write and tell him until it is all over?"

"If you will allow me to wait, I would prefer to do it later. And *your* parents?"

"You will meet them when we visit them in June as is my custom—unless they come to Town for a part of the Season, which I think is doubtful. In a letter I received only this morning, Mother told me they have loaned our town house to cousins who have a daughter who is to be presented this spring."

Wendover and Lady Lillian were silent for a noticeable time while Tony wondered where he could find a house for them at this late date and Lady Lillian examined a sudden fear that Wendover did not *wish* to introduce her to his family.

Finally Tony nodded and again raised that glass of his.

"That is all, my lady," he said in a distant tone. Equally distantly he added, "Unless you know of a topic we should discuss, some point I've forgotten to raise, you may go."

Those prickles under her skin worsened, and Libby hoped she would not disgrace herself by fainting. To be dismissed like a housemaid who had been reprimanded! How dare he? The anger overlaid chagrin so that she managed to turn on her heel and leave the room, carefully closing the door behind herself before she allowed herself to gnash her teeth—and followed that with a desolate sigh, despairing of ever making things right for Lord Wendover.

Tony watched her go, leaving him alone at last. But, with the door shut and no further need to keep up a façade, he suddenly realized how utterly exhausted he was. The moment he had rolled over in bed and looked down into Lady Lily's face, seen her eyes scrunch up tightly as if she could pretend those crowding into the room did not exist if she could not see them, it had felt as if the weight of the world dropped onto his shoulders. And then she had peeked at him.

At the time he wondered why she looked so startled. The door opening should not have surprised her, since she must have hoped to be discovered. She would not have been in his bed if she had not wished to be compromised and he forced to wed her. But she explained that, did she not? She had thought it would be Merwin.

She wished to be found—but not with me.

Tony recalled her comment that she had been unaware that Merwin had left for London. After a very long moment contemplating that, and feeling more exhausted than ever, Tony trudged back up to the corner room where, on the desk put there for Merwin's use, Tony found pen, ink, and paper and sat down to write the hardest letter he had ever had to pen.

What his father and mother would think, would feel,

when they read it, he didn't wish to contemplate. He thought for a long time before he put pen to paper, trying to find a way of softening the blow. In the end he broke the news with his first words. Then, hoping to prevent more resentment toward their daughter-in-law than was impossible to avoid, he listed Lily's reasons for such rash behavior, omitting only the fact she had believed she was compromising Merwin. And finally, he asked that they not attempt the journey necessary to attend the wedding.

Would they have any understanding of his wish they *not* come for the ceremony? Understand that because he felt it a farce, he did not *want* them witnessing it? He could not say that, but his mother was very good at reading between the lines, so perhaps she would guess and explain it to his father.

Tony stared at the finished letter and sighed once before folding it, addressing it, and sealing it.

Later that day the Weatherbees' butler frowned at the pile of letters on the hall table, waiting to be taken all the way into Richmond to catch the Royal Mail. There was, of course, always a goodly number when his lordship entertained. The sending and receiving of letters was an important part of many a tonnish person's daily routine. But this huge stack, very nearly toppling over the edge of the table and onto the floor, was outside of enough!

The butler glanced around guiltily as if someone might have heard the cant phrase running through his mind. No one was there, of course. He looked back. Somehow he must pack all those letters into the mailbag, readying it for the groom. And the groom would arrive at the front door any moment now.

But, thought the gray-haired man as he stowed the post, *this much mail means something has happened. A scandal, in fact. Nothing else could account for this many letters except the hope of being first to spread the word!*

But exactly *what* had titillated the guests, no one

among the staff could guess. Not, that is, until orders were given that early Wednesday morning, they were to prepare the large salon for a wedding. Extra bouquets would be required and chairs set just so for guests, and the kitchen must devise as sumptuous a wedding breakfast as could be managed in the brief time available.

Discussing those orders, the upper servants agreed among themselves that the scandal was that the young lady had been found in the bed of her fiancé. The dressers were pressed by below stairs servants for details, and the valets likewise, but no one knew more than another—except Abley, Lord Wendover's valet, and he was saying no more than that it was a pity that all must be done up in such a scrambling fashion as the circumstances made necessary.

Grooms rode off in all directions with invitations, and each returned word that those invited would not only come themselves, but would bring guests. Word of the wedding spread far and wide, and anyone who knew someone living near the Weatherbees' cottage immediately traveled to join those already visiting in the neighborhood. The small private wedding, witnessed by only those few close friends attending the house party, which was how Lord Wendover had envisioned it, rapidly grew beyond the confines of the salon. He and Libby were forced to agree that it be held in the local church.

As it turned out, even the church was too small for all who indicated a wish to attend. Worse, the wedding breakfast, planned for the gothic entrance hall, had to be moved onto the terrace overlooking the river.

"Pray for a sunny day," said Lady Princeton to her husband when they met in their room, both having decided to change early for that evening's dinner, each meaning to be out of the way when the other came up to change.

Jack, more than a trifle grim that his friend must go through with what he called The Farce, nodded. "On top of all else, poor Tony needs no rain to further spoil the day."

"Has he decided what they will do? Where they will go?"

Jack grimaced. "There will be no wedding journey. The Season is upon us, and the idiots mean to go directly to London where they have the intention of facing down the Ton, by showing everyone how happy they are. Tony's only problem was where to find a house for them. The Hendred town house has been loaned to a cousin, you see, and, at this late date, nothing suitable would be available. I suggested he borrow McMurrey's town house, and Tony instantly wrote Ian. The McMurreys will not be coming down from Scotland this year."

Patricia brightened. "We should have news of the birth of their child any day now, should we not?"

"That," said Jack, giving his wife a quick hug, "is woman's business. Surely you do not think we poor males keep track of such things?"

"Perhaps I am wrong," she mused, "and it is next month." She cast him a quick look and forced away a smile, adopting a demure expression.

Jack, unnoticing of her byplay, frowned. "It is any day now, and Ian is beside himself!" he retorted.

Patricia cast him another look, this one full of laughter, and Jack, instantly comprehending her little trick, tossed her onto the bed, coming down beside her to kiss her silly. He stared down at her. "I have wondered if one or two of us should not ride north to be at hand."

"If you think you should, then of course you must go. I am, however, quite certain Lady Serena will come through her ordeal in fine shape, and the babe as well. Who, by the way, is to be godfather? Was it ever decided?"

Jack grinned. "All of us, of course. We will share that burden for each and every child born to any of us."

"I wonder . . ." said Patricia, sobering.

"Wonder what?"

"Will you ever have that honor for a child of Tony's?"

Jack was silent, and the two pondered the unhappy situation in which their friend found himself. "Someday, surely," said Jack finally.

"Yes, of course," said Patricia quickly. "Lady Lillian will do her duty. Poor lady."

"What of poor Tony?"

"Yes, but it is different for men. She will never know the joy of the marriage bed. *Only* the duty."

"Hmm." Jack put his hand on his wife's waist. "Do you know the joy?"

"You know I do."

They stared deep into each other's eyes. All else faded from their minds as they *both* enjoyed the ensuing interlude. They were almost late for dinner, too, even though both had gone up early to change.

Lady Lillian's wedding day broke with bright skies and singing birds. She put her head under her pillow and tried very hard to return to the arms of Morpheus, who had been kind and sent her pleasant dreams throughout the night. The morning, on the other hand, meant nightmare. Her wedding day!

Sleep was impossible, and Libby, with care not to wake Beth, slid from the bed. She went to the window, uncovered by a maid only a short time earlier, the sound of the rings against the rod waking Libby. Now she stared down into the garden, sad at heart and wondering, for the hundredth time, if there was something else she might have done.

For the hundredth time she could discover no alternative. Besides, one *good* thing would come of this marriage. Lord Wendover had promised to buy Willie his commission. Willie was safe, whatever came to herself.

Movement caught her eye, and Libby stared, frowning. Several men were riding along the lane, but she could not, quite, distinguish who it was who had set off to enjoy the first truly nice day all week. And then one of the men turned a smiling face to say something to the rider beside him.

Lord Wendover. Unmistakably, Lord Wendover.

His lordship felt relaxed and contented enough he could go for a lighthearted ride on the morning of the day that would see him standing at the altar saying traditional vows to a woman he despised! Libby felt tears wet her cheeks. Was the man truly so insensitive he could enjoy riding with friends on the morning of the day that would change their whole lives?

Or was he pretending?

He had asked that she promise to pretend she was happy with their situation. Libby gritted her teeth. It appeared *he* found it agreeable enough! He felt able to go off for a pleasure ride. He could smile at friends.

And if *he* could, then she would not allow him to discover how deeply dejected she was. Nor anyone else. She would show *everyone* how comfortable she was in her marriage!

Beth roused just then. She yawned and stretched before going to peer at the clock on the mantel. "Very soon the maids will come with the bath. We will wash your hair first, and I will brush it dry which will not take long, given how short you've cropped it. I do not know how you dared do it!"

"You should try it. Not only does cropping make it easier to wash and dry, but also I no longer suffer those headaches I used to get. The doctor recommended I cut it."

Beth chuckled. "I doubt he meant you were to cut it shorter than his own!"

Libby's lips smiled politely. "Very likely not."

After a moment Beth asked, "Have you chosen between the sprig muslin and the yellow gown?"

"I decided on the ecru with the heavy tatting."

"I thought you didn't like it. You said it was one of your mistakes."

"But appropriate for a wedding, is it not? All that lace . . ." Libby turned back to the window, hiding a wave of anguish.

Lace. Her great-grandmother's gossamer-fine veil, which she should be wearing over a wreath of flowers in her hair, was stored deep in a trunk in the attic at her home. Nearly a yard wide and two long, the lace was so fine it would float about one at the slightest movement. Libby had never touched it and had only seen it once when the housekeeper opened that particular trunk to air the contents and check that there was no damage due to creasing or age.

The veil had put lovely dreams of her own wedding day into the much younger Libby's head. Now those dreams would never come true. She would never wear that veil, would never touch it. She gritted her teeth—and turned to see if Beth had heard.

Beth was gliding quickly across the room, drawn toward the door by a soft tapping sound. First she peered through a crack and then opened it wide for the maids who carried in a bath and lots of hot water.

"Come, Libby. Today I will be your abigail," said Beth from where everything awaited the bride.

Libby squared her shoulders. It was time. The nightmare was about to begin.

Five

"That went off far better than we might have expected," said Wendover to his brand-new wife. The wedding and wedding breakfast were in the past, and they were seated in Tony's carriage bowling down the Weatherbee drive on their way to London.

"Yes." Libby once again pushed down the lump in her throat. If Wendover could make the effort to be polite, then so could she. "I thought the flowers particularly lovely. Lady Princeton did very well by us."

"Patricia? Not Lady Weatherbee?"

"Beth told me that Lady Princeton took everything in hand from the very beginning. Lady Weatherbee made no objection. I think she felt I did not deserve any extra effort on anyone's part. Lady Princeton did it for you, of course."

"Nonsense. She likes you. She told me so."

"She likes Beth better," said Libby in an undertone.

"Your Miss Browne is a very likeable young lady. You are lucky to have her for a friend."

"You will not—" Libby spoke hesitantly. "—object to having her as a guest at our entertainments?" *Assuming, of course*, she thought, *that anyone will accept invitations from such a scandal-ridden pair as ourselves!*

"Why should I object?" Wendover cast her a mischievous look. "Oh. Because she is the daughter of a Cit? There are those who will object to her birth, but I'm not one of them. She will be an example to our more tonnish young ladies. An example of how one *should* behave."

Libby felt her skin whiten, that awful prickly sensation which heralded a swoon.

Wendover noticed. He placed his hand over her clenched fists. "No, Lily. Please. Forgive me. I did *not* refer to you. Truly!" At that moment he had *not,* but her reaction reminded him of his anger, and the mood was broken.

Libby turned her head aside. Perhaps he had not thought of her when he spoke, but surely it was her nasty trick that had been to the back of his mind. How could it be otherwise? Even if he had slipped when apologizing and used the pet name he had given her when they were still happy in each other's company!

When she neither turned back nor replied, Wendover yawned behind his hand—or pretended to do so. "It has been a tiring few days, my lady. Perhaps you will not object if I attempt a little nap?"

"I, too, could use a rest," said Libby on a slightly strangled note.

The two snuggled into their respective corners, and neither knew if the other actually slept. At least there was no need to pretend there was ease between them when they could, instead, pretend to sleep. She was more exhausted than she knew and, as a result, Libby actually dozed away quite a few miles, rousing only when they reached the posting house where Tony meant to change horses.

Hours later, in London, Libby accepted the hand Tony offered to help her exit from the carriage. She glanced at the façade to the house and continued staring at it as she stepped to the paving. "But this is the McMurrey town house, is it not?"

"Only Ian and Lady Serena use it now, or very occasionally one of Ian's brothers. The old man no longer comes to Town. Ian offered us the use of it since this year it would, otherwise, stand empty. Ian told me that if he was forced to make a run to Town for business reasons, he meant to stay at a hotel rather than open up the house. Now he will stay with us, of course." He glanced down at his wife. "I fear it will not be all out of dust covers since I was able to send word only yesterday, but Ian's staff will have brought in food for our supper, and our bedrooms will be readied. Tomorrow you may see to ordering things as you like."

Libby swallowed. She was to live in a wonderfully tonnish town house which she might order as she pleased! It was too much. She was being *rewarded* for her terrible deed rather than punished! "You must tell me how you like things to go on so that I do nothing to make you unhappy. Nothing *more,* that is."

Since she spoke as they entered the house, Tony was unable to respond, but just as soon as they were introduced by the butler to the footmen and by the housekeeper to the female servants, he asked that their supper be brought on trays to Ian's study and then led Libby to the back of the house and into a comfortable library.

Later, once their supper arrived and the door was shut against any possibility of a servant overhearing him, Tony reminded her of her comment. "My dear," he continued, "you must not make yourself a carpet over which I am to walk." He served her from the platter set before him. "If you feel it necessary to redeem yourself, you must join one or more charity committees and work to help someone else. You must *not* feel that you should walk on eggshells when around me." Holding his own plate, he looked up and caught her eye. "What is, *is*. We must make the best of it. Although this marriage is not what either of us wished, it is a fact, and it will do neither of us the least good to repine."

Once he finished what was obviously a speech, Tony smiled. A slightly forced smile, but nevertheless a smile. "There," he said and served himself. "I have been thinking how I was to say all that ever since we passed Richmond! I am glad it is said. Perhaps we may be comfortable now."

Comfortable, thought Libby. *How?*

"Perhaps," he added, "we should think of this as an arranged marriage such as was common in earlier generations. Then perhaps we may jog along together without too much difficulty?"

"It was certainly arranged!" said Libby, chagrinned.

"My lady—" Tony laid down his fork with something of a clatter. "—you must stop putting the worst possible interpretation on everything I say!"

"I cannot help it. I was so very desperate, but now it is done I feel so very guilty."

He eyed her. "You would do well to do as I have done and accept that the situation is unalterable." *Well,* he thought bitterly, *I am trying to accept it.* "I mean to make the best of it, and I hope you will do the same."

Libby drew in a deep breath. "If you truly mean it, my lord—"

Tony was not completely sure he did, but he hated to see anyone unhappy. Even this woman who had ruined his life!

"—you are far more generous than I deserve." She drew in a second deep breath. "If you will inform me of anything you absolutely refuse to eat, I will put together a few menus that in the morning, I may discuss with the housekeeper—once she has taken me over the house."

"I eat anything except cabbage. I am with Brummell in that respect. There is something so very off-putting about cabbage."

"Very well. I will remember. Do you like sauced meat or prefer it plain?"

"Both," said Tony promptly. "Truly, there is nothing else I dislike, so you must plan as you will."

The two fell silent. Finally Libby could no longer even pretend to eat and rose to her feet. "It is late."

A muscle twitched to the side of Tony's jaw. "But not too late." His voice was firm, perhaps a trifle stern, and his eyes perfectly steady on hers when he added, "I will come to you in half an hour."

Libby had tried very hard not to think about the coming night. Now she felt everything inside herself cringe away from what was to come. Lady Princeton had explained it to her. Which was just as well since she had not had a mother to take on that task. It had sounded rather disgusting, although Lady Princeton insisted it need not be. On the other hand, she had also warned that the first time, it could be a trifle painful. She also said that if Libby relaxed, it would make the whole thing far more pleasant.

Libby wondered how one was to relax in such a situation as her ladyship described. *"Pleasant? That must be nonsense,"* she whispered once she had shut her bedroom door behind her.

The tiny maid waiting to serve her glanced up. She instantly realized it was not herself to whom Lady Wendover spoke. Since the untried abigail, until that morning no more than a promising upstairs maid, was determined to make the very best of this unexpected opportunity, she had asked the housekeeper for advice and then, carrying out each suggestion, carried up fresh warm water, laid out her ladyship's brushes and nightshift, and turned down the bed, which she was, at that moment, warming with a long-handled warming pan.

Libby moved in a listless manner to the dressing table and took off her bonnet, which, although she had taken off her pelisse earlier, she had not yet removed. She ran her fingers through her hair, once and then again.

The maid abandoned the warming pan and approached. "If my lady permits, I will brush it," said the girl.

"Oh!" Libby, startled, looked into the mirror at the maid's reflection. "I was unaware anyone was here. Do excuse me. And your name?"

"I am Finch, if it pleases you."

Libby frowned and then recalled that in some tonnish households it was the practice to have a certain name for each position. The person filling that position, whatever their real name might be, answered to the designated name.

"Finch is an excellent name. And it fits." When the maid looked confused, Libby added, "You are little and perky. Like the bird."

The maid giggled and then cast her new mistress a quick glance. She breathed a sigh of relief when it appeared she would not be reprimanded. In fact, it seemed her mistress was so preoccupied she not only had not noticed the unwarranted response, but was unlikely to give any orders! What to do first?

Finch picked up the brush and, hesitantly and then with more confidence, brushed her ladyship's short curly hair with careful strokes. When she had counted to a hundred she set the brush aside. Still there were no orders. After another moment's hesitation, Finch murmured, "If my lady wishes, I will remove my lady's gown."

Moving very like a puppet, Libby allowed Finch to lead her to the washstand and, once her hands and face were cleansed, permitted the maid to ready her for bed. The warming pan was removed from the bed, and then, with one last look around, Finch removed herself and the pan from the room. Libby was alone.

But for how long?

She shivered, decided it would be best if she were already in bed so that the coming ordeal might be over as quickly as possible, and, when Tony knocked and asked permission to enter, that is where he found her. Only one candle remained lit, and that sat on the table by the door. He lifted it and came to the side of her bed.

"Are you afraid?" he asked. She nodded. "I will be as gentle as I can," he assured her.

Libby opened one eye and watched the door snap shut behind her husband. She shivered and, after she put from her mind the last few moments, she gently tested her feelings about what had gone on between them. First to surface was relief. It was over. And—surprise was an unexpected sensation—not so bad as she'd expected. Not good, but not so very bad.

In fact, at the very beginning, when he'd touched her, leaned over her and—Libby felt her skin heat at the thought—touched his lips to her throat, well it had been—nice actually. "I liked *that,*" she thought, embarrassed by the notion. Lady Princeton had not mentioned anything about actually *enjoying* the marriage bed. . . .

Anguish filled her. If only his hand had not shifted to cover her breast! She had just been beginning to believe that everything would be all right when that odd sensation flowed from his hand to . . . to very embarrassing parts of her body. She had stiffened, then pulled away. . . .

And Tony had sighed, moved away and very soon after that had left the room without a word to her.

Tony lay awake for a long time once he had returned to his own room, a guest room, actually, since Ian and Lady Serena shared the room in which his wife lay.

"Wife!"

Well, she was that. Morally, legally, and physically. Tony grimaced. What had passed between them just now was not rape, but it might as well have been. What he had heard muttered about tonnish brides was true. They felt no desire. Gave a man no welcome. It would be long and long before he returned to such cold comfort as he had found in Lily—No! Libby's bed. He would *not* call her Lily!

Putting this new disappointment from his mind, Tony tucked his arms behind his head. Firelight cast flickering lights across part of the ceiling, and, as he watched them, he turned his thoughts to how best to assure he and his new wife got off on the right foot socially. Their personal relationship must limp along as best it could, but surely he knew his world well enough he could alleviate the social problems caused by their scandalous marriage. When they were private, he decided, he would remain polite. He would do his best to support Lily—Libby!—when they went among the Ton.

But how best to deal with the Ton? His lips compressed and relaxed only to tighten up again. *It is too bad Mother is not in Town,* he thought, feeling just a trifle morose.

His mother would have set Libby's feet on the proper path. In fact, since Libby's own mother was deceased, it was the place of his mother to take Libby around and about and introduce her—but that was impossible. His father had taken a chill, and Lady Hendred was not about to allow him to come to Town. Nor would she come herself when he could not!

There was Libby's grandmother . . . but the old lady was rather frail and unable to trot around the town as would be most helpful. Perhaps, instead, she would hold a dinner at which Libby could make her bow as a married lady—which thought reminded him of another duty which must be performed as quickly as possible.

Tony groaned. He loved society. He did *not* enjoy the royal drawing rooms or Prinny's private parties and avoided the royal family whenever possible, but Libby *must* be presented in her married state. Their too quick and unannounced marriage would set up the backs of the high sticklers in society no matter what they did. If they were to flout that particular convention as well, it would be total disaster!

A little more cogitation and Tony decided that the morrow would see them visiting Libby's grandmother, Ellen, Lady Settle, and his great-aunt, Mary, Lady Sheffield, and they would follow those visits by setting in motion the acquisition of appropriate court dress for Libby's presentation. That, all by itself, he decided, was far more than could be comfortably accomplished in one day—especially since Libby had mentioned she must take time in the morning to see the housekeeper and do whatever it was a woman did when talking to such a person!

It occurred to Tony he need not worry about Libby's abilities in that regard on top of everything else! His wife was not only well trained in that respect, but had already had charge of her father's home for a number of years. She was well able to run this one. He was glad there was something he need not do!

Some moments later, he decided he and Abley would take themselves off in the early morning to decide what to do about his rooms. His possessions must be cleared out, and if there was time, he must instruct the family's solicitor to find someone willing to take up the lease. Bachelor quarters would no longer be required. He must see his man for another reason as well: Some sort of settlement must be established—something that, under normal circumstances, would have been accomplished well before the wedding.

Tony's thoughts returned to memories of the snug rooms in which he had lived for very nearly a decade. Memories that depressed Tony a great deal. He and his friends had had such fun. Even with their differing interests, the Six had remained a tightly bound unit—except for Miles, of course, and now that he was returned to England, he was being drawn back into the group, one of them again.

Thoughts of his friends led him to wonder what his wife would think of them. The Six, as they called themselves, had met in school and developed a mutual support group against school bullies and to help each other accomplish the work that was their supposed reason for being in school in the first place, and also to share the treats Tony's mother shipped to him with great regularity!

Then they went on up to university together—although Miles left soon enough, running off on his adventures. For the rest, Merwin had gone into politics only a few years after they had come down, Ian had become deeply involved in running his father's Scottish border estate and his family's other ventures, Jason had gone to India where he was blinded by an exploding gun, and Jack had bought into a cavalry unit, serving ably until so badly wounded everyone, including Jack himself, had thought he would die.

Tony lay watching the flickering light play across his ceiling, and allowed memories of his friends, of their past and present, to flow through his mind, soothing him, bringing him to a point where he began to feel the calm and sense of contentment in which he usually lived. All was changed, yes, but a great deal remained the same.

The bond among the Six would support him through the ordeal of adjusting to his marriage. They would help in practical ways as well as emotional. For instance, where Ian and Merwin led, the Ton would follow. The very new and untried Lady Wendover would find support for her feet and hands to guide her if she faltered. She had joined their tight little group in an unorthodox manner; but she was now one of them, and as one of them, she would find herself surrounded by friends whether she wished them or no!

Tony smiled slightly as he slid into sleep.

He was still smiling when he woke. The memory of his new status returned but no recollection of his soothing cogitations of the night before. The smile instantly faded.

* * *

"Tell me about your grandmother, Libby. You lived with her for part of each of the last several Seasons, did you not?"

"Yes. It was kind of her to invite me to stay with her when her health is so uncertain. When I wrote her of our marriage, I did my very best to avoid worrying her but—" She cast Tony a quick glance. "—I do not know how our news will have affected her. I so hope she is not cast down. If my behavior were to harm her—" A tear slipped down over her cheek. "—I will never be able to atone for it."

Tears! Tony hated to see anyone cry. His heart went out to her pain. "Libby," he said softly, "this is not like you!" He ran a bent finger up her cheek, taking the tears away. "You are not the lachrymose sort! We can see she is not unhappy."

"But how?"

"We will simply tell her how much in love we are. How it was for that reason that we were led into our impetuous behavior, and the discovery of *that,* well of course it led to an immediate marriage! Libby, she will be happy for us."

Libby didn't look convinced. "She is a twitty old lady, my lord. I have never been able to wrap her around my finger. Not that I have tried so very often, but when I was younger and more thoughtless and there were things I wished for so much, then I tried and failed."

"A gown totally unsuited to your age, perhaps?" asked Tony, teasing.

Libby smiled with her lips, but there was a sad look in her eyes. "That among other things."

"Come now. You must smile properly or she will never believe our story." Tony continued to do his best, which was very good, to lighten his wife's depressed feelings. He actually managed to draw one of her delightful tinkling laughs from her just as they drew up before Lady Settle's door.

The door opened immediately, and her grandmother's butler beamed at them. "My dear Lady Wendover, and Lord Wendover! Welcome! What a great day this is."

"Thank you, Brice. You have heard our news, then?"

"Yes, of course. My lady was kind enough to inform the upper servants when she received word of your marriage. A bit of a surprise . . . ?" he asked with the freedom of an old servant.

Libby was not about to gossip with her grandmother's butler, who was the nosiest man she knew. "Very much a surprise, Brice. Grandmother is well enough to receive us?"

"In the very best of spirits."

It occurred to Tony that very likely no one had been so unkind as to regale Lady Settle with the worst possible interpretation of the facts leading to their marriage, an unexpected bit of tactfulness on the part of the Ton for which he was relieved.

"Come right this way. She is in alt, my lady, happy as a lark. And so full of plans! You will see." They had climbed the stairs while Brice spoke, and now he threw open the doors to the formal salon. "Lord and Lady Wendover," he intoned in proper form.

"Grandmother?" asked Libby a trifle hesitantly once the door was shut with Brice on the outside.

"Come here." The old lady gestured with her stick. "The both of you. Well, don't just stand there."

"We must apologize," said Wendover smoothly, "for our rash behavior."

"So you must. I have put the best face on it I can, but there is still much to do to save your bacon." She glared. "Lillian Margaret Rosemary Temple, just what were you thinking to do things up in such a scrambling manner? And do not attempt to fob me off with some story about a long-standing love that you could not manage to withstand. Such behavior may have done in my generation, but things are quite different now!"

"Have you the full story?" asked Tony, placing his hand on Libby's shoulder and squeezing lightly.

"If I have not, I don't wish to hear more! No pretty tales now!" she warned. "I want the truth with the bark *on,* if you please."

"If it is that we were discovered in bed together, then that is all."

"All? Could it be worse?"

"It might have been, had my bride *not* had the courage to come to me."

"How so?"

"Father . . ." began Libby and then could go no further.

"Did you bring his letter, Libby?" asked Tony. "As I suggested?"

"Yes. I do not see how it may help, but here—" She scrabbled in her reticule until she found it. "—it is."

Tony took it and handed it to Lady Settle. The old woman lifted the lorgnette she wore around her neck and perused it.

"That worm has finally done his worst, has he?" Her ladyship glared at nothing and then turned the look on her granddaughter. "Well, missy? Do you truly think this sufficient reason for playing off your tricks?"

"When I read his letter I fell into such a panic I didn't know what to do. There is Willie, you know. He assumes he'll go instantly into the army as soon as he is free of school, which is not all that far into the future now."

"So you did it for him, did you?"

"In part, yes," said Libby, seeking and finding the courage to add, "but only in part."

"You do not seem terribly cast down by all this," said

Lady Settle to his lordship after glaring at her grand-daughter for a long, thoughtful moment.

"Our marriage is not what I expected, but I am not dissatisfied," said Tony calmly if inaccurately.

"Well said, young man. I don't want to know if it is the truth! You mean to support Libby, then?"

"Both financially and socially." Tony nodded. "Of course I will. She is my wife."

Lady Settle allowed her stiff spine to relax a trifle, although she never ever allowed herself to lean against the back of a chair. Still, some of the starch left her, and she even smiled slightly. "You will have your dowry, Libby. I will see to it. You, Lord Wendover, will order your solicitor to attend mine. The two of them will come to an agreement, and we may sign the papers when they have done so." She scowled slightly. "Very irregular of course!"

Libby's eyes widened. "Grandmother, you will do that for me?"

"Silly child," said the old woman, revealing a touch of affection. "Of course I will." As if to make up for that brief revealing moment, she scowled. "Did you truly believe I would allow my daughter's daughter to suffer at the hands of that scoundrel she married against my wishes? Your brother may come to me when he leaves school. I will see to his commission as well. As to your father," she added in ominous tones, "we will think about that problem." She pounded her cane against the floor several times. "You see, missy? This belief you carry around that you are the only one who can solve problems and that you must do all yourself or nothing will be done is not only ridiculous but insulting as well. You should have come directly to me the instant you knew the worst. I would have sorted it all out."

Libby cast Tony a glance filled with horror. "You mean . . ." She could not go on. Turning on her heel, she ran from the room.

"Let her go," said Lady Settle when Tony made a move to follow. "She will cry out her remorse for tricking you, and having done so, she will do what she must do to right things." Her eyes narrowed. "You, my lord, surprise me. I had not thought you'd so much bottom."

"I believe that must be a compliment."

"Well," said Lady Settle crossly, "you are known for nothing but the cut of your coat and knowing the exactly proper depth to give any particular bow! You make your lighthearted way through the Ton's annual schedule, moving from Season to Season as do the birds and appeared to have little more sense than one!"

"I enjoy tonnish things."

"Hmm. So does my granddaughter. I have always thought her fascination with the Ton more than a trifle overblown, but if it matches yours, then perhaps it is a good thing, since the two of you must rub along together. What do you plan to do?"

"I must organize her presentation at the next drawing room. And frankly, my lady, I rather hoped you would be willing to hold a dinner. Not a large entertainment, but something to show you approve Libby's marriage and support it?"

"I already have that in hand. The invitations will go out by the end of the week. What else?"

"Almack's. She must have vouchers to Almack's."

Lady Settle frowned. "I cannot help you there. It must be *your* well-known address that overcomes any reluctance on the part of the patronesses. See to it immediately."

Tony nodded, half amused by the order and half annoyed. Her ladyship was treating him very like a schoolboy in need of strict direction. "I will visit Lady Sefton tomorrow. She will take our part for my mother's sake if not for ours."

"Very well." Her ladyship's mouth worked. "I am an old woman. Too old. I cannot do as I'd like and take

Libby about with me or see to shutting the mouths of the vicious who will do their best to blacken her reputation and, in the way of things, yours as well."

"I have friends who will support us, my lady."

"Yes, but they are as young as you are. It is the elderly who have ruled the Ton for eons who will do the damage. They forget their youth when the world was not such a namby-pamby place. Deliberately forget, in some cases." Her voice revealed tolerance, yet contained a touch of acid for such self-deceiving behavior. "I must think what to do. . . ."

Tony noticed that her ladyship's eyes drooped and that she leaned heavily on her cane. He suggested that perhaps he should find Libby since they were to continue on to his great-aunt's next and should be about it before it was too late for a proper morning visit.

"Your aunt! Is that not Lady Sheffield?"

"Why, yes."

"Stupid! Why did you not remind me sooner? You will wait so that I may send her a message by your hand."

When Lady Settle began struggling to her feet, Wendover quickly moved to her aid and guided her steps to the small desk standing beside the door. Her ladyship, very quickly, covered several sheets of paper, sanded them and folded them, before applying wax marked with a diamond-shaped seal, a second diamond shape within it.

She handed the letter to Wendover, told him he was to give it to his aunt immediately, and dismissed him, telling him to ask Brice to send in her abigail. "The silly chit is very likely wasting her time flirting with the second footman, so tell him he is not to bother looking in the laundry where she ought to be pressing the gown I am to wear later, but must go directly to the linen room where they like to canoodle. What this world is coming to, I cannot say!"

Wendover passed on the message that her ladyship's

maid was to go to her, and Brice instantly muttered that the wench was likely to be found in the linen room where she had no business being, which comment made Tony smile, glad it was unnecessary to give him Lady Settle's order in full! "And where will I find Lady Wendover?" asked Tony next.

"Ah! I must suppose dear Lady Settle was a trifle testy with her to overset her so?" Tony made no answer, and Brice, denied still more in the way of gossip, sighed. "The poor child," he said, "is in the lady's parlor to the back of the ground floor. You will find your way, my lord, since I must fetch that Betty and send her to her ladyship?"

"Yes, I can find my way."

He did, and ten minutes later they were on their way to Lady Sheffield's. Libby was overly subdued, but Tony reflected that that would not hurt her in his great-aunt's eyes and, during their short ride, did nothing to lighten his wife's mood. His great-aunt was likely to take the hide off them with her unbridled tongue, and the scold would be far worse if Libby set up her back at the beginning by appearing confident or the least little bit smug.

Six

"She is worse than my grandmother," said Libby when they left Lady Sheffield's and were once again in the coach and headed, this time, for a more pleasant milieu.

"Yes. But she came around. As I knew she would. The soiree in our honor which she will host, inviting only the most select guests—"

"And the most boring!"

"—and boring of course!" Tony grinned. "You are correct in that, but we can manage to be polite to them for one evening. It will do much to cut the ground from beneath the feet of the scandalmongers, you know. She is a tartar, but a very well connected tartar. Have you thought at all," he asked, changing the subject, "about your presentation gown? I have had the notion that perhaps a rich blue with a design of seed pearls around the bottom and on the bodice would suit, but if you've already come to other conclusions . . . ?"

Libby turned in the seat to stare at him. "Seed pearl embroidery? But it costs the earth!"

"Yes, but it is important you make a proper bow to royalty. I will send to Mother for the string of pearls that are traditionally passed on to the heir's bride. It is a long single string of perfectly matched pale pink pearls. I think you will like wearing them."

"A family heirloom."

"Yes."

"I will be afraid to wear them. What if the string breaks?"

"I will take them to Ludgate Hill to Rundell and Bridge. If they need restringing, it will be done before your presentation. Come now, Libby. Will blue do or have you a favorite color which you would prefer?"

"You, my lord, are well known to understand what suits one. I would be a fool to go against your suggestion!"

"I have a good eye, but so, too, do you, my lady. I have commented on it before." Tony had expended a great deal of energy soothing the sensibilities of first a testy old lady and then an irascible one. He had very nearly used up his day's ration of tact and was a trifle testy himself when he added, "Now please be good enough to tell me if you would be more comfortable in another color."

Libby swallowed, met his stern eye, and sighed softly. "I like blue. I have always thought I should not wear it since my eyes are brown."

The thought of Libby's beautiful eyes brought a return of Tony's equilibrium. "Your eyes are incredible, and you cannot call them merely brown! For the most part they are the color of the best sherry, yes, but that is surrounded with a faint blue halo that will become more obvious when you wear blue, will it not?"

Libby frowned.

"You have never noticed? Ah well. It must be the right color of blue, of course. We will see. Madame Colette will have samples with which we may test my theory!"

Libby stiffened. "Madame Colette! I have never patronized a modiste of her stature."

"I must remember to set up an account for you," mused Tony. "She will send your bills to me, of course."

"My bills sent to you! But you said I was to have an allowance!"

"Yes, but that is for the bonnet you see in a window

where you haven't an account and vails for servants. It amazes me how many will actually put out their hand for a gratuity when one goes merely for a morning visit! Or perhaps they do not do so to women? You will need pocket money when you attend card parties where you will suffer the occasional loss. You know the sort of thing I mean."

"You are suffocatingly generous," she said, her tone of voice revealing she was more than a trifle overpowered.

Tony was quiet for a moment, his simmering irritation with their situation in conflict with his need to help and reassure anyone he perceived to be in need. Then, gently, his better self winning, he said, "I do no more for you, Lily, than I would for any woman I might have wed. And I can do no less, can I? It is as much for me, for my honor, as for you that I am generous. If that is what you call it."

Libby felt as if humiliation after humiliation had been piled on her that day. Both her grandmother and Lady Sheffield had rung peels over her head, but both had ended by going beyond what one might have expected in order to ease her way. And now her husband was offering her riches beyond her comprehension.

Perhaps, she thought, *his lordship is wealthier than I thought. Perhaps I will not outrun the carpenter, as I have always done.*

But such thoughts flew out of her mind when Tony helped her from the town carriage and handed her up the two steps to the discreet entrance to Madame's shop. Libby had never before set foot inside the door marked by no more than a single name engraved on a simple brass sign screwed to the wall at one side. She had never thought to enter Madame's place of business where only the most wealthy and most discriminating were admitted.

Libby's heart beat faster at the thought of wearing a gown designed by Madame. The modiste was the last word in chic, a real Frenchwoman, unlike so many who put up their sign in London. Madame Colette was whispered to maintain contacts in France, although it was unclear exactly how she managed the trick. She whom Libby merely copied always had the latest news of what was fashionable. Not exact reproductions of designs from across the channel, of course! In fact, for the more modest Englishwoman, Colette was forced to modify them a great deal. For instance, it would never do for an Englishwoman to show her bosom to the degree the feminine members of the French haute monde did at present, and except for the most daring, an Englishwoman would never wear such diaphanous fabrics in public.

The one gown Madame disliked designing was a presentation gown. The modern mode of high waist, straight skirts and the lightest of fabrics did not adapt well to a court dress. When the waist was up under the bosom and the skirt, as required by protocol, draped over large hoops, a woman looked very much like a hand bell with a short handle! Madame did what she could by lowering the waist a trifle, which gave the gown slightly better proportions. Also she insisted the wearer be fitted for the narrowest hoops allowed. Still, in her eyes, the gowns were ugly, and she was never at her best when forced to accept an order for one.

Madame had heard the gossip, of course, and when informed that Lord and Lady Wendover awaited her presence, she bustled into the showroom already talking before she could be seen.

". . . and a riding habit. That goes without saying. Yes, my lord? My lady? Do you not agree?"

Libby looked toward Tony and found him grinning. "Madame, we cannot agree to what we did not hear. Unless you were saying that all my lovely wife requires is a new riding habit?"

Madame's eyes widened. And then she laughed. She flicked Tony with the end of the measurer that hung about her neck. "You! You will tease the great Colette? You are the one, are you not, my lord?"

"Actually not. My good woman, you must have begun talking to us before ever you left your workroom because all either of us heard was that last little bit about a riding habit."

"Ah! You do not tease. Then, if it is not the whole wardrobe to be bespoken, what is it you would ask of me?"

"A great deal, of course. You will make my bride look more a vision than ever. But first of all, as quickly as it may be completed, she requires a presentation gown. You sigh?"

"Ugly. There is nothing one can do. But necessary. One does one's poor best." Madame eyed Libby through narrowed eyes. She prowled all around her new patron, returned to face her, and stared into her eyes for a long moment. "Blue. I have just the blue." She snapped her fingers, and an apprentice came running. "The blue which I said would be difficult to sell. The silk we put on the highest shelf."

When it arrived, Tony fingered it. As he moved it, the bluish green stuff shimmered in the oddest fashion. "The finest silk," he said and unrolled a yard or two, flinging it over Libby's shoulder and laying it across her bodice—

Libby felt her heart race when he touched her there.

—but Tony merely nodded. Madame spoke a soft "Oh la!" and smiled, and the apprentice allowed a very small sigh of appreciation to pass her lips.

"I think it will do," said Tony.

"Is there a mirror?" asked Libby, hesitating. The color really was odd and, looking down at herself, she could not tell if it was becoming or not.

"Come!" Madame had already turned and was bustling off toward the door by which she had entered. "Into the fitting room where I may measure you."

"There is a cheval glass and you may see it there," whispered the girl. "Truly it is wonderful with your eyes."

"I will leave you now," said Tony. "And will leave the carriage for your use. One of Madame's servants will fetch it for you when you are ready to depart. Since you are here, you might as well order two or three evening gowns and several morning gowns to be going on with." He grinned a conspiratorial smile. "A large order will appease Madame's wounded sensibilities that she must make a presentation gown," he explained. "Do not forget the seed pearl decoration! She will approve that as well."

"Of course she will," muttered Libby, beginning to recover herself, "since it will cost a king's ransom to sew all those pearls onto that fine silk!"

"Yes, but well worth it. You will see."

Libby obeyed, but inside where no one could see she quaked at the money she spent that day and wondered if Tony could possibly have any notion just how much it cost to order so much from a modiste with Madame's reputation. For the first time in her life, Libby found she had not enjoyed laying down her blunt—as a man might say when spending his money!

It didn't occur to her to wonder why. . . .

Tony, meanwhile, strolled along Piccadilly and turned up St. James. He was hailed by one friend after another, joshed by this one, bammed by that, and teased by still another. He had expected it, of course, and did his best not to feel put upon or irritated. Still, it was not easy to maintain his normal sunny nature when everyone exercised his wit at Tony's expense. And it was more than a little difficult to suppress those simmering feelings of resentment toward Libby for putting him through such torture!

When he reached his club, it was worse.

Thus it was that he felt a great deal of relief when Merwin joined the group. "Wendover!" said Alex. "I've been looking for you. Do come along now and give me a hand." Merwin led the way outside and gestured to his carriage. Tony entered, and after Merwin gave orders to his driver, he followed Tony in. He grinned. "You, my friend, were looking a trifle harried."

"You saved me from making a fool of myself, Alex! I was very near to offering Jeremy lunch—made up from a bunch fives!" Tony shook his clenched fist in the air. "Blast him for his impertinence!"

"Jeremy?" Merwin's dark brows tilted to a rather satanic angle. "My dear Tony, I wonder who would have eaten *that* particular meal?" He cast Tony a quick mischievous look. "He is a very good boxer, you know."

"I know," said Tony, hunching his shoulders and sliding down in his seat. He shoved his hands into his pockets. "I never could pop a hit in over Jeremy's guard, could I?"

"A very good thing I arrived when I did, is it not?"

Tony tipped his head, staring at the toe of the boot propped on the seat opposite. "I think I might have enjoyed trying! The things he said!"

"But even when all is said and done, it would *never* do to start a mill in the middle of our club's reading room. Would you, instead, like to stop at Gentleman Jackson's for a little sparring?"

"Me? At Jackson's? Alex! You cannot have thought! I would totally ruin my reputation if I indulged myself in such a way."

Alex chuckled at Tony's wry humor and was pleased by the evidence that his friend was feeling more the thing.

"Since we are not going to Jackson's," Tony added, "where *are* we going?"

"Anywhere. Nowhere. Except that isn't true. I told my driver to take us the long way through the park, but I must leave you when we reach Downing Street. The minister wishes to see me, but my carriage and driver are at your command. You may drive on for so long as you wish. Right on to Land's End if you will."

"I believe that will be unnecessary, but, given this rain—" Tony glanced out at the sudden heavy fall. "—I will appreciate it if he takes me home. We are at the McMurrey town house, you know."

"Jack told me before he had to leave Town."

Tony nodded. "You must come to dinner some evening."

Alex sighed. "You are aware I never know my schedule. I dislike accepting invitations and then discovering that at the last moment, I must send regrets. Hostesses do not care to have their carefully arranged tables upset."

"That is never a difficulty for your friends. We understand the problem. Besides, I am only inviting you to take potluck with us."

"My friends understand," said Merwin dryly, "but what of Lady Wendover?"

"Do not be talking nonsense," said Tony just a trifle crossly. "I will explain, of course. I believe we've no evening plans for tomorrow evening or for the one following. Libby will wish to await the delivery of her new gowns before we attend the theater or any other entertainments."

"The day after tomorrow then. We will leave it that I'll come if I can."

When Libby returned to the house, Tony informed her that, if he were free, something one could not depend upon, Lord Merwin would join them for dinner and when.

Libby said nothing, merely nodding, but inside she felt the twinges of a gentle panic. *Lord Merwin.* He would sit at her table. Would join them for potluck, as Tony called it, but no! It must be ever so much more than that. Merwin, after all. The man she had meant to wed! The man who, even now, occupied her thoughts more often than she cared to admit.

Those very odd and exceedingly mobile eyebrows that slashed across Merwin's brow from temple to nose! They suited his narrow face, giving him the slightest of satanic looks, and she found them incredibly intriguing. Her heartbeat sped up. And then, feeling a touch of guilt, Libby excused herself with no more than a glance at her husband.

She went to her room and wrote a note to Beth, inviting her to dine the same evening Merwin was to come—in part because she wished to see her friend, but also to balance her table. Then she spent half an hour with her housekeeper who, often, had served Lord Merwin at the McMurreys' table. Libby found it impossible to believe that his lordship was satisfied with such simple fare as Mrs. Strong recommended. She insisted that several rather complicated removes be added to the menu before returning to her room to change for the evening meal. She had written to ask both her grandmother and Tony's great-aunt to dine, although she knew it would be a most difficult of evenings and she did not look forward to it.

Tony had praised her, however, for suggesting to each lady that they might wish to discuss their respective guest lists and other plans so that there would be no conflicts. "It was most tactful of you, my dear," he had said. "They will both wish to do well by us, but they will also be very slightly in competition, and will enjoy showing each other up in how well they manage."

The two elderly ladies arrived very nearly simultaneously. It was not a problem, however, since Higgens, the McMurreys' butler, had been warned and was prepared to send a footman armed with an umbrella to each lady's carriage. Neither was forced to wait or to endure the drizzle for the few steps to the house.

Libby, who had been ready a good twenty minutes early, felt far more frazzled and unhappy than she had for a very long time. She greeted her guests in proper formal manner and apologized for Tony's absence.

"I will add my own apologies, Lady Settle and Aunt Sheffield," offered Tony, who entered the salon just then. "I do not know why it is, but just when one most wishes to avoid delay, that is exactly when one's cravat refuses to cooperate. I do not know how many I ruined, and I am not yet satisfied." He moved to the mirror over the mantel and pretended to attend to a particularly obstreperous crease, but actually to surreptitiously observe the old ladies' reactions to his playacting. He was content to note that each glowered at him.

"Popinjay!" said Libby's grandmother.

"Whippersnapper," added Lady Sheffield, not to be outdone.

"You look perfect," said Libby, both because he did and because she was irritated by the elderly ladies' scolding tone.

Tony cast her a merry smile, and Libby flushed slightly, although why she did so she did not know.

Her grandmother nodded. "Very proper, Lillian. A wife should always support her husband."

"Bah," said Lady Sheffield, determinedly argumentative. "Tony has always played off the airs of an exquisite and always failed. No, Ellen, you know I have the right of it. Do you remember Lord Lighten? Now there was a man who knew how to dress."

"Styles change, Mary. Styles change. And just as well, I say. Men look like men these days and not painted dolls as they did in our era."

"Nonsense. Lighten was a man's man." Something that could only be called a reminiscent gleam appeared in Lady Sheffield's eye. "Oh, yes. I'll never forget—" Her roving eye happened to light on an absolutely fascinated Libby. "—but we need not go into that now. You, missy, are a sad romp if not worse," she continued in an overly stern voice. "You must not forget for even a moment to be on your very best behavior. One little bit more gossip, just a smidgeon—" She held up her finger and thumb with barely half an inch between them. "—and you, my girl, will find yourself banished from tonnish circles forever."

Even Libby realized that Lady Sheffield's severity was due to the fact she had very nearly been indiscreet about her own slightly shady past. "I will do my very best," said Libby soothingly. "I have never had any desire to become the talk of the town."

The thin line of Lady Sheffield's plucked eyebrows arched; but she forbore to say anything, and Libby's grandmother, hoping to avoid rousing her granddaughter's temper as Lady Sheffield was going on in exactly the right way to do, said, "I have brought my guest list. It is not so very long. My health no longer allows me to hold large entertainments." She opened her oversized reticule and pulled out a folded paper. "Or perhaps you would prefer to wait until after dinner for this discussion?"

"Dinner will not be served for another fifteen or twenty minutes," said Tony. "We've time." He offered sherry, which Lady Sheffield accepted but Lady Settle did not, and then the two gray-haired women put their elaborately coifed heads together and compared their lists. A name was crossed off one. Another name was added. Several names were added to the longer list.

Seeing that the elderly ladies were well occupied, Tony took Libby a glass of the light wine she preferred and, quietly, making a great joke of it, described to her the ribbing he had endured when at Brooks earlier that day. Retelling it, even he could perceive the humor, although he could not forget how angry he had been at the time.

Higgens announced dinner just as Lady Settle folded up her paper and put it away. Lady Sheffield looked up, frowned, and said, "It is about time. I am sharp set, I tell you. Exceedingly so. This is long after my dinner hour. I am unused to dining so late." She was already on her feet and stalking toward the door before Tony could rise and offer his arm. Instead he escorted Lady Settle with Libby on his other arm.

Once the first course was served Tony induced their guests to tell stories of their youth, and the rest of the evening passed off with one old lady doing her best to top the story her rival had just told! Libby even managed to forget for a time that, the next evening, Lord Merwin was coming to dine.

Except that he didn't.

Beth arrived early, and she and Libby had a comfortable coze that lasted until Higgens came in to announce dinner. Libby insisted the meal be put back, and then did so a second time, and still his lordship did not come. Tony was patient until Higgens opened the salon door and gave him one of those *looks*. "Libby," he said, "I warned you he might not come."

"But there has been no note! Surely he would send a note."

"If," said Tony gently, "he is closeted with several men arguing some important point relating to our foreign policy, which is what I think he told me was on this afternoon's agenda, it is unlikely he could get away long enough to do so."

"But how iniquitous. Have those other men no social duties? What of their wives? What of the invitations they must have accepted?"

Tony chuckled. "I see you've no notion of what political wives endure, my dear. Do let us go into dinner before Higgens is forced to report that our cook has taken himself off in a temper. We do not want to discommode the McMurreys by losing them their excellent cook!"

Reluctantly, Libby rose to her feet. She picked at the food so carefully designed to tempt Lord Merwin's palate. She had, actually, changed the menu twice after she first settled it. And now, moping and allowing Beth to entertain Tony, she could not believe her husband's assurances that this was a normal occurrence among political types. Merwin was such a gentleman, so polished in every way. Surely he could not act so boorishly!

But he had. And he behaved similarly on a second such occasion as well. Libby, still unconvinced a gentleman could act so discourteously, concluded Merwin had guessed he himself had been her quarry the night she had slipped into the corner room at the Weatherbees' and that he avoided her for that reason. It hurt but was, she decided, no more than she deserved.

Her new gowns arrived in time for her grandmother's dinner party. Lord and Lady Wendover stood in a formal reception line as directed by Lady Settle, accepting congratulations and best wishes and pretending not to hear the whispered comments floating back to them as one couple after another continued on into the sitting room. Later, thankfully, she and Tony, along with the other guests, left at an early hour—although Libby could not be thankful her reprieve was due to her grandmother's fragile health.

The newlyweds continued on to Covent Garden where they put in a late appearance at the theater. Lady Settle, along with others from her generation, might bemoan the theater lost to fire in 1808 and claim the new chandeliers, hung from hooks extending out from the boxes, made it impossible to view the stage in comfort, but Libby thought the new theater elegant past saying.

"Do not look around," warned Tony. "The whole world is here tonight, and everyone wants a glimpse of us. We would do well to pretend we do not notice."

A number of Tony's friends arrived at their box during the last interval, demanding introductions to Libby. A few were men with whom she had danced in previous Seasons. None seemed to remember her, and she wondered if it was a pretense or if she was truly so unremarkable. But the notion she was nothing special was contradicted by the compliments she received which would have been more than enough to turn her head if she had not been such a sensible young woman. Instead of enduring in silence the most fulsome and extravagant of these, she gave each man such a speaking look he broke off in confusion—except for one young gentleman who merely grinned and redoubled his efforts to put her out of countenance.

The interval ended and, wishing to avoid more of the same, she suggested they leave before the end of the farce. Facing her grandmother's disapproving friends had been draining. She had hoped for a relaxing finish to the evening when Tony suggested they go on to the play, but it was, if anything, worse. At her grandmother's she could counter comments and complaints, but, at the theater the staring crowd was beyond reach of her quick tongue, and she was forced to bear the scrutiny with all the equanimity she could manage.

Lady Sheffield's soiree was, to her surprise, far more easily endured. The guests arrived in a stream and, once the reception line was dissolved, Lady Sheffield kept Libby by her side, introducing her again where necessary and producing such a constant flow of conversation it was impossible for anyone to make the sort of sly comment with which the more vicious wished to attempt to overset the young bride.

The following weeks brought a gradual easing of the quizzing and, because she would not rise to the bait, Tony's male acquaintances soon ceased to tease her. Finally, toward its end, she actually began to enjoy the Season. Not least in aiding such enjoyment was having, for the first time, a wardrobe full of delightful gowns and no need to turn them to hide worn spots or to attempt to change their looks by changing the lace and ribbons or adding an overskirt or some such thing.

And then, too, Tony was careful to escort her of an evening, making it far easier to face the Ton. He only very occasionally left her at some entertainment and only if assured she had a way home so that he could, with unworried conscience, continue on to his club.

He never left early when it was a ball. Tony enjoyed dancing. He willingly admitted he particularly enjoyed dancing with his wife. Furthermore, at those few parties where a particularly daring hostess ordered it, Libby would dance the waltz with no one else! They were very near to making of themselves a second scandal by the number of times they would dance together of an evening.

And then, with the Prince's birthday and the end of the Season only a week away, a letter arrived for Lord Wendover telling that the McMurreys' babe, born very nearly a month later than expected, had finally arrived. Mother and child were doing well, although, if one could believe his letter, Ian was worn to a thread. It concluded by giving the christening date and was written in such a manner that it simply assumed that Tony would trek north to attend it as one of the babe's multitude of sponsors.

Tony, Libby realized, assumed the same thing!

"Perhaps," he said while tapping the folded letter against his chin, "since it is so late in the Season, I will take you to our estate and you can stay with my parents while I attend to this business." Tony brushed the stiff paper back and forth across his other fingers. "I must talk to Merwin at once. And Princeton. And we must contact Renwick. I wonder if Seward is anywhere near," he mused, "so that he may be informed! He will not wish to miss this. In fact, perhaps he could take us north. Travel by water would surely be easier on Renwick than going by land where he must get in and out of carriages and stay at strange inns." He spoke as if to himself and suddenly looked up. "If you will excuse me, Libby, I must find Merwin before he becomes so involved in political business that there is no coming at him until the day is over!"

On those words, Tony rose to his feet and left the breakfast table.

Seven

Tony gave Libby no time to object even if she wished to do so. Which she did. Vociferously.

Oh, not about his going north. That was a very proper desire on his part, but the thought of staying with his parents while he traipsed off elsewhere was so daunting she balanced between fear and anger and, with Tony gone, had no outlet for her emotions. She stalked off to the library where she paced back and forth and could settle to nothing. Not even the latest papers tempted her, newly ironed and neatly folded and put out on the library table.

The library was the room in which Libby and Tony spent most of their private time when at home. Not that there was much of that, but it was a wonderfully relaxing room, and they both enjoyed reading. The various papers and periodicals—social, literary, and financial—were kept there, and Libby usually managed to find time each day to peruse them. She had approached her solicitor—her grandmother's really—asking that he invest for her the bits and pieces of money she scraped from her allowance and the winnings she took home from card parties. She was not surprised that he was astounded she wished to do such a thing. She was merely glad he followed her instructions without making a song and dance about it. She did wonder if he was surprised her investment was doing well!

But today she didn't care a rush about checking it or about news of the arrival of various ships or rumors of new mining projects or offers of partnerships in new manufactories, which usually she studied and sighed and wished she were wealthy so she would have money to invest. Today she was too upset to care.

Therefore, she was relieved when Beth arrived a mere half an hour after she began her pacing. It was always safe to vent her irritation, her fears, to Beth.

"How dare he, Beth?" she asked once they were private in the lady's parlor across the hall from the library. Higgens, after serving tea, had departed, and there was little or no danger of interruption.

"So I was right! I'd a notion you were agitated almost beyond bearing!" Beth set down her cup and saucer and turned back to Libby. "And now, my dear, you must start at the beginning and go on to the end, and then perhaps, when I know what it is, I can answer your question! Who has dared? And what is it he has dared?"

Libby chuckled. "Oh, you! You always make me laugh. Even when I do not wish to. It is Tony. He means to set off for Scotland to visit the McMurreys, and he intends to leave me with his parents! Beth, I am frightened out of my wits by the very thought. How could he be so cruel?"

"You would *prefer* to go north with him?" Beth's eyes widened. "All the way to *Scotland!*"

Libby swallowed. "It would be a difficult journey, would it not? And you, better than most, know I do not love to travel. But *yes*. If the alternative is that I stay with his parents, I will travel all the way to John O'Groats! Beth, they *must* hate me. How can it be otherwise?"

"You had a lovely note from his mother. You showed it to me."

"Doing the pretty, of course. She could do no other if

she has any heart at all. Her son's wife! Beth, she was forced to put a good face on our marriage."

"Have you heard nothing since?"

"Oh, yes. Polite little notes enclosed in letters she sends Tony. His letters are full of news about the various people on their estate and how she and his father go on and how the garden grows. Country stuff. Although he reads them avidly, I cannot believe they truly interest him. All that meandering on about rural people and country doings. Tony is too much the town animal to care for such stuff!"

"Do you think so? Myself, I do not think he is above being pleased wherever he finds himself, and if he grew up with those people, then he may very well like hearing how they go on."

Libby sighed. "Beth, in your gentle fashion you are surprisingly good at making me ashamed of myself! My own experience of living in the country was so very uncomfortable that I suppose I tend to think it true of others as well. Father wrung every shilling he could from the land, and only under the most severe need did he put anything back into it or give so much as good wishes toward helping his tenants. He did not encourage me to play lady bountiful either. In fact, the reverse. So you see, even though I've heard of such things, I've no experience of an estate on which the tenants are considered very much a part of the family. Our neighbors were always kind to me, of course, not blaming me for my father's idiocy, and I enjoyed country entertainments, but still . . ."

When Libby didn't continue, Beth asked, "Have you mentioned to Lord Wendover that you do not wish to go to Lord and Lady Hendred without him?"

"Mentioned it to him! Beth, I'd no opportunity to say a word. He slipped that news in in the middle of his planning, out loud, who would go and how they would travel north. He has gone off to consult with Merwin and

Princeton, mentioned someone named Seward who evidently owns a yacht, and a man who might be more comfortable traveling by sea than by land." Libby sighed again.

"That last, I suppose, would be Lord Renwick."

Libby gave Beth a quick glance. "That was the name mentioned. What do you know of him?"

Beth grinned, a quirky smile that had her eyes twinkling. "Only that he is blind and has a tiger for a pet. Oh, yes. Truly. He is guardian to an eastern prince whose life he saved when in India."

"Elizabeth Catherine Browne, how do you know all that?"

Beth shrugged. "I listen. You were too preoccupied with your wedding to do so, but I overheard Lady Princeton discussing Lord Wendover's friends with another lady. She was explaining why Lord and Lady Renwick were unlikely to attend your wedding. They live year-round at Renwick Towers just north of Lewes. Only the estate is called Tiger's Lair by almost everybody. Because of his tiger, you see."

"That must be nonsense. Who would dare have a tiger for a pet?"

"I only know what I overheard. Since I was not part of the conversation, I could hardly ask, now could I? *You* might, however. The next time you see Lady Princeton."

"The Princetons are out of Town. Tony told me they were forced to visit an ailing relative when they had wanted to be in London to support us. Support him," she amended.

"*Were* out of town. I saw her ladyship only this morning as I came up Piccadilly."

At just that very moment Higgens knocked and, when told to enter, announced Lady Princeton.

"My lady," said Libby, rising. "We had just mentioned

you. Beth saw you this morning walking along Piccadilly."

"Yes, I'd a few errands to run for Eustacia, Lady Renwick. She cannot come up to London very often, so her friends do what they can for her. I came to tell you that Jack and I are sorry we were not here to support you and Tony when you first entered the Ton. Now that we've returned, I planned to hold a soiree in your honor, but the good news from Scotland will have changed everyone's plans. Jack went off immediately after he read Ian's letter to find Alex. I presume Tony did the same?"

"He didn't even give me an opportunity to comment!"

Lady Princeton chuckled. "Very much like Jack! I thought perhaps I might search for a christening present this morning and wondered if you would like to join me in that important endeavor. It must be something very special. It is, after all, for the first child to be born to one of the Six."

"They are a very closely knit group of friends, are they not?" asked Beth a trifle shyly.

"Very," said Lady Princeton, her voice dry as dust. "When one marries within their circle, one finds one is instantly surrounded by friends and that one has obligations one could never have predicted. One might not find oneself *quite* so surprised, except that very often they forget that one has not always been with them and one is at a loss to understand something they take for granted!"

"I don't understand," said Libby, making of it a question.

"For instance, they will each and every one treat your home as if it were their own. They will come and go and never wonder if it is convenient. They support each other and will go to any length to do so. They do the same for their wives, who are fast turning the Six into the Twelve!"

Not this wife, thought Libby. She said in a colorless

tone, hoping she would not reveal her fear, "Tony, as he left, made the suggestion that I should go to his parents while he is in Scotland."

Perhaps it was that very lack of emotion that gave her away because Lady Princeton said, "You will love Lady Hendred. Everyone does. Tony's mother is a wonderful woman. She will take you to her heart and smother you with kindness. Her generosity is proverbial. And she and her husband are so ideally suited it is astonishing. I think everyone who meets them must hope that they, too, may someday have such a marriage!"

"Then, Tony would have grown up assuming it was what he would have," said Beth slowly. Then she shot a quick glance toward Libby, who blushed rosily.

"Tony," said Lady Princeton slowly, "appears quite happy with his bride." She had not quite believed the reports she had received while she and Jack were away from Town but was older than Libby and far better at hiding her emotions.

"Oh, yes, of course he is," agreed Beth—but she had never been able to lie with aplomb, and it was obvious that she didn't quite believe it.

Lady Princeton cast her a narrow-eyed look but made no comment. She turned to Libby. "Will the two of you come with me, then? Shopping always diverts one's mind from other things."

From one's problems, thought Libby. She struggled to repress the sigh that rose to color the notion. "Beth? Would you enjoy helping us find just the right gifts for the infant?"

"You know I would." Beth rose to her feet with alacrity, and Libby went to ring the bell. She asked the footman to see that Finch was sent to her room, ordered fresh tea brought for her guests, and hurried upstairs to change for their excursion.

Beth, realizing she had been precipitate in expecting

to leave immediately, cast Lady Princeton a wary glance and reseated herself. She feared she was to suffer a polite catechism while Libby was absent, and she did not expect to enjoy it!

All was arranged in a surprisingly short space of time. Miles Seward did happen to be where he could be contacted; the Renwicks, including Sahib, the tiger, boarded his ship in Newhaven on the coast just south of Tiger's Lair, and then the others were taken up from a London mooring. The others included Libby. Lady Princeton had talked to Jack, who spoke to Tony, who returned home and discussed the situation with Libby.

"It did not cross my mind you would care to travel north with me," he had said.

"I will not do so if you do not wish it," Libby had replied quickly.

"I have no wishes either way. It will be as *you* wish."

Libby wavered between her fear of visiting Tony's parents without his support and her fear of sailing. Or rather, her fear she would find she was a poor sailor. "I would go to Scotland," she decided. After all, she knew she would find a visit to Hendred Manor difficult. There was the possibility she would make a good sailor!

And she did.

On board she met Sahib for the first time. The big cat took to shipboard living as if he had been born on one. He also revealed more than a little curiosity about the new addition to the Renwicks' circle.

One morning Tony stood near the forward cabin and watched Sahib stalk his wife, who stood, both hands clutching the rail, staring out over the water. Sahib took another silent, slinky step toward Libby. Another. Tony frowned, wondering if he should interfere. . . .

Libby turned. "Oh!" Her hand went to her breast. "Sahib!"

The cat instantly flopped onto his stomach and stretched out. His long tail flipped once this way, once that. . . .

Libby grinned. The grin faded, and Sahib rose to approach more nearly, staring up at her. "You are beautiful, Sahib, but a trifle frightening, do you not agree?"

Sahib produced that strange noise she had been assured was the same as a purr in a cat. He butted her gently with his head.

Libby smiled again. Very tentatively she put her hand on the big cat's head. After a moment she sighed. Sahib bounced her hand slightly, and she looked down. "Life is difficult sometimes, is it not, Sahib?"

The cat moved still nearer and, gently, leaned into Libby. Libby lowered herself to the deck and hugged the huge tiger. A tear escaped and ran down her cheek.

Tony, seeing the glint of sunlight running down her cheek, gulped. For half a moment he wanted to go to her, comfort her—and then, his jaw hardening, he turned away. It was only fair. She *deserved* to be unhappy.

Didn't she?

That evening, when all, including Sahib, lounged on the deck, Libby heard about one of the Renwicks' guests who had not learned to like Sahib. She had fainted with great regularity during the whole of last Christmas's house party!

At least I didn't do that, thought Libby as she listened to the others talk.

"The woman was a ninny," said Jack, continuing the conversation.

"Unkind," said his wife.

"You felt the same way!"

"Unkind in you to remind me!" Patricia laughed and, briefly, touched her forehead to her husband's shoulder.

Libby loved hearing the others banter in such light-hearted fashion, but never felt a part of it all. Very occasionally she even allowed herself to feel wistfully jealous, although she was exceedingly careful to do so when no one was about to observe it!

On the other hand, she found she enjoyed sailing excessively. In fact, she enjoyed it so much she was reluctant to leave ship when they moored in Edinburgh waters where they took to carriages for the remainder of the journey. Lord Renwick had had his own carriage sent north to make proper provision for Sahib's transport. It was a large traveling coach from which the forward seat had been removed and replaced by a special bed on which the great tiger lay. When Lord and Lady Renwick traveled, it was not uncommon for a person, seeing the cat staring out the side window, to wonder if he had, perhaps, had a trifle more to drink than he ought. Or if he had not been drinking, then perhaps he had fallen prone to hallucinations!

They arrived at the McMurreys' huge, rambling old home, more fortress than house, just as evening approached. Ian and Lady Serena, their babe in her arms, stood in the opening where the massive door had been flung open. Lady Princeton shooed Serena inside. "You do not wish to give the babe a chill, do you?" she scolded.

Serena laughed. "Good heavens, Patricia! The child is a Scotsman. Do you think I would dare coddle him in any way? Do come in. And you. You must be Lady Wendover! I am so glad you could come. Ah! Eustacia. You should not have made the effort!"

Lady Renwick, obviously in the family way, just laughed. "Do you truly believe I would miss the first christening among the Six?" She smiled mischievously. "On the other hand, if we had not had Miles to sail us north, very likely neither of us would have managed the journey!"

Libby did her best not to feel left out. The other women knew each other so well, were so comfortable together, they tended, without meaning to, to forget her existence. And why should they not? They had, all three of them, marriages full of love, or so Tony told her when he had described his friends. Tony had not reproached her, although she was certain he wanted to, and Libby could not help but blame herself. It was so obvious that Tony had wished a similar marriage.

Actually, it might be easier for her to bear if he *would* scold her. She sighed softly but not so softly that Lady Princeton did not hear.

"Ah! How we run on. Libby, dear, how inconsiderate we are, ignoring you while we prattle on and on about nothing at all. Worst of all, you've yet to be properly introduced to Serena!" Patricia made the introduction in formal fashion and then explained to Libby that they were in the habit of using given names and that she must become accustomed to such informality immediately, since no one could be bothered with ceremony when the Six were gathered together.

"Please call me Libby, then. I have never cared for Lillian." Hesitating only an instant, she continued in a rush. "May I see the baby?"

Lady Serena laughed. "You may hold him if you wish. Such a lump he is and cares not who has him in hand— just so long as *someone* will hold him."

Libby was enthralled by the tiny bundle and cuddled him close. The babe opened his eyes and stared up at her. She smiled, touched his cheek, and began singing softly, an old lullaby her Welsh nanny had sung to her and then to her brother.

The men entered just then, and Tony stopped in the middle of what he was saying, his eyes glued to his wife.

It had never occurred to him that Libby would like children, but if he could believe the evidence before his eyes, she not only cared *about* them, she knew how to care *for* them! Tony, an only child, had always hoped to have a large family. It was another thing he had put aside as impossible when he found himself forced to wed Libby.

But if she were to wish the same . . .

"Hmm?" he asked, startled from his thoughts when Merwin poked him. "Did I miss something?"

"Only that we are to be presented to our godson! Come along. Don't stand like a stone!"

Tony flushed, but the red faded as they crossed the room to join the others. He approached his wife with caution, unsure of how she truly felt about the infant in her arms. She looked up and met his gaze, her eyes shining.

"A miracle," he said softly.

"Yes." Her smile faded slightly as she looked back down. "A blessing. A new beginning."

"I was unaware you liked children," he said.

"Always. I cared for my brother as much as Nurse would allow. Willie grew to be too much a handful for her when he began running about, and I would follow to see he didn't get into too much mischief. We had wonderful adventures together," she finished just a trifle wistfully.

Ian, overhearing, asked how much younger her brother was.

"There are very nearly eight years between us," she responded, her finger once again touching the baby's soft cheek. "How very small they are to begin with," she mused.

"They grow quickly at this age," said Ian, smiling down at his son. The babe opened his eyes and moved them around. His gaze settled on his father and stayed there.

"He knows you already," said Tony, wonderingly.

The babe squirmed and Ian reached for him. "I believe

he does. Serena," he added, "our son, as politely as he knows how, is suggesting he needs attention!"

Lady Serena came at once, removed the babe from his father's arms and, excusing herself, left the room. Lady Renwick, after only a moment's hesitation, followed. She was almost certain Serena meant to nurse the child, and she wished to learn from her in preparation for her own baby who would be born in only a few more months.

Ian cast a wistful glance in their wake, but, reluctantly, remained with his guests, doing his duty as host rather than going off to enjoy the still novel experience of watching his son indulge in an afternoon meal. Tony, observing his friend's feelings and interpreting them correctly, wondered if he himself would ever have the opportunity to feel that way. After all, there was more involved than merely *wishing* he had a son. Or daughter.

Tony, with a great deal of self-control, had stayed away from his wife's bed.

Libby left her and Tony's suite early the next morning and, with permission from Lady Serena, went off to explore the meandering corridors with unexpected steps up here and down there, and odd nooks and crannies where least expected. The walls completely enclosed three courtyards in all of which a gardener with magical hands had worked wonders. Libby caught a glimpse of them now and again and wondered how one achieved entry to them. And, here and there, she opened a door to look into a room.

She was toward the back of the house when she chose to open still another door. The long, low-ceilinged room was cluttered with a great deal of heavy old-fashioned furniture, but at its far end were three large modern windows, each of which framed one of the most impressive views she had ever seen. A gentle rise beyond the house grew steeper and steeper until one's eyes rose to the purple-covered heights of range after range of hills. Libby stepped into the room, her gaze never leaving the windows.

"Herrre now," exclaimed a cross voice from near the oversized fireplace. Rolling his *r*s, the man continued, "Don't you darrre to leave that door open!"

Libby threw a startled glance toward the voice. "Oh! Sir! I am so sorry. I didn't know anyone was here."

"And wherrre else would I be? Where am I always? Where do I live out the unendurable days of my life?"

The voice growled out the phrases like a litany, and Libby took a better look at the old gentleman who, wrapped in an ancient plaid, lounged in an almost equally ancient leather-covered chair.

When she didn't speak, he asked, "So? Which one be ye? Not that soldier's wife. He wouldn't be fool enough to wed an unfledged flibbertigibbet like you. Nor would that blind fellow. He, too, was once a soldier. Merwin and the sailor ain't wed, so you must be the man milliner's wife. That's who you are!"

"Don't you dare insult my husband! He is a nonpareil, an arbiter of social intricacies, and a wonderfully kind man who does not deserve your snide tongue!"

"Hoity-toity! You watch *your* fine tongue, lassie. I could have you thrown to the dogs and no one would dare to say a word against it."

Libby eyed him. "Why do I doubt that?"

The old man stared up from under shaggy brows. The moment hung in the balance, and then he grinned a mostly toothless grin. "Got spirit, do you? I like spirit in a woman."

"Then, you must love Lady Serena," said Libby.

The grin faded. "Bah. Nothing but trouble, that one. Nag nag nag."

"If she nags you to join the party, which you have not done or I'd have met you, then I will tell her I support her.

You know very well you need not live out a miserable life here in your lair. You've a brand-new wonderful child to watch grow, and you might even find life need not be all that miserable."

"You know nothing about it," growled the old man.

"I know that brooding and feeding your misery only makes it worse."

"A bairn like you. You dare to tell me about life and living? You are barely out of the egg."

Libby turned her eyes to stare out those wonderful windows. Involuntarily she took a step nearer and then, recalling herself, turned back to the man. "I may not have lived so very many years," she said quietly, "but it is long enough to know what misery another can cause those they never in the world would harm if they only stopped to think."

The shaggy brows rose and then fell to half cover the sunken eyes. "Bah. You don't have the first notion of misery."

"I know my father's behavior led me into doing evil. I know my mother's death, which she could not help, led to my father's ridiculous behavior. I know that my behavior has led to misery in one I admire and that I should not have done what I did. I know there is little or nothing I can do to change things, but I will," she finished, standing straighter, "do all I can to alleviate the damage I did."

"So?" sneered the ancient. "What did you do? Manage to forget you promised some lad a dance so you could go off with another better suited to your taste?"

"Nothing so simple. I compromised a man and he married me. Much against his will he married me, and yet he treats me politely. Even with kindness."

"Ah! So that story was true, was it? You married the one man among the Six who thought he was guaranteed a love match?" A burst of ragged laughter issued from the man's barrel chest. A bony finger pointed at Libby, shaking slightly as the chuckles shook the old form. "Nemesis, that's you, lassie! Nemesis!"

Libby's skin got that prickly feeling leading to a swoon. "You mustn't say such a thing! I will not believe the fates could be so cruel to someone so generous!" She reached for the chair to her side and, taking care, seated herself.

"Herrre now!"

There was alarm in the old voice, and faintly, Libby heard the brassy clank of a hard-rung handbell.

"No, you dolt! Not me. Her. That one. See she doesn't fall on her nose in a faint." He continued in a mutter, but Libby was recovering from shock and heard it. "Namby-pamby miss. Pass out for no reason whatsoever. Ah! Ian, do something. My man there wouldn't know what to do if it were written out and read to him!"

"No, no," said Libby. "I am all right."

Ian had only that moment entered the room. He turned, surprised to see Libby seated in one of the large, ornately carved, age-blackened chairs that sat either side of his father's door. "Lady Wendover. What has happened? What has my father done?"

"Didn't do a thing," growled the McMurrey, for that was who the old man was.

"He didn't. Truly he didn't," said Libby, hurriedly, her eyes on Ian. She turned back and curtseyed to Ian's father. "And, sir? You will join us for dinner later, will you not? I would like it very much if you did."

"You would, would you? Ha!" He peered at her from under his brows. "Well, well, we will see."

Libby curtseyed again, then turned to look at Ian, who was standing, solid, silent, and secretly disbelieving, staring down at her. She curtseyed to him, too, and looked toward the door. Ian opened it for her and she fled. Farther down the hall, when she again opened a door, she gave the room a quick searching look to ascertain that she was alone and, finding it empty of other people, entered.

The windows here had not been modernized, but they, too, looked toward the hills. Libby went to the window seat where she curled up to think over the argument she had had with the old man. For half a moment she felt guilty that she had dared speak so to such a venerable figure. But then she recalled how nasty, how snide, he was about Tony, and her spine stiffened.

Man milliner, indeed! How dare he! As if he knows anything about the effort that goes into being an authority on style and dress or having the savoir-faire to know, always, the exactly right thing to do or say in any situation. Tony is a very special man, and the McMurrey has no right to denigrate him!

Her thoughts continued in that vein for some time. In fact, it was only the shadows on the hills that cued her to the fact that if she did not go up to her room immediately, she would not be ready for dinner which, here in the north, was served in the old-fashioned way, both early and without footmen carrying around the plates.

Ian, meanwhile, moved across the room to stare down at his father. "Will you join us for dinner?" he asked quietly.

McMurrey scowled. "Said I'd think on it."

"Please do."

"I *said* I'd think on it." His scowl deepened. "Why are you herrre? Chasing off that minx of a lass! Have to come to dinner to have another touch at her!"

At that Ian scowled. "You would spoil her dinner?"

"Hah! Not that one. That one will always give as good as she gets. She'd do up my appetite a fine trrreat, that one!"

Ian's lips compressed. He would very much like to see his father leave this room and join the company, but he would be very unhappy, indeed, if the old man managed to spoil everyone's appetite but his own! Hopes of moving the man won. "Very well. I will see your place is readied for you."

The McMurrey straightened at that, lifting his head with effort. "Herrre now! None of that! You'll serve like you always do or I'll not set foot out of this room! Can you not just see me spilling a plateful of food in that little lady's lap? She'd neverrr speak to me again!"

Ian chuckled at the picture his father's words drew. "Then, I will take the foot of the table from which I may serve so that you will have your proper place at the head. And, since that will require that my Serena form a new seating plan instantly, I must leave you."

"Why'd you come?"

Ian paused, his hand on the door. "I wished to ask your advice about the old well up in the hills on the east property. It isn't producing as it should."

"It never does when the rains are scant and come early."

"Then, in the years since I've been managing the estate, the rains have always been good?"

"Think back, lack-wit! This year, the last real rain was last autumn. No snow to speak of, either. It has been a very odd year."

"So it has." Ian ignored the insult, as he did all such nonsense from his irascible father. "Very well, the problem will be solved if we open the high pasture into the low so that the sheep may reach the stream there. I will come to escort you to dinner later."

"Old Filbert will see me in. If I come," added the McMurrey in a threatening tone.

For Libby, the days passed more pleasantly after her initial confrontation with the old man. He came to dinner that evening and, the next day, ordered her to his room.

They avoided further talk of a personal nature, more due to Libby's asking the McMurrey about the old days in Scotland than to any desire on his part to avoid controversy, but the telling of tales so pleased him he actually became very nearly jovial on more than one occasion.

As a result, Ian and Lady Serena became Libby's wholehearted supporters. Anyone who could bring Ian's father from his shell and back into the world was, to their mind, worth their weight in gold! After only a little discussion between them, they went, together, to ask Libby if she would be a godmother to the infant.

Libby, utterly astonished, stared at them with her mouth agape. "But . . ."

Ian chuckled the rumbling chuckle that seemed to come from so deep inside him. "Do you feel you are too new to the Six? But I have watched you with my son, and if something were to happen to Serena and myself—"

"May the good Lord forbid!" muttered the babe's nurse, who stood by.

"—a woman with your love of children would be just the proper sort to care for our bairn, would she not?"

"I would be pleased and proud to be trusted with such a role," said Libby after swallowing a lump in her throat. She excused herself and went directly to the McMurrey and asked if he had had a hand in giving her the honor.

"Nae! Might, mind you, if I'd thought of it, of course."

Libby felt tears well up and fought them back.

"Oh, aye, the lad would need a proper feisty woman if the worst happened." He peered up at her through his shaggy brows. "Service is tomorrow."

"I know."

"Service won't last long." He sighed. "And then you'll be taking yourself off, and there will be no one with whom I can fight."

Knowing that for a tale, Libby suppressed a smile: the old man fought with everyone! Instead she said, "We leave the following day. Miles Seward does not feel he can take more time from what I've come to believe is a self-imposed duty."

"The worst sort of duty, that. Impossible to rationalize procrastinating if you are making yourself do it. Hate to admit it, but I'll miss you, lass."

"I would appreciate it," said Libby, "if you would do something for me."

"Hmm? Me?" The McMurrey straightened as much as his bent back allowed. "What can an old and useless man do for a wild young minx like you?"

"You can watch over your grandson for me. You can write me and tell me how he goes on, how well he learns, or when he is ill and when he thrives. It will be our secret, and no one need know how I know when he has done something special, know when he is happy or sad, when he is well or ill. You will write me, and I will write my godson to congratulate him or to chide him gently or to send him appropriate little gifts. Will you do that for me?"

The McMurrey glared at the girl watching him with troubled eyes.

"I will be so far away," she said softly. "The boy will not know me. But he will have a sense of me if he grows up hearing from me in the way he needs to hear and when he needs to hear. Do you see? It is what I did for my brother, but, until he went to school, Willie was *there* where I could see him, could know what he needed and when. Please help me."

Grumbling and mumbling about how everyone wanted something and how there was never any peace in the world and how it would be a terrible nuisance, ". . . but I'll do it," finished the old man.

Libby went to him, hugged him, and dropped a kiss on his thinning hair. "Thank you," she said and returned to her chair.

Ian had entered the room silently somewhat earlier in

their conversation. Now, seeing how moved his father was, he left just as quietly. He would return when Libby was no longer with the McMurrey. Returning to the main part of the house, Ian looked for Tony and discovered him at the old-fashioned clavichord picking out the notes to "Green Sleeves."

"Tony," he said, interrupting, "if I didn't have a woman I dearly love, I think I'd envy you yours."

Tony's hands produced a discord so ugly his face screwed up from the pain of it. He turned on the chair, his arm resting along the top of it. "You would what?"

"Envy you." Ian described the scene between his father and Libby. "She is a very caring soul, I think. Not only has she come up with a means of staying in touch with my son, but has, at the same time, introduced a means of drawing my father out of himself and back to us. You know, until he spoke of it to her, I was unaware he felt old and useless. I must see what I can do to change that."

"You'd no choice but to take over when he withdrew."

"You mean when he became such a sot after Mother died! Yes, but he stopped drinking a long time ago. Perhaps I was having too much fun running things to want to see that I should turn the management of everything back to him."

"Will you? Now?"

Ian bit his lip, his heavy brows drawing together into a frown. "I must get him more involved in estate business, I think, but not in the investment end of things. I've done so much, changing them about and back and forth, until I could never explain exactly what I've done. And I rather doubt he will wish to know. He was never interested in investment—except for the fact it was proof of the growth of the family's wealth! But this is not what I wished to discuss. Tony, are you still so very bitter about your marriage?"

Tony shrugged. "I wanted a love match. You know I always said I'd not wed for any other reason!"

"But you have wed. And the woman you've married is not the featherheaded minx we expected. Nor is she scheming, selfish, and self-centered, which was also what we expected. Can you tell me why she did what she did?"

"For her brother's sake. In part. She admits she feared poverty for her own sake as well. Her father's done his best to ruin the family, you see."

"Tony, I don't want to be a busybody pushing my nose in where it is not wanted, but I wonder if it has occurred to you just how well matched the two of you are."

Tony's mouth compressed, and sadness filled his expression. "Well matched? She dances well and I never need blush for her style." He shrugged. "If it had to happen, then I suppose I am lucky she is neither a dowdy woman nor socially awkward."

"She is also a thoughtful, caring woman. Look deeper, Tony!" Ian nodded to emphasize his suggestion, and excused himself.

Tony turned back to the clavichord and continued picking away at notes and chords, gradually teaching himself to play the ancient song on the unfamiliar instrument. And doing his very best to put from his mind the things Ian had said about Libby.

If he could not have love, the rest was nothing. And how could there be love in a marriage such as theirs?

Eight

There was a good following wind for the return journey to London, and they arrived even more quickly than expected. Then, quite suddenly it seemed, it was the Prince's official birthday, and the Season ended. Libby had spent feverish days crowding in every entertainment she could manage before she must pack and go with Tony to the Hendred estate. Whenever she thought of meeting Tony's parents she panicked. Assurances from Lady Princeton that she would *like* Lady Hendred did nothing to ease her fears, for she knew, deep down inside, that both Tony's mother and his father must despise her. How could it be otherwise?

It was with heavy heart that she entered the traveling carriage for the journey, but even the longest day eventually ends and finally, the carriage pulled up just beyond the Hendred gatehouse. The groom put down the steps for Tony, who climbed down. He turned to peer up at Libby. "Gus will drive you on up to the house," he said in very slightly clipped tones. "I'll be up shortly."

It took Libby a moment to comprehend what he meant. "Tony!" She was too late. The door had closed and the carriage was in motion. Libby lowered the glass covering the window and, her hand on the ledge, watched her husband.

Tony walked rapidly toward a copse nestled against the

honey-colored walls surrounding the Hendred acres. Walls built long ago from the ubiquitous Cotswold stone. A chimney and a gently wafting strand of smoke could be seen beyond the trees. She stared until the carriage rounded a curve and she could no longer see him.

Who, she wondered, *lives there. . . . Someone Tony loves a great deal. . . .* "More than he'll ever love me," Libby muttered and was saddened by the thought.

She sighed. It had not been the most pleasant of journeys. Tony had been preoccupied and uncommunicative. Libby had fretted about meeting her new relatives, but was relieved that her husband would be with her when she did so. And now that the moment was upon her, *he* disappeared, and the situation she had avoided by going to Scotland would occur.

She must, after all, go alone to meet his parents.

"How dare he?" she muttered. But incipient anger dissolved into anxiety, and biting her lips, she turned her eyes forward. Unfortunately, she stared out the wrong window and missed the first possible view of the house. The coachman, a more sensitive man than his colleagues would have guessed, had slowed for a moment so that she would have a longer look. But once beyond the vista provided by a cut through a wooded area, he flicked the reins, urging the team back up to speed.

Libby, having no notion as to why he had pulled the horses to a walk, settled back into her seat and felt very nearly as low as at any time since receiving her father's letter. His *last* letter! He had not sent her so much as a note in response to her communication telling him of her marriage. She sighed again, softly. It was all of a piece, was it not? He simply did not care enough to make the effort. He thought of nothing but mad schemes to make his fortune.

The carriage moved into another curve and, for the first time, she saw her husband's home. The lowering sun shone along the south-facing façade. For a moment, when the light struck them just right, the windows glowed a fiery gold, and the mellow Cotswold stone appeared warm and welcoming. Or it might have done if Libby had been in a mood to see it that way. Instead of taking advantage of the view, her gaze settled upon what seemed dozens of people gathered, obviously, for no other purpose than to meet her.

Even though, when sorted out, the crowd consisted of only eight people, she shivered. Her carriage swept up to the front door. Footmen instantly surrounded both it and the one that followed, pulling the luggage from the tops and backs. The terrace, up a few steps from the drive and situated all along the front of the house, also seemed overly full of people, one of whom, a liveried footman, approached, opened her door, and waited to hand her down. Libby experienced a failure of nerve. For half an instant she cowered back into the squabs, but then, lifting her chin, she accepted the offered hand and descended.

"Tony?" called a little woman with streaks of white running back through dark hair worn in a simple chignon. "He isn't there?" she continued when only Libby stepped down. "Oh, that silly boy! Of *all* times to hold to old habits," she added, as she moved quickly forward in a step-and-hitch movement that didn't seem to discommode her a bit. "*Just* like the boy and how thoughtless of him to let you come on by yourself! You must be terrified to face us and Tony not here to support you! My dear child—" She held out her arms to Libby. "—welcome to your home."

When Libby didn't move, Lady Hendred chuckled. "Oh, my, you do not even know who I am, do you? I'm Tony's mother, of course." She took a last step and encircled Libby in a wonderfully comforting embrace. And then she held Libby a little away from her. "My dear child! I have looked forward to this moment for so very long." Her eyes twinkled. "Perhaps ever since I looked down into my son's cradle and wondered what sort of woman would be his wife. But do not stand here!" she exclaimed and bustled toward the door. "Come in! Come in!" She urged Libby along with her. "I very much fear," she whispered, "that I am not the only one who has longed to meet you. You *must* be introduced, you know. The servants insist." In a confiding tone, she added, "Do not worry. I'll support you."

As they crossed the threshold Lady Hendred changed in some subtle manner. Not that she became the least bit less sincere or comforting, but there was suddenly an authority to her that had been missing. "Ah, Bickles!" she said. "This is Lady Wendover. Quickly now. Do let us get on with it and be done with it as soon as may be. And, my dear," she said, rising on her toes to whisper into Libby's ear, "do not worry if you remember only one or two names. The servants will remind you whenever it chances you must deal with one or another of them. Just until you are comfortable with them, I mean. So many of them. Ah yes, Mrs. Bickles . . ."

The continuous gentle flow of words enclosed Libby in a warm blanket that surrounded and protected her and, much to her surprise, comforted her. She managed to say all that was proper to the butler and his wife and a few words to the staff after they were presented, but she was exceedingly glad that it was over quickly and that everyone was dismissed and an order given that refreshments be brought to the small parlor overlooking the knot garden.

"My dear, I apologize for my son," said her ladyship once they were seated.

"He didn't even say where he was going," said Libby, hurt and more than a trifle bewildered.

"Oh, how I will scold him! But, you see, my dear, it has been a habit with him ever since he went away to school. The instant he is within the gates, he goes to say hello to his old nanny. I used to feel rather jealous, which was silly, of course. Nanny Richards has grown rather frail the last year or two, so it has become even more important to him that he see how she goes on. You will forgive the boy, I hope?"

"There is nothing to forgive," Libby said, although she was not entirely certain she meant it. Her fear that Lady Hendred would treat her coldly was obviously misplaced, but this welcoming woman with her warmth and smiles and the limp about which nobody had warned her was so far from what she had expected that Libby was having a great deal of difficulty adjusting. "I am the one in need of forgiveness."

"My dear child! Why?"

Libby stared. Had Tony not informed his parents of the reason for their marriage?

"Ah! You mean because you tricked Tony into wedding you! But, my dear, from everything I hear, and I have many friends who write the most ridiculously long letters—I am forever having to pay extra to have them delivered, you know, so it is as well I've little else on which to spend my pin money, is it not?" She blinked. "Where was I? Oh!" She smiled and continued, "I remember. From all I hear, the two of you are so well matched it is impossible that the marriage not thrive!"

Libby smiled, although it was a trifle wanly. "You will understand if your son does not quite accept that?"

Lady Hendred sobered instantly. "Oh, dear. My poor child! Has he been unkind to you?"

"No!" Libby's eyes widened in horror that her ladyship suggest such a thing. "Never! You must not imagine anything of the sort! But it can surprise no one that he resents that he was forced to wed where he'd no notion of wedding!" Libby's fears prodded her into adding, "And you. How can you not take exception to it for his sake?"

Lady Hendred tipped her head to one side and studied her daughter-in-law. "I see. I had not thought of that problem. My dear, may I give you some advice?"

"Of course." Libby responded instantly, although, also instantly, she felt a protective shield go up. What would the woman say to her?

"I see that you feel guilty, but you must do your best to forget the reason for your marriage. I suspect you have apologized over and over and atoned in any number of ways and done everything you could to pander to my son's well-being." Lady Hendred's features revealed a mischievous streak. "It does no good to treat them like gods, you know. Men then begin thinking they *are,* and then where are we poor females? You put the past behind you, my dear, and we will carry on as if you and Tony met for the first time when in leading strings and have grown up together, forever expecting to wed each other!"

"I don't think I *can* do that, my lady . . ." said Libby—and stopped when her ladyship shook her head vigorously. "My lady?"

"If you cannot call me Mother, which I would like very much—" She smiled a wistful smile. "—then please call me Winnie. I cannot be 'my lady' to my daughter-in-law! But why can you not go on as if your marriage were a totally normal one?"

Libby bit her lip. She stared at Lady Hendred.

"Ah! That ridiculous guilt! You cannot rid yourself of it, is that it?"

"Oh, but it is not ridiculous! Did Tony not tell you that it was only an accident that he was in that bed? I had thought it Lord Merwin's room. And it was! Only his lordship went off to London, which I did not know, and gave his bed to poor Tony, who had been sharing with a man who snores, so it was Tony who woke up with me at his side."

"Lord Merwin?"

"Yes." Libby sighed. "I will never forgive myself. Tony is much too nice a man to have such a thing happen to him."

Lady Hendred blinked at the notion Lord Merwin was *not*. "It is all very well," she said, "for a mother to hear her son is a nice man, but, my dear, do you really think you'd have preferred marriage to Alex?"

Libby didn't respond instantly since she was no longer sure of anything. "I took great care in choosing a man who would have all the qualifications I needed. His lordship fit every requirement."

Lady Hendred tipped her head in a birdlike way characteristic to her. "You made a list of qualities you felt your husband should have and then looked about for a man who embodied them?" Her tinkling laugh filled the room. She looked up as the door opened allowing entry to her husband and son. "Oh, my dears! I love this woman! She is wonderful."

Libby rose to her feet when she realized Lord Hendred followed Tony. She glanced toward Tony and then to his mother. Lady Hendred held out her hand to her husband, and the man came forward instantly to take it between his own. "My darling," said Lady Hendred. For a fraction of an instant the two formed an entity needing nothing, no one. Then Lady Hendred recalled where they were. "My darling, your daughter-in-law."

Lord Hendred, too, seemed to return from a long way away. "My dear child! Welcome to Hendred Manor." He beamed at Libby, but almost immediately turned back to his wife. "You are all right?" he asked softly. "You have not overdone?"

"I am fine. You worry too much," said Lady Hendred just a trifle crossly. She smiled, taking away any sting there might have been.

"Of course I worry. How can it be otherwise? But if you say you are fine, then I must believe you. My dear," he added, turning back to Libby, "I hope you like the rooms my wife prepared for you and Tony." He turned just a bit, not releasing his wife's hand, but so that he could look at Tony, who had remained a little apart. "Son, we've redone the lavender suite. A husband and wife should have a place where they may retreat and be private. There are the bedrooms and dressing rooms, of course, but we chose it because there is also a small study and a reasonably well proportioned sitting room. I think it is sufficient and that you will be comfortable, but if you need more space, then you can have the rooms across the hall. They will be made up in any fashion you choose. Just tell Mrs. Bickles what you want done with them."

Lady Hendred assured herself that the men wanted no tea, having already indulged in a more potent brew, and that Libby wished no more. "And now I am sure you both wish to go up to those rooms and have an opportunity to refresh yourselves. I do not care how well sprung a carriage is, or how tight against the dust, one still feels in need of a wash and a change. There will be fresh water and by now, surely, your trunks are unpacked and all made ready for you. Tony, I would have a word with you. Shall we say half an hour, my dear?"

"Of course, Mother," said Tony, his tone as languid as ever. He turned to look at Libby, who rose, instantly, to her feet.

Some minutes later, after climbing a flight of stairs, then traversing several halls joined by a few steps up *here* and a few more going down *there,* they arrived at the door to their suite. "I will leave you to look around," said Tony politely. "Choose whichever room pleases you. It will not matter to me. There is something I must do." He bowed slightly, waited until Libby entered the suite, and then walked off down the hall in the way they had come.

Libby stared at the empty doorway, sighed and, feeling exceedingly depressed, moved slowly through the rooms, making an uninterested, although necessary, exploration of the suite. Eventually, she settled beside a small round table near a window in the room her maid had already decided must be hers, and having seen both bedrooms, Libby agreed. These walls were papered, a dainty pattern with nosegays of violets, their color matching the draperies and upholstery. The other bedroom, she had noted, was far more masculine. Shades of lavender dominated, but the furniture was heavier, the wood darker.

She opened her mind to the view out her window, and its magic soothed her. Gently rolling hills were broken up into small fields by walls built of stone, the scene accented here and there by small wooded areas. It was a gentle landscape and very lovely, the scudding clouds dropping moving shadows across the multicolored fields— here the green of pastureland, there the lighter green verging on yellow of ripening grain, and, very occasionally, farm buildings nestled into nooks and crannies, against the woods here, and up the hill from a stream there. Very pastoral. Serene.

Gradually, Libby's roiling thoughts settled, and she could think more calmly of the last few hours, days and months.

First there was Lady Hendred. Call her ladyship Mother? Libby couldn't, even though she wished it were possible. She had often and often felt the lack of a mother in her life. Her grandmother had not often been available, and Nanny, from the time Willie was born, had been far more interested in the heir than in Libby, who was merely a female and, in the scheme of things, not so important. Libby sighed. Was it any wonder she had become self-sufficient, that she had got in the way of thinking—as her grandmother accused—that she must do all herself?

As she had asked herself before, Libby again wondered what she might have done other than she did. She would not have gone to her grandmother when she found herself in difficulties because not only had Lady Settle given her no hint that she was wealthy enough she would be able to help, but she had never indicated she would be willing to do anything special for either of her grandchildren. Besides, Grandmother was not a well woman, had, for years, been something of an invalid. One did not impose problems on those suffering the stress and strain of a debilitating illness.

It seemed there was nothing she could have done differently. Libby sighed softly. If she had not been so preoccupied! If she had only been less self-involved! Then she would have realized Merwin had left the Weatherbees', and then things *would* have been different. But she *had* been preoccupied and hadn't noticed. And therefore Tony—innocent Tony—suffered.

So.

Since there was nothing she would have done differently, should she accept Lady Hendred's advice and attempt to put behind her how her marriage began? Try to pretend theirs was a normal union and that they had as much chance for happiness as any couple did?

And if she did?

Libby sighed again, this time far more deeply, because even if *she* did, Tony would *not*. So how would it change anything? *He* would continue to regret that he had had to give up hopes of a love match such as his parents enjoyed. As brief as the interval was when Tony and his father had joined Lady Hendred and herself, she had seen how close the two were, how much they cared for each other. And now she had seen them together, Libby realized how much Tony had lost and could sympathize as, before, she had not.

"Which gown shall I press for later?" asked Libby's maid.

"Hmm? Oh, Finch, you startled me. For dinner? Something simple. Since we have just arrived, there will be no company, and this is the country so an elaborate toilet would be out of place." Libby turned back to her window, her thoughts returning to what had become a circle leading nowhere. She was so very tired of it all. Was it even *possible* to put it behind her?

To think of Tony and *not* feel guilty? To think of Tony and merely appreciate the wonderful man she had discovered him to be? To think of Tony as she would of any man she admired? As she did him? To appreciate and admire him and, if she were lucky, learn to love him?

Or *would* that be a lucky thing? Would it not be still more terrible to love a man who could never think of one without also thinking of the trick played on him? Who would never in a million years feel love for such a woman?

Libby's maid returned from the room set aside for the work of abigails and valets. Over her arm she carried a gown made up of the blue Tony had convinced Libby she could wear successfully. The gown had the smallest possible train. An underdress went with it, made up in a very pale blue with a floral pattern embroidered on it. Libby wondered if it was suitable. Was it not, perhaps, a trifle dressier than required for a family dinner in the country? On the other hand, did not her first dinner with her husband's family require something just a trifle out of the ordinary?

And besides, what was there in her wardrobe, other than day gowns, that might suit better?

Libby decided to leave well enough alone. She would see what Tony thought when he first set eyes on her. It would be revealed in his expression. And, since he always knew exactly what one should wear for any possible occasion, he would be right.

Tony stood over his mother and stared down at her. "You cannot know. . . ."

"I know you are unhappy which makes me unhappy for you." She stared at him, compassion in her eyes. "But, Tony, I believe that if you would only allow the past to stay in the past, you would find you have made a very proper marriage."

"Even if begun so utterly . . . ?"

"Even if begun so *improperly?"* she said, filling in the word her son was unwilling to say. "You needn't curl your lip in that ridiculous manner," she scolded. "Of course it was improper. Tell me, Tony, what were your feelings toward Lady Lillian *before* she made her desperate bid to save her brother and herself?"

Tony frowned. He tapped his quizzing glass against his chin and actually did his best to recall those days at the Weatherbees' before he had been tumbled into scandal broth. "I found her a trifle brittle, but I admired her sense of dress and enjoyed dancing with her. I still admire her taste, and she is a delight on the dance floor. You would say that those accomplishments are sufficient for a good marriage?"

"Sarcasm." Lady Hendred sighed. "Tony, you have become bitter which is something I never thought to see. Is there nothing else you like about the woman?"

Their recent trip north slipped under Tony's guard and into his mind. He recalled Libby's love and gentle care of Ian's son, her odd and unexpected relationship with Ian's father. Ian's unbelievable claim of envy. . . .

No! He wouldn't think of that particular bit of nonsense! He stared over his mother's head, remembering, instead, that it had occurred to him that perhaps it would not be impossible to have the large family he wanted—but only if he could bring himself to bed his wife!

Tony thought of her neat figure, thought of how smoothly their dance steps fit together. His lips compressed. The idea of bedding her was not the difficulty. The problem was how to explain to her what he wanted.

How to ask that she give him children. Lots of children. Libby loved children. Surely she wanted her own. Surely she would understand and accept that he must return to her bed? That is, if she knew it was necessary that he must do so in order for them to have children. He had been told most young women did *not* know.

Perhaps he had erred in not going to her again after that first time. So that she would not have gotten into the habit of thinking he would *not* come. The longer he waited, the more impossible it seemed to even *suggest* he wanted his husbandly rights!

"Tony!"

"Yes, Mother?" he asked, startled from his thoughts.

She sighed. "Never mind. We will talk again another time." Tony bowed slightly and turned to go. "And, Tony . . ."

"Yes?" He didn't turn back.

"Do remember that we love you."

Tony turned, smiled his sweetest smile, and returned to her side to drop a kiss on her hair. "And I the both of you. You know that." Then he left, quickly, before she could say something else to keep him there. He had too much to think about and needed to be alone while he cogitated.

But his thoughts merely circled, getting nowhere.

Tony, normally ebullient and naturally happy, suffered from an unaccustomed moroseness and found he did not like it. Not one little bit. He wanted his comfortable life back. He wanted the old days when all he need worry about was whether his tailor cut his coat just right or the problem of finding answers to the problems set him by Lady this and Lord that concerning matters of taste and Ton! But it was not to be. Somehow, someway, he must, as he recalled telling Libby, make an adjustment to what *was*.

If only he could!

Tony strolled through his favorite gardens, checked up on his favorite spaniel bitch—and discovered she had just had pups—and then sneaked through the kitchens where he stole a tart and an apple. He was rather late returning to his room. His valet was nervous that they would not have time to do a proper job of dressing and actually had the temerity to scold his master!

"Enough Abley. It is no one but family." Tony's morose mood deepened. "I do not care how I look."

Abley's eyes started from his head. *"Not care?"*

Tony laughed, but there was no humor in it. "Must I repeat myself?" He was stripping off his travel-stained garments, which he had not bothered to remove earlier. "What have you set out?" He glanced at his bed. "My best evening clothes? Nonsense. The dark coat and pearl-colored trousers and—"

"But, my lord, it is *not* just family."

"Not?"

"Mr. Leath—your father's valet, you know—was kind enough to inform me your mother has asked in your nearest neighbors so that she may introduce your wife to their notice. It is not," he repeated, "merely family!"

"Does my wife know?"

Abley blinked. "I've no notion, my lord. I believe her maid has been busy since our arrival, pressing and hanging and otherwise unpacking for our stay."

Tony grimaced, then sighed. "You had better go knock and tell—what is the chit's name?"

"Miss Finch, sir?"

"Tell Finch there will be company. Tell her Lady Wendover should wear something neat but not too elaborate. The blue with the embroidered underdress would be suitable."

Abley disappeared and returned to say that that was what Lady Wendover had planned to wear this evening. He had, he said, detected a trifle of frost in the impertinent chit's gaze, but had forborne to scold her. "It would," he finished, scolding his lordship instead, "have taken too much time, and we've little enough as it is!"

"Enough of your sauce." Tony spoke more sharply than usual, and after a glance, Abley decided his master must have eaten something that disagreed with him when they had stopped for a nuncheon on the road. After all, he himself had felt a trifle queasy after indulging in what might have been an overly large portion of a very rich squab pie.

Finally Tony picked up his quizzing glass and hung it by its ribbon around his neck. Without bothering to check in the cheval mirror standing in the corner of his room—such an unusual deviation from practice that Abley once again could not believe his eyes—Tony stepped into the sitting room where he found Libby waiting for him. He hesitated and then shut his door quietly. "You are ready to go down, my dear?"

"Yes. But I've a complaint, Tony. Please don't insult my maid again by sending impertinent messages by way of your valet!"

"Ah! You were aware we are to have company to dinner this evening? That my mother has invited in the neighbors to meet you?"

Libby paled. She reached for the edge of the table standing by the fireplace. "Company? I thought it merely family."

"You meant to wear that gown when it was no more than family?" asked Tony politely.

"You think I should not?"

"The train, my dear," he said with the faintest hint of a sneer. "A trifle much for just family, is it not? Quite right, however, for the sort of country do m'mother has in mind."

Caught up in the sort of sartorial dilemma that intrigued her, Libby forgot she was angry. "But, Tony, what should I wear when it is only the family?"

Tony rapidly reviewed his wife's wardrobe, which he

knew almost as well as he knew his own. He grimaced. "I see the difficulty. We should have ordered gowns proper to the country before we left London. I apologize."

Libby smiled. "That is one of the things I like about you, Tony," she said a trifle shyly. "When you have erred, you apologize and do not try to pretend nothing is wrong or try to bluster your way around the problem."

Tony flushed slightly. "I do not think it something for which I deserve a compliment!"

"But it is. It is rare for a man to feel so secure in himself that he can accept that he has made a mistake. More often than not, or so I have observed, a man feels he has somehow diminished himself if he perceives that others think him less than perfect!"

Tony was about to pooh-pooh her observation when it occurred to him he had noticed the same problem now and again. He nodded. More in charity with her than he had been for some time, he offered his arm. "Come, my dear. We'd best go down before we are unforgivably late!"

The evening passed off easily. Libby had spent most of her life among just such people as populated the Hendreds' neighborhood and knew just how to go on amongst them. She carried it off with just the proper mix of the reserve due her status and modesty proper to her age, but seasoned her manner with just a hint of humor. Tony, as was usual when he observed his wife in a social situation, felt pride in her poise and intuitive handling of even the most difficult guest, who, in this case, was Lady Manderfield, the oldest and most peppery lady at the party.

This particular elderly lady was not the only dowager in the Manderfield ménage. There was also her deceased son's dowager wife and then her grandson's wife, which meant there were three Lady Manderfields in a family noted for its irascibility—especially toward each other—which led to all sorts of problems for a hostess attempting to make a proper seating chart for a formal dinner! Luckily, on this particular evening, the two younger generations had not yet returned from London where they had spent some weeks enjoying the latter half of the Season.

Libby was surprised to discover how much she enjoyed the evening and put it down to the fact it had been a very long Season during which she had been under a great deal of pressure, walking a very narrow line in order to compensate for the scandal she herself had caused. Here, at Hendred Manor, she merely met new people, most of whom were disposed to treat her well. She chose to discover what she could about them, and since most people enjoy talking about themselves, she relaxed and felt at ease.

When the last guest was gone, Lord and Lady Hendred stood with Tony and Libby in the great hall talking. It became obvious they were waiting for Tony to say good night and take his wife upstairs. Tony, who had meant to go back out to check on his spaniel bitch, realized it would seem more than a trifle odd if he did not go up with Libby, said what was proper, offered her his arm, and started up the stairs.

When they were beyond hearing of the older couple, Libby frantically searched her mind for something to say. Tony, also uncomfortable, tried to ease the situation. "The evening went very well. I had many compliments on my wife," he said.

Unfortunately Tony's voice was touched by sarcasm, and Libby hastily choked back a desire to cry at this sudden shadow on the evening. She wished he were sincere, but his tone made it impossible to think that. The silent caveat that such compliments were *despite* the manner in which he had acquired her had Libby feeling very nearly as unhappy as she had just previously felt very nearly contented!

It never occurred to her to ask *why* she wanted him to be proud of her!

* * *

During the days following the party Libby, willy-nilly, became better acquainted with Tony's parents. Tony found excuse after excuse for taking himself off, which left her no choice but to do the pretty—as some of her friends called it—by the older couple. Not that she found it difficult. They were too easygoing and too polite for it ever to be difficult, but she soon discovered that Lord and Lady Hendred needed none but themselves. The depth of their love for each other spilled out over those around them, making all feel liked and wanted, but, if there was no one else about, they were very obviously perfectly content to be alone together.

Libby discovered two things. One discovery surprised her greatly, and that was that she felt more than a little pity for Tony. He must, given their preoccupation with each other, have grown up thinking himself rather unnecessary to either of his parents! The second discovery was no surprise at all. After meeting Lord and Lady Hendred, she acquired a strong craving to experience such a love! Because of that yearning, she finally understood why Tony resented her so much. He had grown up wanting such a love. *Expecting* it!

"How," she muttered, "does one fall in love? How does one make another fall in love with one?"

Unfortunately she did her muttering while strolling through the gardens. Just on the other side of the hedge by which she walked, Lady Hendred was working in the herb garden which supplied ingredients needed for the unguents and medicines she made for her well-stocked stillroom and also, of course, provided herbs for the kitchen.

"My dear child, is that you? Do join me," called her ladyship through the leafy barrier between them.

Libby felt heat flow up her neck, but even though she

was embarrassed that she had been overheard, she walked on and around the end of the hedge. She studied the careful plantings, some surrounded by ten-inch-high, well-clipped miniature hedges and others laid out in narrow plots carefully set off by narrower strips of stone.

"I know nothing about herbs," said Libby, after walking along the garden to join her mother-in-law. "I regret admitting my ignorance, but I know nothing about supplying a stillroom either. Will you teach me?"

"Yes, of course. But not just now. Tony says you go on to the Renwicks' and will be leaving soon—"

Which was the first Libby had heard of it!

"—but when you come home for a month or two over Christmas, we will begin studying the topic seriously. Did I hear you ask how one fell in love?" she added, abruptly changing the subject.

Libby, who had hoped to avoid this, grimaced. "I never have, you see. But then, I'm not entirely certain I would *know.*"

Lady Hendred chuckled. "My dear child! Believe me, you will know." She pulled another weed and sat back onto the lawn, her bad leg extended to one side and the other bent. She peered up from under the wide-brimmed hat that shaded her face. "Please sit down. Unless you fear for your gown, of course. I dressed for work so do not think of stains and dirt!"

Libby lowered herself to the dry grass. "This is an old gown. I've always thought it nonsense to wear one's best when one means to traipse around, poking into this and that and perhaps wanting to go where one should not!"

"Very sensible. But as to making someone fall in love with you, you do mean Tony, do you not?"

Libby blushed. Had she thought of Tony? Or was it Merwin she had had in mind? But these days she rarely thought of Lord Merwin. . . .

"You see, my dear," continued Lady Hendred gently,

"Tony told me that you rather expected to have married Lord Merwin. Are you still certain his lordship would have done for you?"

Libby frowned. She recalled those occasions when she had expected his lordship to dinner and he either had not come or had come late. Sometimes he had arrived just before the tea tray came in. She sighed. "I don't know. When I planned to . . . to . . ."

"To wed," said Lady Hendred placidly.

"To wed—" Libby cast her a look that expressed her appreciation for the help. "—I thought very carefully about the men attending the party. First, I decided who could best help me help my brother. That was the important thing, of course. But I also wanted a man I felt would . . . would . . ."

"Would provide you with the opportunity to show what a good hostess you can be?"

Libby smiled. "I hadn't considered that, but yes, I do feel I might shine as a political hostess. But what I meant is a man who . . . who . . ."

"Who appealed to your senses, perhaps?"

Libby blushed rosily. "Oh, dear. It sounds so terrible when put that way, but yes, I guess that *is* what I mean. I had rather thought of it as a man whom I did not find off-putting!"

Lady Hendred nodded and smiled when Libby's blushes became hotter still. "My dear, do not feel chagrinned! It is perfectly normal. Do not think otherwise." She sobered and, when she continued, spoke a trifle wistfully. "Do you find that Tony does *not* appeal?"

"Tony is a wonderful man. He has treated me far more gently than I deserve. And, although he says it is because he does not wish the Ton to think him a fool and a dupe, I think it is because he is naturally kind. And thoughtful. And so very knowledgeable." She frowned. "I suppose I

have not really stopped to think about whether he . . .
he . . ."

"Appeals?"

Libby nodded.

"My dear, since the two of you are wed, it might be
a good idea if you *were* to think about it, do you not
agree?"

Once again feeling the heat of a flush, Libby nevertheless nodded. "You are correct, of course." She bit her
lip. "If you'll excuse me?"

"Of course, although I did not mean to chase you
away!" Lady Hendred bit her lip as she cast her daughter-
in-law a speculative glance. She nodded, as if to herself.
"If you have not wandered down to the lake yet," she said,
"I believe you would find that the belvedere on the rise
on the far side of it is quite a pleasant place. Take the path
through the nut grove and bear left down the hill. You'll
see it as soon as you are clear of the rhododendrons." Lady
Hendred watched Libby go, bit her lip once more, and wondered if she had done the right thing. . . .

The grove was cool, and Libby tarried under the trees,
putting names to those she could and wondering what
particular nut might be produced by others she had never
before encountered. But trees paled as an excuse to avoid
thinking, and she continued on her way. The path wandered through rhododendron shrubbery and led her around
the end of the silver-colored lake, nary a ripple marring
its surface. Once she crossed the humpback bridge over
the stream that fed the lake, she entered another glade,
this one of relatively young trees, although old enough
to provide shade as one climbed the hill on a track curv-
ing around and up.

Libby was very slightly out of breath as she approached the back of the belvedere. She had set a pace

that was rather fast for the grade, but had enjoyed the feel of her skirts swishing against her legs and the energy flowing through her body. She stood some yards from the arched entrance while she caught her breath and admired the structure. It had been repainted recently, and the white was brilliant against the blue of the sky and the dark green of well-clipped shrubs around the base. At this season, color was provided by deep pink rose-covered vines that climbed latticework set between the Doric columns holding up a domed roof.

All in all, it was a delightful little building, and after appreciating its careful design Libby entered. The room was brightly lit, sun streaming in the three windows set into the lake-view side of the building. For a moment, Libby blinked, regaining her vision.

Then she did. "Oh!"

Across from the door was Tony. He had seated himself on a bench, crossed his arms on the sill of the wide window facing the lake, and laid his head on them. He straightened and looked over his shoulder.

"Oh," he, too, said—but the word sounded very different from when Libby said it.

"Should I go?" she asked.

"Go?" After a moment he turned slightly. "No, of course not." He gestured languidly toward the window next to his and the bench under it. "Sit down if you will."

Libby hesitated, wondering if she should. He had taken such care to avoid her that she felt it must be an intrusion to remain now. Still, he had invited her to stay, so she crossed to the bench. She seated herself, her eyes never leaving Tony's face. "My foolishness has made you very unhappy, has it not?" she asked quietly.

"Unhappy?" He stared out over the lake. "I suppose it must have done. It was all right while we lived in London. At least I didn't notice it there."

"It was returning home and seeing your parents, their

love for each other, which reminded you what you had lost," she said.

He nodded. "Yes."

"I lost it, too. Except I never knew it existed." She sighed.

He turned to look at her. Really look at her. "You aren't happy either."

She smiled. It wasn't much of a smile, and it faded almost at once, but it was a smile. "I have met your mother and father, Tony. I have seen what a marriage should be."

He laughed. It wasn't much of a laugh, but it was a laugh. "The high sticklers find their relationship disgusting, you know. The very highest have said it makes them no better than animals."

"Nonsense. The *animals* are the men and women who pretend to be oh-so-decent but have mistresses in keeping or take lovers."

He straightened and turned to stare at her, a shocked look in his eyes. "Libby! You should not know of such things!"

"Should I not?" she asked wistfully. "Grandmother didn't seem to think it wrong when she lectured me on the subject."

"Oh. After we were married."

"No. It was when I first came to London several years ago. She assured me that it was better that I not dream impossible dreams, but that I know the worst of what my life might be."

"Dreams?"

"Doesn't every young girl dream of her knight in shining armor who will come to her rescue and keep her safe?" There was a touch of humor in her voice.

"Does she?" asked Tony. "I didn't know." He smiled one of his quick smiles, but it faded instantly. "I guess I'd not have fit any girl's dream, then. I'm no knight. Not even in rusty armor!"

"Nonsense. You are the very best sort of knight for modern times!"

Tony cast her a disbelieving look.

"But, Tony, you *are*. We don't have real dragons anymore, only social dragons, and who is better than you at fighting off that sort? I mean," she added, in some confusion, since she had never quite thought of him in this way, "that is what you did, did you not? For me? When I was such a fool?"

"I did it for me as much as anything," said Tony, looking out over the water, a tinge of red darkening the skin just above his cravat.

"Yes, but the thing is, you *could* do it and you *did* it. Don't you see? That is far more important, in this day and age, than the ability to rescue a maiden from a tower or a dragon or what you will!"

He eyed her for a long moment and then, sounding astounded, asked, "You truly believe that, do you not?"

"But it is obvious." She put out her hand, then hesitated a moment before actually laying it on Tony's arm. "You are *just* the sort a woman would have in her dreams, Tony. Don't ever again think otherwise."

He turned to stare out the window. "I have always thought a soldier like Jack or a big handsome man like Ian was the sort about whom a woman dreamt. I'm nothing special, Libby."

"You are, too! Lord Princeton is all very well, I suppose. Lady Princeton seems to think so anyway, but I find him rough and not at all interested in important things. In fact, he is rather impatient of those social niceties, those politenesses, which make life go smoothly and happily, is he not? And Ian McMurrey is *too* big. I always felt like a child when he was around, and it was very uncomfortable. But you, Tony, you always know exactly what to say and do in any situation. I like that. It is very important. Without men like you, who are examples for the younger men to look up to and emulate, the whole of society would become nothing but a zoo full of wild animals."

Tony blushed. "That, too, is important, is it not?"

"Too?"

"Well, Merwin works very hard in the government, and is responsible for all sorts of important things, is he not? Men like Jack go off to war and die or are wounded to keep us safe here in England. That is even more important. I've always been just a little ashamed I do nothing at all."

"But you do. That is what I've been saying!"

"Yes. It isn't like dying in war, but it does need doing. Thank you, Libby."

"You are welcome, but what have I done that deserves your thanks?"

He turned to look fully at her. "You, too, are something important in our world, Libby. You have the ability to make a man look at things from a different angle. As you did just now for me. And as you did in Scotland for the McMurrey."

"But that is nothing. Anyone can do that."

"Anyone?" He shook his head. "Libby, did no one tell you how long it has been since the old man came to the table for dinner?"

She blinked. "Should someone have done so?"

"My dear, it was years!"

"Surely not."

"Truly."

"But what did I do?" she asked, bewildered.

For the first time in days Tony laughed a happy laugh. "My dear Libby, if you do not know, then I haven't a notion who could explain it to you. Or perhaps, if he *would,* the *McMurrey* could! But my guess is that the old curmudgeon would get pleasure from *not* explaining. Have you no idea?"

"None at all. I did nothing special, I assure you. I

didn't plan to lure him from his den for the simple reason I was unaware he lived in one!"

Tony cast her a quick glance and then looked back out over the lake. "You were also very good with the babe."

"I have always had a knack with babies. I like them and I think they know that."

"You should have your own," mumbled Tony.

"Hmm?"

"Nothing," he said, responding just a bit too quickly.

Did he actually hint that I should have his children? But that would mean . . .

Libby felt her skin heat and was glad Tony stared from his window. She stared from hers, and they were silent for quite some time. Then a pair of swans came into view from around the bend in the lake, and Libby gasped softly.

"Beautiful, are they not?" whispered Tony.

"Yes," breathed Libby.

Again they sat silent, but this time with a unifying feeling of awe. The swans passed silently by their windows and continued on until they disappeared into a small cove just to the side of where the lake narrowed and the bridge could be viewed.

"That was lovely," said Libby.

Tony took a watch from his fob pocket and snapped it open. "A lovely way to end an interlude," he agreed. He spoke more briskly when he continued, "We must return to the house, Libby, if we are to be dressed in time to leave for the Manderfields'. I cannot think how the youngest Lady Manderfield was able to plan such a formal dinner so quickly. They only returned yesterday!"

"According to your mother, she was determined to honor us before her mother-in-law could arrange something at the dower house. Do both the elder Lady Manderfields live in the dower house?"

"No. They cannot abide each other. The eldest of the three ladies, the one you met, has an apartment in a wing of the main house separate from the rest of the household. She has her own kitchen, her own servants, even her own front entry. She rarely entertains these days, so she is no longer in competition with the others as she once was. I am very glad I don't live in that family. In fact, I have wondered—" He cast her a mischievous look. "—if it were not the brangling among the women that leads to the early deaths of their men!"

"Tony!" Libby was half shocked and half amused. She returned his playful look. "Well! If that is directed to me, I will inform you, my lord, that you need have no fear of an early death. I never brangle!"

Lady Hendred, watching for them, called out the window as they approached the house. "Children! It is so good to see you laughing. Do come in and tell me the joke!"

Tony took Libby in by a side door and straight to his mother's sitting room. "You look as if you caught the sun today," he said, studying his mother's pink cheeks.

"As Libby knows, I spent time with my herbs today. Did you find the belvedere?"

Tony glanced from his wife to his mother, noted the pink was an even deeper color than before. "She did. We saw the swans," he said, suddenly quite certain his mother had sent Libby to him. *Now, why . . . ?*

"Such beautiful creatures," said Lady Hendred, nodding. "Now off with you. You won't be ready to leave, and we will be late. That would never do when you are the guests of honor!"

Tony, poker-faced, bowed. He offered his arm to his wife, who was prettily flushed. Surely the two women hadn't plotted together. . . .

"Tony," whispered Libby when they were safely in the hall. "Could your mother have known you were there when she suggested I might like the view from the belvedere?"

Tony, relieved to know his wife, at least, was doing no plotting, shook his head. "How could she have known?"

Neither voiced the thought that Lady Hendred might not have known, but she might have made a good guess! What the young couple would have been still more disturbed to know is that her ladyship had had information whispered into her ear that disturbed *her*.

Lord Hendred entered the sitting room just then and frowned to see his wife frowning. "My dear. What is it?"

Her ladyship's frown faded, and that mischievous look took its place. "My dear, have you ever had any sort of fatherly discussion with your son on the very important topic of how a man keeps his wife happy and content?"

Lord Hendred's ears burned. "My dear!"

She sighed a soulful sigh. "How remiss of you, my love!"

"But . . ."

"My very precious love," said Lady Hendred, "those two are not only not happy in their marriage bed, they are spending no time at all in their marriage bed! You'd best talk to your son!"

For several days, every time he looked at his wife, Tony felt his ears heat. On this particular occasion, they were drinking tea with his mother. Tony, preoccupied, allowed the conversation to drift over and around him. Instead of listening, he cast the occasional surreptitious glance toward Libby.

Can my father possibly be correct? Are all women actually the same and the common view among my friends wrong? Are ladies no different from those other women with whom a man sows wild oats? Does my own mother actually enjoy . . .

But at that point, after a quick embarrassed look at

his mother, Tony could go no further in his thinking. For too long he had assumed that tonnish ladies, if they were truly ladies, were too delicate, too sensitive perhaps, to enjoy lovemaking. He could *not* think of his mother welcoming his father to her bed!

But Libby . . . ?

What of Libby?

His ears were so hot he *knew* they were as red as red.

Nine

The journey to Tiger's Lair was accomplished with far less tension than was the trip to Hendred Manor. Libby had met the Renwicks, knew, in fact, all the Six, some of whom would also be visiting in Kent. She even knew Sahib, and, although she could not be completely comfortable with the beast, she enjoyed watching him, the sensuous strength of him and the beauty of his fur, the glowing intelligence within his great eyes, and, when he was at his most benign, she liked touching him. . . .

There would be other guests, of course, for leavening. Tony had mentioned Lord Hayworth, for instance, who was Lady Renwick's uncle and another family she knew as acquaintances. The visit would be just the sort of entertainment she most enjoyed. *Except for a ball, of course, which was the most pleasurable of all!*

To help them ignore the jouncing of the carriage, Tony told her more about his friends, stories of their school days and how they had grown up and each gone off in different directions, making lives for themselves, but, at the same time, somehow retaining that special closeness that bound them into a unit.

"Even Miles, who ran off at an early age," he said.

"Did he go to sea? He handles his ship with such intuition and ease and I wondered . . ."

"Not then. He explored Europe in all sorts of disguises

since it was dangerous for an Englishman to travel in many areas. He admits he sent back reports to the Home Office. The first time he did so was because he ran into something too important to remain a secret. After that, if there was something he felt our government should know, he'd get a message through. Eventually he drifted around the eastern end of the Mediterranean and into Egypt. There he went up the Nile passing as an Egyptian! I'd have thought it exceedingly uncomfortable," concluded Tony thoughtfully as he tapped his quizzing glass against his chin.

"Exceedingly! I have always thought having adventures terribly foolish. Not, I suppose, that one can always avoid them. I mean, if we were held up by highwaymen as my grandmother once was, that would be an adventure and not very nice, but we would not have gone looking for it. I cannot understand how one could actually *want* to have them."

Tony nodded. "I never think of adventure without thinking of the dirt and the discomfort. If one goes to be a soldier, one expects such things as a matter of course, but one is doing something important. To go looking for trouble for no reason is outside of enough!"

"But you like Mr. Seward, do you not?"

"Yes. He has a way of making one laugh even when one doesn't wish to. And I'd trust him with my darkest secret. If I had one. But he isn't *comfortable*, Libby. He must always be up and doing."

"And he has the ring?"

Tony gave her a quick glance. "Who told you of the ring?"

"Ian McMurrey. I overheard him and Lord Merwin plotting to get it back. Have you ever had it?"

"Oh, yes. But—" He cast her a quick look."—if you'll not reveal it, I'll tell you a secret."

"Mum's the word," she said, smiling, "but I think I can guess."

Tony turned and plied his glass, staring at her through it. "You could not."

"Yes, I could," she insisted. "Because I would feel the same way. It is a rather nasty looking little ring of no particular value and, if you had to wear it at all times, why, how could you plan a wardrobe around such a silly little trinket?"

"You *have* guessed!"

His expression made her chuckle. "But I said! I would feel the same way."

The miles passed quickly, and far sooner than Libby expected, they were being welcomed to Tiger's Lair.

"I have given you a suite in the west wing," said Lady Renwick as she led them up to it. "Dinner will be in an hour, and the company will begin gathering in the blue salon in half an hour or so. I'll leave you now," she added after a glance around to see that all was as she had ordered.

Their maid and valet had arrived some hours earlier, which was a very good thing, since all was ready for them to change. But Libby discovered a cozy-covered teapot awaiting their arrival. It was set on the table in the sitting room, and she called to Tony.

Her husband appeared in his doorway, his cravat dangling from his hand, his coat gone and his vest unfastened. Libby stared. She had never before seen her husband in dishabille—or rather, she had, but not to really look at—and she found she was far more profoundly affected than it ever would have occurred to her she might be.

"Libby? You called to me?"

"Oh! Oh, yes," she said, speaking quickly. "But it is only that I thought you might like a cup of tea. You see? It has been provided for us, and I, at least, am very thirsty. A very thoughtful notion, is it not?"

As she spoke she tore her eyes from her husband and,

with great care not to rattle them, set out two teacups. Tony noticed her agitation but was unsure of its cause. He came forward slowly, taking the cup and saucer she held out to him and seating himself in one of the chairs set beside the linen-covered table. He watched her pour her own cup, saw her hands tremble ever so slightly and, raising his quizzing glass, stared at her bent head. When she began to look up, he dropped it.

"Yes," he said belatedly. "A very good notion." But his mind was occupied with frantic thoughts, unlikely hopes, and interesting questions—none of which he could bring himself to voice.

Libby was also more than a trifle preoccupied. What was the meaning of that frisson that passed through her when Tony first appeared? Not disgust, which one might have expected, seeing him so untidy and all. She would have recognized that emotion. No, there had been no revulsion. In fact, nothing negative in any way, but still . . . What did it mean?

"That was very good," said Tony setting down his cup. "And just what was needed. But we'd best hurry now, Libby."

"What? Oh! Yes, of course." She set down her barely touched cup and rose to her feet. "Yes, we must, must we not?"

Tony looked at her cup and frowned. Had she not said she was thirsty? But there was no time to discuss her problem, whatever it might be. They must, as he had said, rush their toilet in order that they not be late.

And they did. Although not late, they were the last to enter the salon. Sahib rose to his feet as they came in, and, as was her habit, Libby stared at the great beast. "He is so beautiful," she murmured.

"Very," said a strange voice at her side, and she turned. "I am Lord Hayworth," said the stranger, introducing himself. He bowed in the old-fashioned manner of his youth.

"I am Lady Renwick's uncle and I am wooing Lord Renwick's aunt." He sighed a lugubrious sigh. "Do you think that if I changed my way of dressing, she might be more forthcoming?" he asked. His eyes gleamed wickedly—the only sign in his otherwise innocent expression that he might be jesting.

Libby eyed his green coat and lighter green cravat. "Perhaps you should not have matched the coat to blue trousers?" she asked with her own features firmly under control.

"But biscuit color is so boring," he complained. "And black would not have done. Not at all. Brown, perhaps? A foxy sort of brown?"

"Just the thing," she agreed, tongue in cheek.

He grinned. "You'll do, missy. You'll do." And, just like that, he wandered off.

"I *like* the things he wears," said another voice Libby did not recognize. She turned to discover who spoke. She found herself staring at a rather startling young man. If Lord Hayworth had been oddly dressed, this young man was exotic in the extreme with his blue silk coat made up tight and high to the throat, his somewhat baggy white trousers caught in at the ankles and—a quick glance revealed—he wore red shoes with pointy toes, too. The costume was finished off with a wide red sash around his middle. "I am Prince Ravi," he said, holding out his hand in western fashion. "I do not believe we've met?"

Libby introduced herself. "My husband, Lord Wendover," she continued, "told me something of your history. He said you are Lord Renwick's ward?"

The boy frowned. "He is Savior and Keeper. It is his duty to see to me," said the boy, his head at an arrogant angle. "I do not understand this nonsense about wards and such stuff."

"I believe it is much the same thing, actually. Just different ways of saying it, perhaps," said Libby.

The lad tipped his head. More quietly, he responded, "Perhaps that is it. I admit I do not always understand your very odd language." He changed the subject. "You are only newly married, are you not?"

"Not so very long ago. A few months now." She cast him a wary glance.

"If you were in my country and were my wife, you would live with my other wives in a special set of rooms where you could have everything you wanted, but could never leave them. I, your husband, would visit you there." He grinned. He lowered his tone. "I think I rather like your western ways better," he said, "but it would never do to allow my people to hear me say so."

"How long have you been here?" she asked, and continued talking to the boy for some time. While she did so, she watched Sahib, who seemed to watch her back, occasionally blinking benignly. Once Sahib turned his great head and looked toward the group in which Tony stood talking, but then looked back at Libby. He appeared to be thinking deep thoughts, and Libby wished she had some way of knowing if they were favorable—or *not* as the case might be!

Dinner and the evening passed off as smoothly and as pleasantly as Libby had expected, although the after-dinner guests assembled in the salon were mostly women. She had had another conversation with Lady Renwick's uncle. His lordship was the first gentleman to return to the salon after dinner. In fact, one of the *few* men who joined the ladies!

Those of the Six who attended the party disappeared entirely.

"You've all read Ian's letter?"

Princeton wafted a glass of port under his nose, enjoying the aroma. "I read it last night, Jase. And I think Miles read it this morning. Tony?"

"Jase gave it to me a few moments ago. I am shocked!"

"When will Ian arrive? Did it say?"

"Toward the end of the week. He'll stop a day or so in London and then come on down. Miles, can you remain so long?"

"For this? Try to be rid of me!"

"Do you think Ian has proof of this infamy?" Tony flicked the letter, which he had just finished rereading, with his fingernails.

"This time he has. His despicable lordship made a serious error when he lost his temper with that poor woman in Reading."

"She is lucky she survived."

"Yes. Dixon may have thought her dead. She's permanently crippled, however, and has no means of supporting herself."

"But she is willing to identify our contemptible lordship? Willing to play a part in bringing the man to heel?"

Renwick grinned wickedly, thinking of the longer letter Ian had asked him to destroy lest it fall into the wrong hands and Lady Serena's father get word of his plans to remove Serena's mother from her husband's clutches. "For a consideration, yes."

"I recall something Ian once said about the temperament of a woman of Lady Dixon's ilk," said Jack. "Does Ian think Lady Serena's mother will agree to leave her husband and come away to live with them?"

"If she will not come for her own sake, then she will when—" Tony spoke soberly, lazily swinging his glass by the ribbon. "—she discovers she is not actually married to the beast, that he is a bigamist."

Renwick nodded. "Ian will use that information as a last resort if Lady Dixon is stubborn. He will put his proofs and statement in a safe place, including a signed and witnessed testimony from this new victim. He has accumulated quite a lot of information to his fine lordship's disparagement. Unfortunately he has very little proof, so none of what he has, by itself, would do much damage. *En toto,* however, it is quite interesting."

"Then, we hold ourselves in readiness to confront Lord Dixon," said Miles, his eyes shining with the thought of being up and doing.

"Will you write Merwin?" asked Jack. "Will he not wish to be here as well?"

"I dictated a letter to Eustacia earlier today. She was utterly shocked at what Ian has discovered and wonders that Lady Serena managed to grow to be the woman she is with that awful man for a father."

"I believe Ian once told me of a grandmother who had a large hand in raising her to be the strong independent woman she is," said Tony, still swinging his glass.

Tony spoke idly, his mind only half occupied with their discussion. The other half was playing with a notion. But did he dare ask about the very personal topic on which his father had lectured him. He knew his married friends shared a bed rather than requiring two bedrooms, as was common within the Ton. Still, was that an indication that his father had actually meant what he seemed to convey by his rather convoluted discussion ranging from the language of flowers to reminding Tony of the difference between agape and Eros in the Greek lexicon?

Tony's ears heated up at the thought of making love to his wife. To avoid thinking about it, let alone about how to frame a question concerning marital relationships in such tactful words a friend might feel free to answer, he forced his mind into other channels. If he didn't think, then his blood would cool.

"Then, it is decided. Tomorrow we will picnic by the river," said Eustacia. "I will have the fishing equipment looked out."

"Then," said a new voice, "you may fish from a window in the summer house. We do not require the sort of excitement we suffered last year!"

"When did you return?" asked Eustacia of her husband's aunt. She blushed, startled into rudeness by the sudden interruption. "Oh, forgive me!"

"I will consider it," said Lady Blackburne with a smile, "if *you* will forgive me for frightening you. I arrived something over an hour ago. I asked that I not be announced." She grimaced. "Brighton is already, this early in the summer season, unbearably crowded, and the Pavilion is as ugly as it ever was. The travel itself was accomplished as smoothly as possible. I will admit his lordship's carriage is particularly well sprung."

"Lord Hayworth was certain you would find it as smooth a ride as could be provided. And the tooth?"

Lady Blackburne shrugged. "We will not speak of my tooth, if you please. We will merely be glad it is no longer a problem." She stared a trifle rudely at Libby. "I do not know your guest, Eustacia. Why have you not introduced us?"

"Ah! I think being *enceinte* must have a deleterious effect on the brain. At least, it seems to have one on mine! Libby, I apologize." Lady Renwick made the introduction.

"Of course. The new bride. You are not quite so young as I expected."

Libby blushed rosily. "Should I apologize?"

"Not to me," said her ladyship. "Now, Eustacia, how many will attend your picnic?"

Libby felt as if she had been snubbed and wondered why. Neither Lady Renwick, Lady Princeton, nor Lady Serena had treated her badly, and, as the wives of Tony's friends, they had more reason to resent her than did Lady Blackburne, who, so far as Libby knew, had no connection to Tony at all. She sighed softly and looked up to find Sahib staring at her.

The tiger had entered quietly in Lady Blackburne's wake and settled near the door. Now he approached the window, moving slowly toward Libby. Libby felt her breath quicken and her nerves tighten. The big cat stopped only a yard distant and opened its mouth in that intimidating although silent roar.

"Sahib! What are you doing in here? Where is Jase?" asked Lady Renwick, noticing the beast for the first time.

Sahib turned his head toward her ladyship, growled slightly, and then turned back to stare at Libby.

"Why does he look at me that way?" asked Libby nervously.

"I don't know," said Lady Renwick, more than a trifle concerned by Sahib's odd behavior. "Sahib, down."

The cat sank to his haunches and then down to lay sprawled against the highly polished wood floor. His white fur, marked by faint black streaks, seemed to gleam as well. And he still didn't take his eyes from Libby's face.

"He won't hurt you," added Lady Renwick after a moment. She glanced around and, just a trifle fretfully, said, "I wonder where Jase has gone that Sahib is not with him."

"I'll go see," said Libby, thankful for an excuse to escape Sahib's steady gaze. But when she rose to her feet, so did the tiger. "Oh, dear."

Lady Renwick bent forward slightly and put a hand on the tiger's neck, digging her fingers in until she had a grip on the skin there. "Off you go. Sahib will stay. Won't you, Sahib?" she finished on an interrogatory note. The tiger looked up into her ladyship's face, seemed to sigh and, again, flopped to the floor. "There. Now, if you will do that little thing for me, Libby, I would appreciate it very much. The men have very likely gone off somewhere together, but, for some reason, these days, I prefer to know where Jase can be found!" Her hand rested on her swelling abdomen, and she blushed rosily.

Libby didn't hesitate. She left at once—and sent the Renwick butler back into the room to explain that the men had, indeed, gone out together. Riding. Libby wondered at that. A blind man, riding? And Lord Princeton, with his limp—did he ride? But then she recalled seeing Lord Princeton on horseback when they were at the Weatherbees' house party.

Libby decided to take a walk. She was in one of the many rose gardens surrounding Tiger's Lair when the men returned, and Tony, who had decided he really must come to some decision concerning the regularization of his marriage, happened on her there.

"My lady!" he said, coming around the end of a hedge that protected one of the gardens.

"My lord?" Libby blushed and looked down at the path.

Tony, remembering his decision, cleared his throat. "Will you walk with me?"

"Of course." After a moment she added, "I'd like that." They strolled toward the arch in a hedge at the far side of the garden. "Lord Renwick's butler told me that you men went riding after a forum in the study. Forum is a strange word. What does it mean? If you would not mind explaining it to me of course."

"Forum?" Tony welcomed the excuse to put off a discussion of babies and how one went about getting them. "It is what the Six call a special sort of meeting. When one of us has a problem—" He had a sudden vision of himself calling a forum to discuss *his* problem and blushed rosily. "—we call everyone together to ask for help in finding a solution. It is from the Latin, and, since our first such meetings were held when we were all at school together, and Latin was an important part of our life, that is what we called them."

"From the Latin?"

"In ancient Rome it was what they called their parliament."

Libby, enlightened, said, "Ah!"

Tony chuckled. "I suppose you think it strange that we hold our own little parliaments?"

"Who is prime minister?" she asked, with a sly glance from the corners of her eyes.

Tony tipped his head and tapped his chin with his glass. "I had never considered our group in that way, but I suspect Renwick is PM and McMurrey our Solon."

"Solon?"

"Solon was a Greek and a wise giver-of-laws," explained Tony. He had never thought himself particularly learned, but Libby, with her questions, made him think that perhaps he actually knew more than he had ever suspected.

Libby nodded and, after a moment, asked, "Then, is someone the Loyal Opposition?"

He laughed. "We might even be said to have that. When we need it, Merwin acts as devil's advocate, raising potential problems to whatever someone proposes as a solution."

"And your place, Tony?"

He shrugged, sobered. "Me? I guess I'm just there. I don't do much of anything special."

"I doubt that very much."

"You do?" He cast her a startled look. "Why?"

"Because I am quite certain that whenever there is any problem that involves the Ton, it is to you they turn for advice."

Tony felt his ears burn. "But that is nothing special!"

"And I would guess that the others feel the same when it comes to what they know. One rarely values what seems easy."

Tony thought about that as they strolled toward the

house. He held the door for his wife, a side door he rarely used, and halfway down the hall noticed a comfortable-looking parlor into which he ushered her. "I think I understand what you mean. Jack could never see why a person had trouble learning to ride. Not that any of us had difficulty, but there are very bad riders, you know. He simply couldn't see why. It is as you said, is it not? Because riding was so easy for him, he didn't value it as a special talent. He thought it something everyone should do."

"He must have felt awful when he didn't know if he'd recover the use of that leg. The thought of being unable to ride must have upset him a great deal."

"But he couldn't ride, didn't you know!" Tony nodded when she frowned.

He was telling Libby about their problems with Jack a few months previously when Sahib looked into the room. The big cat stared from Libby to Tony and back again. Then he entered, nosed the door shut, and lay down in front of it.

Libby moved a trifle closer to Tony. She was no longer interested in Jack and Patricia's history. "Sahib acts so strangely! He frightens me, Tony. He stares at me and stares at me, and I do not like it."

"You mustn't fear Sahib, Libby," said Tony, taking her hand in his. "Truly. He is very sensitive to a person's problems, and, on more than one occasion, he has aided my friends in his rather odd fashion. I don't think he'll harm you. When he stares at you, maybe he is just trying to understand you."

"Understand me? But he is an animal, Tony. Do animals understand people?"

"Have you never had a pet, Libby? A dog, who seemed to know when you were sad and needed comforting, for instance?" She shook her head. "I did. A spaniel. One of her descendants had pups recently." Tony had a sudden thought. "Do you think you'd like one when they are weaned and house broken? A pet to keep you company?"

"A pet?" Libby repeated thoughtfully. "My very own?"

"Of course your very own."

"I'd never thought to have a pet. A spaniel?"

"The one I think you'd like is a beautiful dark red. When she is adult she'll have the silkiest hair and long boots growing from the back of her legs. Her ears will drag on the ground, almost!"

Libby laughed. "How can you know all that when the pup is still with her mother?"

"She will be just like her mother. I am sure of it. Shall I write and have her saved for you?"

"Yes, please," said Libby, realizing that Tony really wished her to have the little dog. She wondered why. "But why do you wish to give him to me?"

Tony frowned. "I hadn't asked myself that. Why? Well, I think because you've never had a pet and everyone should, once in their life, have their own dog or cat. Someone to talk to and to tell secrets to. You know."

Libby shook her head. It was her turn to frown, which changed to a surprised look. "Or—" She blushed. "—perhaps that is how I treated Willie? I used to talk to him a lot, tell him things, and discuss things with him. Do you suppose it is because you had no brothers or sisters you felt the need for a pet?"

"Perhaps," said Tony. "But I still think you'd like one of Sunshine's pups."

"So do I," she said, knowing it was what he wanted to hear. But, although she said it, she wasn't all that certain. She remembered her aunt's smelly spaniels and was less certain, but not about to harm the rapport between them by telling Tony she had no wish of a pet.

Libby rose to her feet and looked down at Tony. "I'd better go up now. My hair has grown enough that Finch wants to try a new hairstyle, and it may take some practice to get it right." She turned toward the door, and Sahib rose up on his front paws, his mouth opening in a silent growl. Libby paused, then glanced at Tony, a look filled with both dread and a plea for help.

Tony, too, rose. "Sahib, what is this? You know us."

Sahib rose to stand on all four feet. He snarled. When Tony took a step toward him, the big cat raised a paw, very much as if he were telling Tony to come no closer.

"Tony, no. He might attack you," she said when Tony moved forward and Sahib made it quite clear he was to come no nearer. Libby clutched his arm. "Tony, let's just sit down again. He didn't bother us when we were seated. Please?"

Tony stared at Sahib, and Sahib stared right back. After a long moment Tony turned to Libby, seated her, and sat down beside her. "I don't understand. Sahib has never acted this way before."

"I don't like it when he stares at me in that daunting way. I wish he'd not do it."

Sahib blinked, stared for just another moment, and then laid his great head down and closed his eyes.

"Tony," whispered Libby, "it is as if he understood me!"

"Nonsense!" But Tony eyed the tiger for a moment before turning back to Libby. "But it does seem we must stay here awhile yet! So . . . Tell me about how it was when you were young. If you didn't have any pets, and your brother is so much younger, what did you do?"

Libby looked back to those early years when she had been ignorant, when Nanny had protected her from any knowledge of her father's obsession with making a fortune—even though he was incapable of making a rational assessment of the projects in which he invested. She smiled, thinking of the fun she had had, Nanny a great one for encouraging the use of one's imagination. Libby told Tony stories of the long ongoing games Nanny and she had invented, and then, when Willie was old enough, the two of them had played the same sort of games.

"Nanny would read to us about knights and princesses and dragons and castles, and then we'd make up our own adventures. Or sometimes she'd read about traveling in foreign lands. And then we'd make up games where we had to fight off bandito hordes or pirates. . . ."

Libby talked for a long time and, finally, realizing it, blushed and asked, "But what about you, Tony? Before you went to school? Did you play the same sort of games?"

Tony told of riding his pony and playing with the grandmother of his latest spaniel. ". . . When I have children I will want them to have their own dogs," he said and then realized he had mentioned what, in his mind, had become a forbidden subject. He broke off in embarrassment.

Just then they heard the distant sound of the gong, reminding guests it was time to dress for dinner. Sahib raised his head and looked over his shoulder. He heaved himself to his feet, ambled to the door where he raised up on his hind legs and, using his forepaw, pushed down on the door handle, pulling it open a trifle as he did so. Putting his nose in the crack, he opened the door still farther and pushed through. He was gone.

Libby and Tony stared at each other. Then Libby giggled. "I wasn't aware Sahib had to worry about dressing for dinner!"

Tony chuckled. "Dress for dinner? But of course. He must check the tails to his coat for creases."

They stared at each other. And then they laughed. And laughed some more. Partly, of course, from the humor, but still more from relief that Sahib had left them of his own accord and that they, too, were free to go up to their suite. Feeling more relaxed in each other's company than they ever before had felt, they made their way up to their rooms.

* * *

The next day the picnic party crowded into a variety of vehicles. The dogcart was most popular, but the gig, with difficulty, held four, and a couple of the men actually sat on the back of the farm wagon brought in to use to haul baskets, fishing gear, rugs and everything else someone happened to mention as essential to a comfortable day by the river.

When they arrived, bumping across the last bit of rutted lane to the small summerhouse Renwick's grandfather caused to be built beside a particularly placid section of the river, they discovered that Jase had ordered a marquee raised which would provide a larger area of shade than the small building could do. Both, however, were open to the gentle breezes, and both provided some sort of seating for those who preferred *not* to sprawl comfortably on the rug-covered grass.

The wine was hung in nets in the running water to cool, the baskets placed in the shade next to the summerhouse, and the men began sorting out the fishing gear. Prince Ravi plucked his favorite rod from those provided and moved upstream. Eustacia watched him take up a position almost exactly where, a year earlier, she had fallen into the river and, except for Lord Renwick's courageous action, would have drowned. She shivered at the memory of Jase diving into the river to save her. Jase might have drowned as well. How could he, blind as he was, have dared to attempt that rescue? What if *he* had died? She placed her hand over her swelling middle and turned away, not wanting to think of what *might* have been.

"Are you cold?" asked Libby, noticing the shiver.

"No." Eustacia, her hand still protectively over her babe, sighed. "I was thinking of the past. Of the last time I was here and I fell in. Jase rescued me or I must have drowned, but it just struck me that *he* might have as well. A terrible thought." She forced a smile. "And not one for a bright and sunny day such as this."

"It didn't happen," said Libby encouragingly. "But . . ." She shook her head. "No, I must not ask. You do not wish to discuss it."

"If you mean to ask how a blind man could rescue his wife," said Renwick's voice from behind her, "then you should know I'd a great deal of help. Prince Ravi's man gave me direction, and when I reached the riverbank he jumped in to help me get her ashore."

"And," said Eustacia, "became very ill as a result."

"A very brave man," added Renwick. "He couldn't swim, you see."

"A tale out of one of those novels one sees everywhere," said Libby, more than a little awed by the story. "A very proper heroine, an equally proper hero. A situation filled with terror! And *not* a story bound by marble covers and *told by a lady* but a real story . . ."

". . . *also* told by a lady," said Eustacia, chuckling.

Libby chuckled. "Well, yes, but you know what I mean!"

"There might have been a tragic ending, but there was not," said Renwick, his hand extended for his wife's. She put hers into his, and pulling her near, he moved his arm to clasp her around her waist. "Instead of a tragedy, it was a beginning leading to a very happy ending." He lifted his free hand to Eustacia's face and touched it lightly, found her mouth and drew a smile there. She smiled in response. "That's better," he said. "Lead me to one of the benches in the summerhouse, will you, my dear? If they are not all occupied?"

Libby watched them go, their heads tipped toward each other revealing an intimacy she envied. She didn't fault Lady Renwick for shivering when thinking about the incident. What if one had died and the other lived? Given the love they obviously felt for each other, that would have been the worst tragedy of all!

As she unfurled her parasol, she looked around and

discovered that Tony was downstream watching a couple of the men fish. At the moment, her emotions in a tumult, she dared not join him. Instead, she moved upstream, stopping some little distance from the prince, who concentrated on his casting. Taking care she not disturb him, she seated herself on a stone and marveled at the control the young man had of his casting.

The day was beautiful. And peaceful. Libby absorbed the peace for a bit and then turned back to watching the fisherman. A few moments later Prince Ravi pulled in a nice-sized trout.

"Very nice," she said.

He turned, his teeth white against his skin. "It is, is it not? A beauty. I hope we catch enough that Cook will prepare fish for tonight's dinner. I have learned to like it."

"I tried some of the curried vegetables served at dinner last night. I think I would like them if they were not *quite* so highly seasoned."

His grin widened. "I will order my cook to prepare a milder dish. Tomorrow. I will have him provide the two of us with parathas for breakfast. They are a little like your griddle cakes but thinner and with a curried vegetable chopped up fine between two of them. You will like them. Even my lady likes them, but not just now when she carries the babe. She says she—" He frowned slightly. "—does not even like the smell. I do not understand it."

Libby chuckled. "Women take strange fancies when *enceinte*. You and I must eat our breakfast early or eat late so that we do not disturb her."

"Or we may dine on the terrace. I do that when the weather is good. Will you join me there? At nine in the morning? I would like that. It is early, I know, but I must begin my studies at an early hour. My tutor insists," he finished and made a moue of disgust.

"Nine is an excellent hour for breakfast in the country. Thank you very much for the invitation," said Libby, hoping she would not disgrace herself by finding the prince's food inedible.

"You—" His eyes sparkled with humor. "—are thinking you will go away hungry. Do not fear. I will see you do not!"

Libby cast him a rueful look. "Should I apologize?"

"No. I remember how I detested your English food when first I came to England. I thought I would starve and gave my cook two jewels and said he would have more if he managed to feed me well." He drew in a breath and blew it out. "And I am very glad, Lady Wendover, that we have had this little talk. I have not done as I said I would! I must remember to reward the fellow, since I did *not* starve, as I truly feared I might!"

"Yes, we should always fill our promises."

As they spoke, the prince put the fish on a line. "And I promise you a feast fit for a maharani. It is a promise I will keep. Come now," he added with unconscious arrogance, "we will return to the others."

Libby noticed that the food had been laid out. Tony saw her approaching with Prince Ravi and came to meet them. "Ah," he said, "that is a nice-sized fish. I believe it is the largest caught today. I am informed that we will have barely enough for dinner this evening."

"I will catch more after we eat. It is the wrong time of day, but the river is well stocked. I do not despair of adding to our catch," said Ravi. "But now I am hungry. I," he added a trifle plaintively, "am always hungry. Lord Renwick says it is because I am growing." He looked at Tony. "My lord? Do you think I am growing?"

Tony chuckled. "I remember when you first arrived. You, my lad, were a mere tadpole, and now you are all long legs and arms and—" He lifted his hand to the level of the top of Prince Ravi's head. "—I would guess you are very nearly as tall as I."

The prince sighed. "Yes. Very nearly. But it is Mr.

McMurrey I wish to emulate. I hope I grow a great deal because I've a long ways to go to be so tall as Mr. McMurrey!"

"I wish you luck in that," said Libby, smiling.

Prince Ravi scowled. "You do not believe I can do it."

"Do you wish the truth?" He hesitated and then, ruefully, nodded. "Then, no. I think you have a different sort of build. I think you may grow to be as tall as Captain Seward or perhaps so tall as Lord Princeton, but *not* so tall as Mr. McMurrey!"

"Not captain, Libby," said Tony. "Miles is just a plain mister."

Libby cast him a look. "Miles Seward isn't just a *plain* anything!"

Tony chuckled. "You got me there, Libby. I would have to agree that Miles is something else, indeed!"

Prince Ravi smiled, but there was a sad look about him as well.

"You have a special reason for wishing to be so tall as Ian?" asked Tony.

"I would be the tallest person at my father's court. It would add to my prestige, you see."

"Better to be the smartest and best educated person at your court, I would think," mused Libby.

The boy nodded. "That too, of course, but—" The princely arrogance returned. "—I do not worry about *that*."

They had reached the others, and a footman took Ravi's fish from him, adding it to the others. Tony led Libby to the table on which the food was arranged and filled a plate to her order. He settled her on a rug under the marquee beside Patricia and Jack and went to fetch his own dinner. Libby, as had become a habit when with the others, fell silent, withdrawing into herself, although watchful of those around her. She could not be easy with Tony's friends. She could not rid herself of the feeling she had entered their closed little world under false colors and didn't deserve to be included.

Now, as she listened to the banter, she wished with all her heart she did belong. She sighed softly. Lady Blackburne, sitting nearby, noticed. "Lady Wendover, I fear you've caught a trifle more sun than is proper. You better remain under the tent this afternoon."

Libby nodded submissively, not too happy with the notion, but once the others wandered off, she discovered Lady Blackburne and Lord Hayworth were an entertaining duo who kept her laughing until it was time to tumble back into the various forms of transport and be carried back to the house—where Sahib greeted their arrival with a roar heard throughout the whole of Tiger's Lair.

Libby saw Lord Renwick brace himself, and then suddenly, there was the big cat prancing toward him and rubbing up against him, first on one side and then the other. The tiger made an odd sound, and Libby looked at Lady Blackburne, who stood at her side.

"It is like a cat's purr. I know it does not sound the same, but he does that when he is pleased. And he is very pleased whenever Lord Renwick returns after being gone for more than an hour or so."

"He is so very beautiful, but I cannot be easy with him."

"Many cannot. I, too, find him rather fearful and freely admit I am thankful he leaves me be."

"I only wish he *would* ignore me. He stares at me. And occasionally he has even growled at me."

"Oh? Growled?"

"Yes. Last night my lord and I were talking together but then decided to go up to our rooms, but Sahib would not allow us to leave the room in which we sat."

"Were there others in the room?" asked Lady Blackburne sharply.

"No, it was just the two of us."

"Hmm."

"What does that mean?" asked Libby.

"I wonder . . ."

"Wonder what," Libby asked after a moment.

"Do you suppose . . . ?"

Libby, impatient to know what her ladyship thought, glared at Lady Blackburne, who, catching the expression, smiled, shook her head, and wandered off. "Well!" said Libby, staring after her.

"Well?" asked Patricia.

"No it is not. Not well, I mean. What, I wonder, did she mean by that?"

"By what?"

Libby explained, watched a smile form in Patricia's eyes and spread to her whole face—and watched her lips compress. "You don't mean to explain either, do you?"

"No. Except to say you needn't be concerned about Sahib. He goes his own way, but he will not harm you. To the contrary!" She, too, nodded and walked off.

The Renwick's butler came into the hall that had gradually emptied of all but Libby. He moved in stately fashion toward the oversized brass gong his lordship had shipped back from India and, picking up the mallet, gave it a sharp whack. The rolling tone of the brass echoed around her, seeming alive in its intensity. Libby moved toward the stairs. It was time to change for dinner, and, once again, her maid had had no time to practice the new style for her hair that had grown from its exceedingly short crop!

Dinner passed in its usual fashion, talk among the guests not restricted to those at either side, but flowing freely around the table which was sized so that all were comfortable but could be intimate with all the others. On this particular evening, the men did not linger over their brandy, but quickly joined the women in the Blue Salon, Ladies Blackburne and Renwick's favorite.

Charades were organized, a game Libby loved and

Tony tolerated. Tony, paired with Libby, discovered that when one had the proper partner, one with an excellent imagination and the ability to coax servants into finding the most outrageous of props, charades could be hilariously funny. In fact, Libby's endeavors inspired the others to greater efforts, and everyone produced more elaborate performances than were their norm. The evening broke up late, the men retiring to Renwick's study and the women, for the most part, to bed.

Libby, far too wide awake to even think of going to her room, wandered into the back of the house where she found what she discovered was a sewing parlor. To the side of one chair was an oversized workbasket, and to the side of another a tambour frame, the work well forward. Libby held her candle higher but was too far away to determine the design. She moved into the room, lit two candles and a lamp, and took a better look. The greater part was rolled onto the bar. What remained showed a mass of flowers and, rising out of them, a geometric design Libby guessed continued up the panel. Having decided that, she felt at loose ends and wandered the room. She discovered a small bookcase, chose a collection of verse, and returned to the chair by the tambour.

At the other side of the house, the men decided it was time to break up their evening, and most headed straight for their beds. Tony was reluctant to go up. His room was too near Libby's. And Libby was a temptation he found harder and harder to withstand!

Deciding to stroll down to the stables, he headed for a back door. The hall he entered passed the breakfast room and then several small rooms devoted to various occupations. There was a music practice room, a room Lady Renwick used as an office where she did her accounts in privacy, and then finally a door out of which light poured. Tony glanced in and saw his wife. For a long moment he stared at her and then, on a whim, entered the room.

"It is good, your book?" he asked softly.

But as softly as he spoke, he startled her. She straightened, and her hand flew to her throat. Then, seeing who it was, she relaxed. "It is a collection of poetry that has not come my way. I've found several old favorites and some I've never before read, but which I like very much indeed. I was memorizing this one." She lifted the book.

"Which one?"

"It is by a poet called Blake, whom I've never read, and about a tiger. *Tiger Tiger burning bright* is the way it begins, and it goes on for several verses. It is as if he knew Sahib! Except, of course, that Sahib is a different color." Her gaze flew beyond Tony as a movement caught her eye. "And there—" She sighed. "—he is."

Tony turned. The great tiger stood in the doorway, eying them. Slowly, sinuously, Sahib moved a few paces into the room. He stared at Tony, then at Libby and then back at Tony. Then he opened his mouth in that way he had, a sort of silent snarl. Tony jumped and moved closer to Libby.

Libby was glad to have him near. And then she recalled Lady Princeton telling her she need not worry about Sahib's strange behavior. She said as much to Tony.

"She didn't explain?"

"Neither Lady Blackburne nor Lady Princeton would do more than smile and assure me it would be all right. But, Tony, he stares so," she complained.

"I wonder . . ."

"Now, don't you go doing it as well!"

"As well?"

"That is exactly what Lady Blackburne said. 'I wonder' and then no more."

Tony chuckled but, after a moment, sobered. "There is a tale told that Sahib plays cupid now and again. Jase will not explain what he did, but he and Eustacia claim that if it were not for the tiger, they'd very likely never have managed to get around to getting married. I know he was there when Jack and Patricia came to terms, and Ian and Lady Serena claim he put a paw into their marriage as well. Do you suppose he is taking a hand in ours?"

"What nonsense. He is an animal."

The tiger lifted his head and growled.

Libby swallowed. "Well," she said, feeling very brave, "you *are.*"

Sahib blinked, appeared to nod, and then laid his head back to the floor.

"Sometimes you would swear he understands every word," said Tony, watching Sahib.

"Surely it is merely an accident. . . ."

"Yes," agreed Tony, a doubtful sound to the word, "but sometimes I have noticed the same thing with my dogs. Oh, not often, but often enough one must wonder just how much they do understand of what one says."

"As you know, I've never had a pet, so I'd not know. I think—"

The tiger lifted its head.

"—it must be—"

Sahib growled softly.

"—a very special thing," she went on quickly, "if it is so!"

Sahib stared at her, his beautiful eyes blinking slowly. Then he laid his head back down.

Libby sighed. "Maybe I will be forced to change my mind," she said a trifle ruefully.

Tony smiled. "One must admit that Sahib is a very special creature. I don't know if all animals are so intelligent, but one is forced to believe he is." He fell silent. "Libby . . ."

"Yes?"

He fiddled with his quizzing glass, sighed, and said, "Oh, nothing."

"Nothing?"

"Well, nothing important." He wondered if that lie would come home to him!

"Hmm." When Tony said nothing more, she said, "I am to breakfast with Prince Ravi tomorrow. I hope I can eat his food. We are to eat on the terrace since the smell bothers Lady Renwick. Tony . . ."

"Hmm?"

"Will you come, too?"

"Do you want me to?"

"I'd not have said so if I did not. Prince Ravi is only a boy, but there is something about him that disturbs me. Every so often it is as if he were another person entirely."

Tony nodded. "I know exactly what you mean. Every so often he changes from average boy to royal prince. It is disconcerting, is it not?"

"I suppose it is that. A sort of arrogance which sits oddly on such young shoulders."

"Hmm."

Again silence ensued. Tony yawned. "I should go up to bed." He rose to his feet and then hesitated. "Do you suppose Sahib will let us leave if we ask him politely?"

The reference to the last time Sahib had chaperoned them made Libby giggle. "You try."

Solemnly Tony bowed to Sahib. "My lord of the jungle," he said, "may we be excused from your presence?"

Sahib blinked. He seemed to consider Tony's words and then looked at Libby. Libby rose to her feet and went to stand beside Tony. Uncertain whether she was playing a game or if she was serious, she curtseyed. Sahib climbed to his feet, stared at them for a long moment, and then took himself off. Libby and Tony glanced at each other and then hurried to the door, peering around the frame to see Sahib stalking down the hall, his tail lashing slightly from side to side.

"Is he angry?" asked Tony.

"I don't think he is exactly happy. I wonder what he expected of us?"

Tony, thinking of how Sahib had managed to get his friends' marriages on track, had a notion, but it wasn't one he dared speak aloud. Instead, he offered his arm, Libby took it, and the two of them hurried off to their suite.

Once there they each hovered in their sitting room, neither quite certain why. Finally Libby offered, "Well . . . good night now."

"Hmm? Oh. Well. Yes. Sleep well, Lily."

Libby went to sleep with a smile on her face and that "Lily" ringing in her ears. Maybe . . .

Just maybe . . . ?

Ten

Despite the early hour, Tony looked as elegant as usual when he joined Libby and Prince Ravi for breakfast. "This looks excellent," he said, studying the table with his quizzing glass.

Prince Ravi laughed. "I think your wife does not agree. Do be seated so that she may be served and learn that my food can be very tasty, indeed."

Much to Libby's surprise she liked it. Most of it. In fact, Prince Ravi's cook had judged her tastes so well, she rather feared she made a pig of herself. "Do you," she asked the prince, "think he will teach me the trick of such flavors?"

Ravi instantly sobered. He shook his head. "Lady Renwick's cook has asked, and he refuses to show her a thing. I might order him to do so, but—" Ravi shrugged. "—he is a cook. It is very strange with cooks, is it not? He might run away or kill himself rather than obey me. I do not understand it."

Libby had heard tales of tempermental cooks from London hostesses and had some experience with the McMurrey cook when she and Tony borrowed the London town house. "I, too, do not understand, but cooks seem to be exceedingly possessive about their work. Like an artist?"

"The very best are artists," said Tony, idly moving rice

from one side of his plate to the other. He, unlike Libby, did not care for Indian cuisine.

Libby noticed, changed the subject to Prince Ravi's studies, and very soon the meal ended and she and Tony strolled into the garden. It was a pleasant interlude—until Tony's stomach growled, embarrassing him.

Libby, giggling, excused him, suggesting he raid the kitchen.

Later that day Ian McMurrey and Lord Merwin arrived. They had picked up Miles Seward, who was walking down the drive, so that the three walked in the open front door with Miles hallooing.

"Where the devil is everyone?" he shouted.

Others of the Six poured from the Renwicks' private wing of the mansion in which Lord Renwick's study was situated. Ladies Wendover and Princeton appeared at the top of the stairs. Lady Renwick came through the green baize door leading to the servants' quarters, and Lady Renwick's uncle, Lord Hayworth, held open the salon door for Lady Blackburne, who held before her a rather large vase full of roses.

"Ah. More of the Six," the last said. Her ladyship turned on her heel and returned to the salon where she deposited the vase on a table between the front windows and rearranged several of the blooms. The others followed her, and soon all were gathered in the salon.

"You did not bring Lady Serena and the babe?" asked Eustacia of Ian.

Sahib stepped forward a few steps until he faced McMurrey. The big cat voiced his habitual silent welcome and then seemed to peer around as if looking for something. When Ian spoke, the big cat lifted his eyes to his face for all the world as if he were listening.

"Serena decided she and our son would stay with my father, who takes a great interest in his grandson. Lady Wendover," he added, turning to Libby, "I haven't a notion what you did; but you have given my father a new interest in the world, and we thank you for it!"

Libby blushed, glanced at Tony, who smiled and nodded approvingly, and blushed still more hotly. "I don't know that I did anything," she said. "I am glad if I helped, but truly, I don't know what I might have done."

At that Lady Blackburne nodded *her* approval. She admired modest young women who did not put themselves forward. Not that she was ever such a one herself, of course. "Well," she now said, "if the two of you are here to stay, I'd best have a talk with Reeves."

"All has been seen to," said Lady Renwick. "A letter arrived for Jase which told us we were to expect them, so I ordered their rooms prepared." She turned to the men and missed Lady Blackburne's chagrinned look. "Your usual rooms, of course."

Lord Hayworth, who did not miss it, moved toward Lady Blackburne and, taking her elbow, led her quietly from the room. He tucked her arm into his and strolled with her, talking quietly of this and that, until they reached the large conservatory at the back of the house. Once there he set her before her potting bench, shoved a flat of newly sprouted seedlings in front of her, and, without another word, took himself away.

Once out of her ladyship's sight, however, Hayworth did a more than adequate hornpipe, nearly shocking a maid into a spasm. He grinned at the girl, patted her on her head as he passed her, and went on up to his room. He rang for a pot of tea and, once it arrived, sat drinking it while he plotted ways and means of convincing his love he needed her far more than Lord and Lady Renwick needed her—which was her ladyship's primary reason for not accepting his proposal.

Ian, meanwhile, answered questions concerning his son's well-being until he laughed and raised a hand in a fencer's defensive gesture. "In my trunk is a long letter from Serena. I believe she has documented the boy's every moment. If you ladies will only be patient, I will retrieve it, and you may read it when I am not by." He chuckled one of his deep-chested laughs. "I love the lad with all my heart, but I may wish him to the devil if he is going to take up Serena's every moment and all her interest! I am jealous, you see." He shook his finger at Eustacia. "Take it as a dire warning, dear lady! Do not forget your husband when you've your new love in your arms!"

"You exaggerate, my lord," said Eustacia. "I watched you with the boy when we came to his christening! You are as obsessed with him as is Serena!"

He grinned. "Well, perhaps. If you say so." He glanced around at his silent friends. "But enough talk of the infantry!" He sobered. "A forum, do you think?"

Renwick nodded at Ian's request that the Six hold one of their special meetings. His fingers lightly on Sahib's head, he led the men to his study. "You stopped in London?" he asked, once all were seated and holding a glass of port.

"Yes. Where Miles had better go once we are finished here. Someone at the Horse Guards wishes to see him. Something he has evidently put off as long as he dares," said Ian. "Or perhaps *longer* than a prudent man would dare?" He threw a laughing glance toward Miles, who grimaced. Everyone knew Miles avoided dealing with authority whenever possible. "Anyway, I spent the day in town, and Merwin and I were on our way, on the next tide." He grinned. "If you are wondering how that can be, I hired a boat. I was intrigued by the stories you told about sailing up for the boy's christening and decided to try it. I am amazed how easily one travels by water and am considering the notion of buying a yacht."

"Wait until you've experienced your first storm," said Miles, his voice surprisingly lazy. "Or until you become lost in a fog or have been becalmed and find yourself drifting on the current toward a cliff face, the sails not so much as rustling."

"It is true I've sailed only in fine weather. Nevertheless, I have never come south more comfortably or arrived more rested."

Miles was too interested in Ian's plans for Lord Dixon to abide any more chitchat. "How," he asked, "are we to beard our beast in his den?" Sahib growled, and Miles turned to look at him. "Excuse me, Sahib. Let me rephrase that. Have you a plan for taking Lord Dixon down a peg?"

Everyone chuckled, and then the men put their heads together to plot their next move in Ian's campaign to free his wife's mother from her father, who was a tyrant and a bully and a nasty piece of work altogether.

"My investigator has discovered several pieces of information which will, I think, do the trick. The latest involves a young woman and the news that our fine lordship is indulging in some sort of skullduggery where the local workhouse is concerned."

"Skullduggery?" asked Renwick.

Ian's deep voice deepened. "It has to do with removing the young children who fall into his hands via the poorhouse and putting them to work in northern factories. I had heard rumors that a few mill owners would buy such children, but tended to disbelieve it. Now I must." A muscle worked in his jaw.

Ian drew a breath. "In addition, his fine lordship has changed his habits. He never left home if he could avoid it for as long as Serena can remember. Now he does. Every week or so. And what he does while absent from home—" Ian's lips compressed. "—well frankly, you don't want to know the details, but, as I wrote you, he very nearly killed a young woman in Bristol only two weeks ago. She is too frightened to confront our man directly, but she has made a deposition that was witnessed by a gentleman whose signature means a great deal." Ian sighed. "It all adds up. I think it will be enough."

"From what you told us before," said Wendover, swinging his glass, "I think he will give in to your wishes merely because he knows people believe that where there is smoke there is fire. He will not want word of any of this bruited about."

"Yes, threats of casting the bits we have onto the winds and allowing word to scatter like the dried seeds of the thistle will, I dare say, frighten him into accepting the inevitable."

Silence followed Ian's conclusion. Finally, Renwick asked, "Then, we start tomorrow, early, and return the same day?"

"If my mother-in-law can make herself ready to depart that quickly, we can manage it in one day. It depends entirely on her ladyship."

"You do not mean to punish Lord Dixon in any way?" asked Miles, frowning.

"I wish I could, but to do anything of the sort would reflect badly on Serena and her mother, would it not?"

"I hate it when injustice goes unpunished." Miles spoke with an intensity he rarely revealed, his deeper emotions nearly always covered and concealed by his insouciant surface nature.

"I think there *will* be punishment," said Tony, surprising the others. Discussing the principles underlying his personality was as out of character for him as allowing true emotion to show was for Miles. "Perhaps a more dreadful punishment than any we could contrive."

"Nonsense," said Miles, "Ian means to do nothing!"

"But that is just it. Ian has said the man's foremost desire in life is to retain his position in his community, and if word of even one strand of his infamy got about, that would be endangered. We will demand that he change his ways, of course, but he is the sort who cannot live without avenging himself for every imagined slight, a man who must have his way in all things. He will *want* to act and, at the same time, *fear* to do so. He will be on tenterhooks, wondering when one of us will reveal something by accident—or *on purpose* as he might do for the pure mischief of it—will he not?"

Miles smiled. It was not a nice smile. "I will threaten to do just that if he allows one more child to fall into the hands of those damn mill owners!"

"And I might promise to speak out if I hear of another woman harmed by him," said Jase, who had a horror of men who took advantage of anyone of lesser strength or station.

"I wonder if the man is capable of controlling himself," mused Ian in his deep rumbling voice. "But would you hear of it if he does *not* behave? And if he behaves badly and gets away with it once, then I fear he'll grow worse than ever. No, we will offer no threats. Instead, we will allow his fear to fester and grow within his own mind. In the long run, fear will do more to control him than anything else."

"Perhaps, once in a while, one of us should check to see he's behaving," said Miles through gritted teeth.

"Miles, you cannot right all the wrongs in this world. Not singlehanded."

Miles grinned a wolfish grin. "Ah! But there are six of us. Together, the Six could do a great deal!"

"I am no crusader," said Tony, rather horrified by the notion.

"Are you not?" Miles still grinned that wolfish grin. "Then," he asked, a sly note to his tone, "it is not true, what I have heard, that after Brummell's yours is the most feared quizzing glass in all of London?"

"Oh, well!" Tony felt the heat of a flush rise up into his ears. "That is nothing."

"Is it not?" asked Ian, a smile in his voice. "Have I not

heard of a dowager who no longer browbeats her daughter-in-law, and that change occurred after facing your glass on only two or three occasions!"

"But we cannot know how she behaves at home, can we?" asked Tony, frowning. "Sometimes I wonder if I do more harm than good." He tapped his chin with his glass, staring into space. Then he sighed. "It is so hard to know what is right."

"Nonsense. Right and wrong are very clearly set before us," said Miles sharply.

"I cannot agree," said Tony slowly. "Almost nothing is black and white. Rarely is a situation without shades of gray." He shook his head, bringing his gaze into focus. "Why are you all looking at me that way?"

Lord Renwick laughed. *"I'm* not looking at you."

"No, of course not," said Tony, embarrassed by Jase's easy reference to his blindness. "But those others are."

"Perhaps they are surprised that you've grown so philosophical in your old age," said Renwick, chuckling.

"Philosophical? Me?" Tony looked horrified. *"Never."*

Everyone, even Tony himself, laughed at that.

The next morning the men left for Lord Dixon's estate before the women rose from their beds. Libby had no notion of how early they were off, since she was the only married lady who slept alone. Lady Blackburne, who also, if rather reluctantly, slept alone, knew, but that was because she was an early riser herself. She and Lord Hayworth, who rose early to breakfast with his love, waved them off.

"I know it is best I do not join them," said Lord Hayworth wistfully, "but I am feeling quite blue about it." He sighed, then focused on Lady Blackburne and, speaking mock sternly, demanded, "Distract me, woman!"

Lady Blackburne cast a glowering look his way before pursing her lips and putting her mind to the problem. "Perhaps you would escort me into Brighton. There is shopping I must do which can be done nowhere nearer.

I should have managed it when I was there before and cannot think why I did not!"

Hayworth chuckled. "I don't suppose having a tooth drawn had anything to do with it? The fact you did not feel *quite* the thing?"

Lady Blackburne had the grace to flush slightly. "That might have had *something* to do with it."

"So I should think! Very well, my lady. Brighton it is."

While his lordship and her ladyship laid plans for the uncomfortably long jaunt into Brighton, Lady Renwick made her own for an outing to Lewes. When she, Patricia and Libby met over the breakfast cups, she laid the suggestion before them. Libby had already decided to ride and was not tempted, but Lady Princeton thought that it would be a fine day's entertainment. *Perhaps,* she added in glowering tones, the shops would distract her from the trifling concern she could not help but feel for their menfolk, who, as it were, meant to confront an ogre in his den.

Libby waved the others off and went to put on her habit. Lady Renwick had suggested a particular destination, and Libby jogged along happily until she reached the stretch of river recommended to her as particularly lovely. Once she and the groom assigned to go with her reached the river, Libby dismounted and, leaving the horses in the care of the groom, walked along the bank for a space, idly thinking about this and that but nothing in particular.

She had turned and was returning to the horses when it crossed her mind to wonder if the ladies were finding all they required in the village shops. Lady Princeton had said that if she could find silk stockings, she would buy several pair, and Lady Renwick had named a book she meant to get at the bookstore. Or she would order it if it was not available, as was likely the case. They also meant to stop in at the very nice hat shop that Lady Princeton remembered from a visit just before Christmas.

Libby's thoughts were totally speculative and utterly without envy and, suddenly, it occurred to her she had done no shopping—*none whatsoever*—for weeks now. Nor had she had the least desire to do any. She had not missed it!

Libby stopped in her tracks, trying to understand what was different, why her compulsion to buy things had vanished. In fact, had not another quarter day recently come and gone? Her heart pounding, Libby returned to the horses and, far more rapidly than she had begun her ride, she returned to Tiger's Lair. The groom, shaking his head over the foibles of tonnish ladies, trotted along behind.

Libby didn't even bother to remove her hat before seating herself at the small desk in the sitting room of the suite given over to Tony's and her use. She made a series of quick calculations. She stared at the result, and, more slowly, she started over. The answer was very nearly the same. Libby blinked. Was it really possible she had so much money in hand?

It seemed it was. Libby rang the bell, and, once her order was understood, the secretly astounded butler provided her with the last newspapers and one or two recent journals.

Libby laid them on the table in her sitting room near the comfortable love seat, but embarrassed by the notion that Tony might return and see them there and wonder at her interest in them, she gathered them up and took them into her room. There she relaxed in a lady-sized armchair near her window.

Libby heeled off her boots in a manner that would have shocked her maid, unpinned and threw her hat onto the bed, and only then picked up the first paper. Having the house to herself was perfect. She needn't worry about contravening convention by ignoring her hostess and the other guests. There was time to pore over every article she found relating to shipping, canal building, mining, and other forms of investment, which she would have had to read surreptitiously and in bits of stolen time if there had been others around to notice what she did.

After something over two hours of careful study and still more careful reading between the lines, she found that for which she searched. Returning to her desk, she took out a clean sheet of paper and looked at the pen. She frowned at the nib, searched for a new one, did not find one, and decided to use what she had. The questions she asked her grandmother's solicitor—her own now—were many. She hoped he had the resources to discover the answers for her since she was *not* like her father and would *not* invest where she hadn't sufficient information.

She rewrote the letter twice and, just before she sealed it, remembered one further question. She glared at the page, nearly filled with her small neat writing, and glanced at the clock, which told her it was far later than she would have guessed. There was no time to rewrite it. She sighed and put the question as a postscript, squeezing it in along one edge.

It would have to do. She sealed it and took it down to Reeves, the Renwicks' butler, for inclusion in the following day's mail pouch.

Ian stared at the man seated across the desk from the Six. Sahib stirred restlessly under Renwick's hand. Miles scowled, his fists clenched. Jack lounged against the wall beside the door, his crutch under one arm and his arms folded across his chest, and Tony sat, one leg across his other knee and his quizzing glass swinging from the end of its ribbon.

"You cannot come in here and accuse me of such nonsense," said Lord Dixon defiantly. "I'll bring suit!"

Ian's brows rose above his deep-sunk eyes. A smile spread slowly. "What an excellent idea!" he rumbled. "My lord, you should do just that very thing. What fun when we bring evidence against you and the mill owners with whom you deal. You are aware, of course, that the buying and selling of human flesh is illegal?"

"No such thing!" growled Lord Dixon. "You can't say I've sold anyone."

"Can we not? I wonder. Would the courts agree?" Ian's elbows were on his chair arms, and now he put his fingers together, tapping them gently. "Lord Merwin, you must immediately check into the exact penalties for such behavior. Would not this suit be a nice change for the judges, something a trifle different from the usual brought before the courts? Then, of course," he went on in musing fashion, "there is that woman in Bristol and—"

Dixon half rose from his chair at the mention of still another evil to be laid at his feet.

"—I am assured she will testify, assuming she is promised protection from your well-known desire for revenge against those who defy you. Have I forgotten anything?" he asked rhetorically.

"He must answer for the children," said Miles. "How any man can be so cruel and uncaring as to send innocents into the hell which is a mill I will never understand."

Lord Dixon's lip curled. "Surely—" He spoke coldly. "—you do not believe your so-called innocents have any sensitivity? Not only are they barely a step above animals, but they are good for nothing else."

"They are children," said Ian quietly. "Living beings. They look to those set over them to protect them. When the protectors will not, what can they do?"

"Bah. Living beings? Living *trash!* Useless. Expensive. Worthless. Except to someone like a mill owner!"

"I see you've convinced yourself you do no wrong. I doubt very much you can convince others. I wonder what the other men on the poorhouse board truly think. Assuming they know." Ian smiled thinly when Lord Dixon blanched. "But even if they do, when they find others disapprove, will they not find the courage to stand against you?"

His lordship's fists clenched at Ian's suspicion the other men on the poorhouse board knew nothing of his dealings with the mill owners, but he did not attempt to convince those confronting him he had acted with full knowledge and support of the board.

The conversation followed various paths and, gradually, tangled Lord Dixon up in his own words, but when Ian said he meant to remove Lady Dixon to Scotland, Lord Dixon began to bluster. Loudly. His eldest son opened the door and looked in. He glanced from man to man, then back to Ian, the only one he recognized. And only then did look toward his father. "You called?"

"I did not," shouted Dixon. "Out. *Out!*" he bellowed. "Go away!"

Sahib rose to his feet and would not lie down when Renwick pressed his hand against his back.

Serena's brother's brows clashed. "And if I won't?"

"You'll go or I'll have the hide off your back!"

Dixon's eldest son's lips pursed. Then he shrugged. "Yowl," he said, sneering, "if you want me." He closed the door.

Sahib sank back to the floor.

But after the intrusion of his son, Dixon seemed somehow to collapse. He pulled a handkerchief from his pocket and mopped his brow and, holding it clutched in one hand, stared wildly around the room. "You cannot take my wife away. What," he mumbled, "would people say."

"They would say," said Ian, gently "that she wishes to visit her new grandchild."

Dixon straightened. Some shadow of his old arrogance returned. "Yes. Of course. So they would. Very well. I give her permission to go." A sly look slid over his features. "For three weeks."

"You have not been listening," said Ian patiently. "She is going, yes, but she will not return. She will live with Serena."

"You cannot come between a man and his wife!"

"But," said Ian, his voice very quiet in the otherwise silent room, "you are not man and wife."

For a moment, Dixon did not comprehend Ian's meaning. Then he paled, shrank back into his chair. "How did you . . . ?" He shook his head. "You . . ." He shrank still farther into his chair. "There is no way. You *cannot* have discovered that." His eyes rolled, and he whined, "Papa promised. He said it was over. He said I was to forget it."

"The world has forgotten," said Ian politely. "For your true wife's sake it is better so. Too, if your real son were to inherit, as is his right, his feeblemindedness would require that he have a guardian for the whole of his life, after which the title and lands would revert to the king. Worst of all, although he, too, is unworthy of the position he will hold, the man you call your heir would be labeled a bastard."

A cunning expression narrowed Dixon's eyes. "You forget. So, too, would your precious wife. Serena is no more legitimate than the rest!"

"But for her it would change nothing. She is my wife, and I shall protect her. You know I not only could but would."

Again Dixon drooped, staring at nothing at all. The room was silent. Finally his lordship looked up. "What would you have me do?"

"You will sign certain papers I have brought with me which I will add to certain other papers I possess. I will take Lady Dixon away from here, provide a home for her, and keep her in funds. You will never attempt to see her again."

Lord Dixon looked around, desperately seeking an escape. "Has it occurred to you that you or—" He was blustering again. "—any one of you, might suffer an accident?"

"Threats?" Ian chuckled. "My lord, you'd best pray nothing by way of murder or even an accident occurs to any of us. I am not such a fool that I've not left my various proofs in a safe place. All will be revealed if you decide to avenge yourself on any one of us."

Dixon fisted his hands and pounded on his desk. "Devils!" he roared. "How dare you?"

Renwick tightened his hand in the loose skin at Sahib's neck when the cat indicated an intention to rise. He was unsuccessful, and the big cat not only stood, but opened his mouth to emit a roar that instantly silenced Lord Dixon.

When Sahib again subsided, Renwick answered Dixon's question by asking his own. "How dare we be concerned for those weaker than you? Concerned for those you bully and control by means of fear and threats you act upon just often enough no one dare cross you? How dare we feel concern for those you would harm? In other words, how dare we interfere in your, mmm, *pleasures?* My lord, it is incumbent on any gentleman to protect the innocent from evil, is it not?"

"Bah!"

Ian sighed and took up the lecture Renwick dropped. "Have you," he asked, "had your own way for so many years you feel you've a right to do exactly what you please no matter what devilish thing it is?"

"Bah, I tell you!" Again Dixon raised his voice to a roar, but with one eye on Sahib. "You, not I, have the devil in you! I curse you. All of you."

Ian's temper began to fray. "You may," he said, "curse us up and down the length of England if you wish. But you will sign these papers." He took them from his pocket. He did not, however, release them into Dixon's hands. "Will you not, my lord?" For the first time there was something of a threat in Ian's tone.

Again silence fell, a pall smothering the room. Lord Dixon stared at the papers as if they were snakes threatening to strike.

After a long moment's silence, the door opened once again. "Father? Are you certain I should not call for aid to throw these men out? I can have the groom and the footman and the gardener called in, and my brother has just returned."

Ian turned to look at his brother-in-law and chuckled. "We must be a formidable lot that you need so many."

"Go away," yelled Lord Dixon, interrupting Ian. "I don't want you!" He reached toward Ian. "Give me your damn papers. I'll sign." He turned to his son. "Tell your mother to pack. She is going on a journey."

"Mother?" The young man revealed his confusion. "But she never goes anywhere. You always say she is better here where you can know exactly what she does, where you can keep her up to the mark, but never allow her to know exactly what is expected of her so that she will never be quite certain of her position. You told us that when we marry we would be wise to do likewise."

Ian's jaw clenched. "Still more reasons to take Lady Dixon away!" he muttered. "You, my lord, are the monster Serena has always called you."

Softly as Ian spoke, the young man standing in the doorway heard his rumbling comment. "Monster? *Monster?* No one calls my father a monster!" He lifted a long-barreled pistol and aimed it. Jack, lifting his crutch, gave the arm a cruel hit. It flew up. The pistol went off, but the ball soared harmlessly over Ian's head.

Lord Dixon slapped his hand to his brow. "Now," he blustered, "I suppose you'll have my heir up for attempted murder. On top of everything else?" There was a cruel twist to his lordship's lips, an evil glint in his eye when he turned his gaze toward his heir. His son blanched as he backed from the room.

Ian eyed the older man. "There, there," he said in a deep, soothing rumble. "You will feel better now that you've frightened your son half out of his wits, will you not?"

But Ian's brother-in-law was no longer there to hear him, and later, it was discovered that the lock on the household money box was shattered, the money taken, and Dixon's supposed heir gone off to Bristol with the intention, it was believed, of taking ship to the new world. In the meantime, Dixon signed the papers.

After a long, soothing conversation that did not reveal he intended her visit to last forever, Ian convinced Lady Dixon that she really truly did wish to visit her grandson. Actually, that was not so very hard to do, but convincing her that Lord Dixon had given permission was very difficult, indeed!

Ian was not, on this occasion, forced to explain the illegality of her marriage. He still hoped to keep it from Lady Dixon, only revealing it if she refused his invitation to remain under his roof for the rest of her life. If she decided she was morally obliged to return to her home and her husband, he would use it as his final weapon in his battle to save her from misery, and his wife from worry.

So . . . unto the evil day, and all that.

Eleven

"What *does* that creature think he is doing?" asked Libby when, once again, she discovered she and her husband were, as it were, being held prisoner. Alone. Together.

Tony thought he knew, but he wasn't about to express what he suspected. He was a trifle ambivalent, unsure that it was what he truly wanted. After all, what he wanted was a love match, was it not? But with Libby? Who had cheated him into this marriage? On the other hand, the big tiger had played cupid to good effect when nosing into his friends' affairs, so perhaps he could make it happen. Tony felt torn in both directions and put aside his thoughts on a subject about which he could do nothing.

"After the day we had," he said, "I haven't the energy to raise my voice in protest. Why, do you suppose, is it so difficult, so very tiring, to do a simple thing like stand around holding up a wall while your friend argues with a devil?"

Libby put her hand on Tony's arm. She was surprised by the hardness of the muscle under his coat and only then noticed his fist was clenched. "Was it so very awful?" He didn't respond. "I cannot imagine it was anything like the simple and humorous tale Mr. McMurrey told at dinner. Can you not tell me more? Or is it a secret?"

"There are secrets which I may not tell—" He cast her an apologetic look. "—but the worst of it was the man himself. First he blustered. Then he threatened. At one point he seemed to shrivel into nothing at all and *whined* like a spoiled child. But the most awful thing of all, I think, was when his eldest son appeared and, if Jack had not been quick, would have shot Ian in the back."

"Shot him!"

"Yes. In the back! He had secreted the gun in the rather old-fashioned full skirts of his coat, and when Ian said something to his father which he didn't quite like, he actually raised the gun, pointed it at Ian's head, and fired. Except Jack pulled his crutch up in an arc and hit his arm a good thump, raising it up. The shot went high."

"But that would have been murder!"

Tony nodded.

"You might have been killed!" She blushed at the personal note and added, "All of you!"

Libby felt such shock her hand involuntarily tightened on Tony's arm. He put his free hand over hers and patted it. Suddenly, at the same moment, they both realized they were touching each other in a manner other than a conventional one acceptable between any tonnish man and woman. Almost reluctantly Tony lifted his hand from hers. Equally halfheartedly Libby loosened her grip and brought her hand to her lap where she carefully folded the one he had touched inside the other.

Tony cleared his throat. "Hmm. Yes. Well, that was about the end, I guess. Except once old Dixon agreed to Ian's demands concerning Lady Dixon, he took himself off, and it took Ian the better part of an hour to convince Lady Dixon she could come away and leave that awful man."

"And now she is upstairs fast asleep, happily awaiting tomorrow when Mr. McMurrey and Mr. Seward will sail away with her on the *Nemesis*. Tony, you would not believe the state of the poor woman's wardrobe. I helped Lady Blackburne put her to bed, you see. Her night wear! When I found the gown in the drawer, I thought it some old rag put there by mistake, but then I realized all her unmentionables are in terrible shape, mended to the point it is difficult to see how another stitch could be set to advantage. I got two of my night shifts and a robe and gave them to her. I hope you do not think it was out of line of me?"

"If you did it in such a way you did not embarrass her in front of Lady Blackburne, I would guess it a very good thing! It is all of a piece, is it not? Lord Dixon does all for show. Since no one will see his wife's night shifts, why worry about the state they are in?"

"I wonder what the washerwomen had to say about them?" mused Libby.

Tony laughed. "*I* wonder if that ever occurred to our villain. Or perhaps he forced his wife to do her own washing."

Libby turned an appalled look his way. "Surely not!"

Tony shrugged. "Frankly, I would put nothing past the man. He is a monster. I remember thinking at one point that he had no notion that anyone other than himself had feelings. That everyone beyond himself is merely a puppet with whom he may amuse himself in any way he wishes."

"What an odd man he must be." She sat silent for a moment and then added, "I feel rather sorry for him, I think."

"Waste of time," said Tony in his most languid tones.

"I should not feel that way simply because there is nothing I can do? I don't think anyone controls his emotions to that degree. But think, Tony, he will never know true friendship, let alone love. He will go through life alone, believing the whole world against him, and, in a way, it will be. No one of any sense can do other than distrust such a man. Even those who play the sycophant for fear of him would, figuratively speaking, stab him in the back, given the opportunity."

"Or perhaps *not* so figuratively. If they dared! I see what you mean," said Tony slowly. He stared at her. "You are very sensitive to how others think and feel, are you not? I mean, what you did for Ian's father, for instance. And you understood Lady Dixon's fears more than any other lady, did you not? I mean, when we arrived with her this evening. And—" He grinned a quick grin, lightening the moment. "—you won over my mother almost instantly. She likes you, you know. She told me I'm to treat you properly or she'd have words to say to me!"

Libby blushed. "But, Tony, what did I do? I don't recall doing anything special at all."

He smiled and, acting without thinking, touched her cheek with one gentle finger. "Libby, you don't *have* to do anything special. You simply *are* special."

Libby felt her heart quicken. She stared at him, tension around her eyes giving her a strained look. "Do . . . do you truly believe that?"

"Of course." Tony was more than a trifle astounded to discover that he *did*.

As they stared at each other Sahib rose to his feet and left the room. He shook himself and then, on silent pads, stalked off down the hall. It was some moments later when, embarrassed by the intensity of the feeling stretching between them, Libby glanced away from Tony, looked around, and registered that the big cat was gone.

"Tony! Sahib has gone away."

Tony glanced at the doorway. "So he has."

Tony contemplated the meaning of the cat's departure and decided Sahib thought enough had been accomplished between Libby and himself for one evening. Deciding to take the cat's example to heart, he rose to his feet.

"Perhaps we should go as well," he said. "I believe it is about time for the tea tray to come in, and it would be impolite if we were not there when it arrives."

* * *

Libby had a long talk with Finch that evening as her maid prepared her for bed. ". . . if you would rather not," she said, "I will ask Lady Renwick if there is a maid who could go with her ladyship and return with Mr. Seward after Lady Dixon has reached Scotland. She will be so alone, Finch. The only woman on a boat full of men. Even with Mr. McMurrey there—her son-in-law, you know—I fear she will be exceedingly uncomfortable."

"Of course I will do it, my lady, if you wish it," said Finch, pulling the brush through Libby's short curls still again, "but who would do for you while I am gone?"

Libby grinned a rather sour grin. "Finch, who did for me before you became my maid?" She watched Finch's reflection in the mirror, saw her hesitate for a moment in her brushing, and then register a sudden suspicion. Their eyes met in the mirror. Libby nodded. "That is right," she said. "I did for myself. My father had rid us of every possible servant by then to save a few pounds here and a few shillings there. If I could do for myself *then,* I can do so for the two or three weeks you'll be gone."

Finch bit her lip. "You *will* have me back, won't you?"

"We suit, Finch. At least you suit me. I will be glad to have you return to me."

Finch drew in a deep breath. "Then, my lady, if you would not mind that she'll be a trifle awkward, there is an under housemaid who would be pleased to do for you. She has ambitions, you see, and anything she could learn while I'm gone would be to her advantage. She's quick. You'll not have to tell a thing more than once."

"Very well. See if you can arrange it before you go. And, Finch . . ."

"Yes, my lady?"

"When you pack for yourself, pack a small case with my extra shifts and other items of clothing which do not show. I fear Lady Dixon has little or nothing of that sort she will wish her daughter to see. You might see that what *should* disappear does before she reaches Scotland?"

Finch's eyes widened. "Throw her things overboard?"

Libby smiled. "Yes. Exactly what I had in mind. If necessary, you may tell her you washed them and laid them out to dry where the men would not see them and that a breeze blew them into the sea!"

Finch grinned and began brushing Libby's hair with firmer strokes. "I will do just that, my lady. No reason to embarrass the lady more than one needs!"

"Exactly."

Libby closed her eyes. She was very glad the two problems were settled with no more difficulty than that. Lady Dixon would have a maid with her, and the worst of her wardrobe problems would be quietly solved. And with that, Libby went to bed that night with only the other, much larger dilemma, on her mind. Her own!

Is there any way at all I might nudge my marriage into better heart? And, if there is, how can I ever discover what it is?

The next day, which included the sadness of *departing* guests, brought several *new*, one of whom was exceedingly welcome to Libby. Lady Renwick, at Lady Princeton's suggestion, had invited Miss Elizabeth Browne to join the party.

"Beth!" exclaimed Libby, hearing her announced in Reese's rolling tones. *Beth!* she thought, *I can talk to Beth.* She turned from Lord Hayworth with whom she had been speaking and rushed across the room, pulling her friend into a warm embrace. "I was unaware you had been invited!" She tucked her arm through her friend's and tried to turn her toward the door.

"A moment, Libby," said Beth, her voice very slightly

chiding. "I must greet my hostess and—" She glanced around. "—my host?"

Libby felt her skin heat. "Oh! Of course." She introduced Beth to Lady Renwick, looked around the room and, feeling as if every moment were an eternity, introduced her to several other people, Lady Blackburne and Lord Hayworth among them. "Now you must come up and take off your bonnet and pelisse," said Libby.

"I have given her the room at the end of your hall, Libby," said Lady Renwick. "On the opposite side of the house. I think you will find it comfortable, Miss Browne, but if you do not, be certain to tell me?"

"Do call her Beth," said Libby.

"Certainly, if she prefers," said Lady Renwick.

For the second time, Libby blushed. This time furiously. Lady Renwick, she felt certain, was subtly informing her that she had encroached by assuming her ladyship would wish such intimacy so quickly. "Yes, well, I see," she muttered, and tugged at Beth's arm. If she did not escape soon, she felt certain she would melt into a smear of butter from the heat of embarrassment.

"I have never seen you so flustered," said Beth, once they had closed the salon door behind them.

"I know. It was the shock. Hearing your voice. It was so unexpected—" She squeezed Beth's arm. "—and so very welcome."

Beth didn't say anything, merely squeezing Libby's arm in response, waiting until they were alone in her room to ask the question burning words against the wall of her mind. The instant her door closed, she asked, "Libby, are you so very unhappy?"

Libby blushed still again. "Unhappy? Not at all. Whatever gave you such a notion?"

"If I was wrong, then I am glad, but if it is not that, why are you so agitated?" She watched Libby pace from one side of the room to the other and back again.

Libby swung on her heel. "Oh, Beth," she wailed, "why did you let me do it?"

Beth's eyes widened. "You *are* unhappy."

Libby shook her head. "No. Only confused. Exceedingly confused. Beth, I have come to the conclusion that Lord Merwin would *not* have suited. After all my planning, all my scheming to marry the perfect husband, I would have chosen the wrong man!"

"Why?"

Libby frowned. "I didn't understand how preoccupied political men were with their work. They never think how important it is to maintain a proper social position. I have been trying to understand just how certain women manage to weave their lives into those of their political husbands, and I have concluded I would have enjoyed planning and managing those wonderful political dinners and soirees, but I would *not* have wanted to gain the respect of political men by learning all the boring ins and outs of every current political dilemma! Those women *do* know. They actually seem *interested* in it all!"

Beth nodded. "Yes, I have always thought you would only like being wife to a highly placed official in Treasury or some person equally involved in finance! You are fascinated by it, but the relationships among the various countries and the diplomatic scheming would not interest you at all."

"Why did you never say so?"

"Libby," said Beth slowly, "would it have done the least little bit of good?"

"You mean I had the bit between my teeth and wasn't about to veer from my course."

"Yes."

Libby sighed. "Sometimes I think I am a fool."

Beth laughed. *"That* is rather strong, but you *can* be exceedingly stubborn."

"Yes, well . . ." She returned to her pacing.

After a moment, Beth asked, "What is it, Libby?"

"I don't know!" She swung around to face Beth. "If only I *knew!*"

"Quick. What is the first word to come into your head?"

It was a game a young teacher at the school where they had met would play with them, and, occasionally, it had brought to light problems they would never, otherwise, have known they had.

"Libby, you didn't respond properly," Beth added when it became clear Libby was picking and choosing her words. "Now, truly, what was the word?"

"Love." Libby's hands flew to cover rosy cheeks. "Beth, I have not blushed so much in one day since I was first at school and did everything wrong!"

"Why does the word love bother you?"

"I want it." The blush deepened.

Beth sobered. For a long moment she was silent, and then, very quietly, she asked, "Lord Merwin?"

Libby looked startled. "No! Of course not. I have said we would not suit, have I not?"

"Then . . . ?"

Libby moved to the window and stared out. She picked up the end of the drapery tie and fiddled with the fringe. "I have met Lord and Lady Hendred."

"Ah! Is it true, then, that they are obsessed with each other?"

"Obsessed? Is that what is said? I would not have called it *that,* but they are certainly very much in love." Libby leaned her shoulder against the window frame, half turned toward Beth. "I want that same tie between Tony and myself, a sort of wonderful rope of feeling which loosens and tightens but never breaks."

"Loosens and tightens?"

"I don't know how else to say it. They are aware of each other even when they are not together. They each have preoccupations, interests, of their own, as well as interests together, and they do not have to sit in each other's pockets, but they like nothing better than to be together discussing all the things they have done separately and—" Libby threw up her hands. "—I *don't know* how to describe it. If you ever see it in a couple, you will recognize it. And," she added, actually looking Beth in the face, "very likely you *will* have the opportunity to observe it. I believe Tony's friends' marriages have the same quality, although perhaps not to the same degree."

A mulish expression Beth knew well settled into Libby's features.

"*I want it,*" she said.

Beth sighed. "So?"

Libby sighed. "That's just it, is it not?"

"It?"

"I don't know how."

"How to get it?"

"How to make Tony fall in love with me," wailed Libby.

And then she ran to Beth's bed, threw herself across it and sobbed and sobbed. Beth seated herself beside her friend and gently smoothed her hair, patting her shoulder now and again, and waited. She had occasionally endured these storms in the past. She suspected Libby had been storing up emotions, tamping them down, ignoring them, and doing so for weeks. Finally, the pressure had built until they had to burst out. It was her friend's way. In a moment or two she would roll over, apologize for being so maudlin, wipe her eyes and take a deep breath. And then she would admit she felt a great deal better.

Libby rolled over. "Oh, what a watering pot you will think me. I am so sorry, Beth. You have just arrived, and here, the very first thing I do is sob all over you!"

"But you feel better, do you not?"

Libby, surprised, said, "Why, yes! I *do* feel better."

Beth smiled gently. Libby was *always* surprised by the fact that releasing emotions she kept too tightly bottled up also released tensions of which, prior to her tears, she had been unaware.

"But," Libby added, a sad look in her eye, "I've no more notion than ever how to go about making him fall in love with me."

"Are you in love with him?"

Libby blinked. "Me? In love? With Tony?"

"Are you?"

A slow smile tipped Libby's lips and brought a sparkle to her eyes. "Beth, why have I never asked myself that?"

"I don't know. Now you have asked, do you know the answer?"

"Yes."

When she didn't add to that, Beth demanded, "Well?"

"What?" Libby, who had been staring rather dreamily at nothing at all, cast Beth a startled glance. "I said yes, did I not?"

"Yes, you know the answer!"

Libby's dreamy look intensified. "I meant yes, I think I just might actually be in love with him. I think that is why I become so angry when he denigrates himself in some way, making himself look small in comparison with his friends. Why I want to scold him and why I tell him how wonderful he is! And maybe that is why I have come to actually look forward to those occasions when Sahib corners us in a room together and will not let us depart!"

"Sahib? Is that not the name of Lord Renwick's tiger?"

"Hmm? Oh, yes. You will meet him when we go down to dinner."

"I will *what?*"

Libby cast Beth a glance with just a touch of irritation in it. "Will what what?" she asked rather unintelligibly.

"Did you say I would meet the . . . Oh! I am a fool. You meant I'd meet Lord Renwick before dinner."

"I meant," said Libby patiently, "that you would meet Sahib."

Beth's eyes popped. She swallowed. Hard. "Sahib is brought into the salon?"

Libby nodded. "And the dining room and the breakfast room and—" She cast up her hands. "—just everywhere."

The big gong standing in the front hall rang, a bit faint at the end of their wing with the door shut, but the sound could be nothing other than the warning it was time to dress for dinner.

Beth drew in a deep breath. "Well, then. If I am to be introduced to a real live tiger, perhaps you had better leave. What, my dear Libby, is the proper style of dress for an introduction to a tiger?"

Libby's lips twitched. "I don't know that society has spoken on that particular point. On the other hand, you will also be introduced to a real live prince, so perhaps you might keep that in mind when you choose your gown."

"A prince? The Indian boy?"

Libby nodded. "Prince Ravi. He prefers bright colors, so your cherry-colored gown with the bright pink ribbons might be suitable."

"Lillian Margaret Rosemary Temple, you know very well I gave that gown to my maid the instant you told me it would not do!"

Libby, half out the door, grinned at her friend. "Not Temple, Beth. I will have you remember I am Lady Wendover." She was about to go on when she looked back, a trace of a frown on her brow. "The lovely pale yellow would be appropriate. The one with the exceedingly delicate lace you removed from that old gown of your mother's?"

Libby shut the door and proceeded down the hall to her own room—at which point she recalled she had sent her maid off to Scotland and had not arranged for a substitute. She sighed as she wondered if she could reach all the hooks and tapes her dressmaker deemed necessary, decided she could not and, entering their suite, pulled on a bellpull. She was surprised by the prompt appearance of a young girl who positively quivered with excitement at the prospect of maiding a real lady.

"I am Tibby, if it please you," she said, bobbing a curtsey. "Miss Finch arranged that I be ready when you need me, if you do not object, of course. I will do my best," she finished shyly.

Libby expressed her satisfaction with the arrangement, silently hoped the child would not be careless with the fine fabrics from which her gowns were constructed, and led the way into her bedroom.

Lord Hayworth finished arranging his cravat and chose a truly beautiful if overly large ruby stickpin. Very carefully he inserted it in such a way it compressed one particular fold of the dark blue linen. He stared at it for a long moment before nodding. The deep red of the ruby, the dark blue of the cravat, and the lovely bright yellow of his coat made a wonderful statement. His lordship grinned. What it said, of course, was very much up to the ears that heard it speak!

He glanced down. Dark blue trousers and highly polished slippers with yellow stockings clocked in red. Everything was matched to perfection. His own particularly odd notion of perfection, of course, but nevertheless, thought out to the very last jot and tittle!

His lordship glanced at the clock on the mantel, nodded once again and, giving one or two quick orders to his valet, stalked from the room. Lady Blackburne would be in the blue salon. She was always down early. He would go to her, and he would corner her, and he would, for the forty-seventh time, ask that she agree to wed him.

He did, and she said no—also for the forty-seventh

time. Before he could bring forth new arguments in favor of his suit, Miss Browne and one or two other guests appeared. Lord Hayworth sighed lugubriously, which drew a roguish look from his inamorata before she moved forward to greet the early arrivals.

Lord Wendover entered and glanced around. He seemed disappointed, but joined the group around Lady Blackburne. Lord and Lady Renwick, Sahib stalking between them, arrived next. Prince Ravi and his tutor soon followed and then, quickly, most of the remainder of the party arrived.

Reeves entered with a tray of glasses and passed quietly among the guests. He offered a glass to Lord Hayworth, who declined and continued watching the others.

Lady Wendover entered, glanced around and, when she saw her husband talking to Lord Princeton, appeared to relax in some indefinable way. She didn't attempt to join her husband, but strolled through the room, gradually approaching the group in which Miss Browne was the center. Lord Hayworth drifted closer.

". . . and that is all I know," finished Miss Browne with the faintest of shrugs.

"But did no one say how long they were alone together?" asked one young lady, flicking a quick glance toward the other side of the room where her mother had her head together with another matron's. Her mama would not be happy to know her daughter knew anything at all about Lady Martha's attempted elopement with an impecunious poet who wrote the most indelicate and titillating verses in honor of Martha's eyebrows. Miss Loughton had had an opportunity to peruse those verses and understood very well, indeed, why her friend had run off with the man. She shivered delicately as she quoted one particular verse. ". . . So romantical," she finished and adopted one of the classic poses indicating a heartsick and languishing female.

Beth, eying her critically, decided Libby could do it

ever so much better and, feeling someone new at her side, looked around to find her friend at her elbow. She raised one brow in silent communication. Libby nodded. The two withdrew as quickly as good manners allowed, but were immediately accosted by Lord Hayworth, who had endless curiosity about people and who found the young Lady Wendover a curious young lady, indeed.

"You, Miss Browne," he said, "obviously have news concerning the Ton's latest scandal. I would hear it!"

"But I do not. Certainly no more than has been in the columns."

Hayworth arched a brow. "Will a wedding follow the lady's escapade?"

Beth shook her head. "They were followed immediately and separated long before she could have been compromised."

Lord Hayworth, remembering at the last instant that he spoke with very young women and one of them unwed, bit back the comment that that was nonsense—assuming the two were alone in the carriage. He asked.

"Oh, no. She took her maid, of course."

"Ah. Not totally lacking in sense, then. She returned to the Ton for the last of the Season?"

"The Season was nearly over, so she went to reside with her grandmother in Bath for the summer. The old lady is not well and needs someone young to fetch and carry."

Lord Hayworth shook his head. "Mistake that."

"A mistake, indeed," muttered Libby.

He cast her a quick glance and recalled that Lady Wendover had, herself, faced scandal and had had the good sense to *face it down*. He nodded. "Yes, you were very wise, my dear. Very wise, indeed. I congratulate you on your good sense."

"My lord husband's good sense, you mean," said Libby and grimaced slightly. "I fear I am too much the coward to have done what I knew was the right thing to do. He knew and had enough courage for both of us."

Once again Hayworth nodded. "Good man, Lord Wendover. Very good man." On that he wandered off, joining Lady Blackburne, who spoke with another matron about roses.

One of his questions about the young lady had been answered: she was in love with her husband. A new question rose to plague Lord Hayworth. Did Wendover know his wife loved him? Hayworth tucked the subject to the back of his mind and paid strict attention to how one best treated mildew on rosebushes. Luckily, since he had heard the lecture before, he was not forced to suffer for so very long. Dinner was announced long before Lady Blackburne finished her usual discourse on the subject.

Twelve

Lady Wendover wandered disconsolately around the Renwicks' music room. She had practiced a new piece of music at the well-tuned pianoforte for more than an hour and feared she would never manage all the running half notes. Her fingers trailed idly over the harp's strings, allowing the softest of purring notes to rustle through the room. She plucked a violin string and touched the flute that lay in an open case beside it and recalled the exceptional quality of the duet performed a few evenings previously by Lady Blackburne and Lord Hayworth on those same two instruments. She had been intrigued by the nearly flirtatious glances that passed between them as they played.

Before her marriage, it had not occurred to her that people of the age of her ladyship and his lordship felt the pangs and longings of the young. First to enlighten her were Lord and Lady Hendred, who, no one could deny, were deeply in love. And now Lord Hayworth and Lady Blackburne revealed warm feelings for each other.

How did I, wondered Libby, *reach the great age of twenty-three unaware that love not only exists, but that the poets are exceedingly misleading in that they never speak of love lasting the whole of one's life?*

She mused briefly on her father's loss of her mother, wondered if he had once felt for his wife those tender emotions these people felt. And, for the first time since she had become aware of his financial escapades, she felt sorry for him.

So, her thoughts continued, *how does one go about putting that sort of love into one's own life?*

"Blast it, Sahib, don't push me."

Libby turned on her heel. Her cheeks flamed to see that her husband, about whom she had just been daydreaming, was backing into the room. The tiger butted him gently in the knees so that he moved another few steps toward her. She giggled.

Tony turned. "Ah!" He glanced behind him and saw that Sahib had slid to the floor, a long, sinuous rope of living flesh, relaxed, but at the same time, alert. The beast blinked benignly up at him. "Sahib brought me here. Do you suppose he wishes us to indulge him in some music? A duet, perhaps?"

Hoping her cheeks would not color up again, Libby looked at the tiger and frowned. "Somehow I doubt it. Do you recall the other evening when Lord Hayworth played his flute? Sahib got up and left the room."

"Yes, but he seemed to enjoy the piano music before that."

"Perhaps that, but when Miss Loughton sang his tail twitched, and I would swear that his ears folded down."

"Hmm. But then, I'd have shut my ears if it were possible, and if I'd a tail, I would have switched it back and forth in a most impolite fashion. Her voice—" He grimaced. "—is not the most felicitous of those I've ever heard!"

Libby smiled at his wry tone. "I know. I felt rather sorry for her."

"I am not surprised, because you do feel sorry for people, but if you are going to feel sorry for every tonnish maiden who hasn't a musical bone in her body, then you will waste a great deal of time. And, if you do mean to waste emotion, then waste it on those of us who must listen to performers such as Miss Loughton! Or you might not waste it and put it to better use appreciating those who *do*."

"Who do?"

"Who have *talent*. Someone like you, yourself, Libby." Smiling, he touched her cheek. "I like it when the roses bloom in your cheeks!"

Her gaze dropped from his, and her cheeks felt still hotter. "I never think of myself as musical," she said and glanced at the pianoforte. "In fact, I know I am not. I have worked and worked on that piece Lady Blackburne brought back from Brighton, and I wonder if I will ever manage the trick of it."

Tony moved to the instrument and picked up the music, studying it. He frowned. "Hmm. Here—" He pointed. "—and here . . . ?"

"Yes. And—" She reached over his arm and pointed farther down the page. "—there. I cannot seem to catch the tempo properly." Realizing how close they stood, she carefully withdrew her arm—and then, a trifle, herself.

Tony didn't seem to notice, but merely seated himself, settled the music, and using only his right hand, played the notes of the first passage that Libby found difficult. He tried it over again. And then a third time. "There is a difficulty with the fingers not wanting to go *there* when they've just been *there*."

"Exactly. I tried starting with my fingers and moving my thumb under to reach that note—" She hestitated half a moment before, daringly, she put her hand on his shoulder so that she could reach to point. "—but it didn't help. In fact, I believe it only complicated things a little farther on. I think—" She smiled impishly, but where he could not see them, the fingers that had touched him, curled into a protective fist. "—I might manage if only I'd another two or three fingers!"

Tony slid to the end of the bench, moving his hand up an octave, and suggested she sit.

Remembering that she was determined to woo her husband, Libby slid carefully onto the bench. Soon, though, she forgot the odd feelings his presence roused, and they spent the next half hour working out a way that particular run of notes could be managed and without the acquisition of more fingers! Once they had done all they could, Tony stood up and asked if she would play the piece for him.

"Oh, Tony, it isn't ready to be heard by anyone."

"I, surely, am not just anyone!"

She smiled up at him shyly. "Oh, no. Definitely you are not! If you will be kind when I make mistakes, as I will, then I will try."

Her smile caught Tony unawares. He could not draw his eyes from it. If she had not turned back to the music, he wondered if he would have managed to restrain himself from leaning down and kissing her! The music caught his ear, and he glanced over her shoulder, saw her flinch when a wrong note resulted in a most discordant chord. He put his hands lightly on her shoulders, squeezed gently, and she tipped her head to touch her cheek to his hand. He took it as a sign he might leave his hands there and did, very much liking the feel of her under his palms.

Libby, concentrating hard on the unfamiliar music, at first found comfort in his touch. But, as she continued, she came to a passage that was not so very difficult, and then his touch intruded on her consciousness. And would not be chased away. She found she was hitting more wrong notes than right and lifted her hands.

After a long moment, Tony lifted his.

For another long moment neither moved.

Behind them Sahib made a rather odd noise. Tony turned. Libby swung around on the piano bench. Sahib stared from one to the other and, again, made that odd sound.

"Tony," asked Libby, speaking slowly, "why would Sahib sigh?"

Tony didn't have the answer to that. He might make a tolerably good guess, but he wasn't about to express a mere suspicion. Especially when it might embarrass Libby and make it impossible for him to be comfortable with her.

Things—although he wasn't certain what he meant by that—were going very well. More slowly than Sahib could approve, perhaps, but well. No, Tony wasn't about to discuss any guesses about Sahib's odd behavior.

Lady Blackburne watched the new gardener walk away. He had listened politely to her orders and then explained that Lady Renwick had, just yesterday, suggested the very same thing. Her ladyship felt a sense of loss and a suspicion she had become of no use. It was a very unsettling feeling, the notion that she was not needed.

"What is it?" asked Lord Hayworth softly.

She spun around. "Oh. You."

"Yes. Me."

They stared at each other. "What is it?" asked Hayworth again.

"Eustacia . . ."

"What about Eustacia?" he asked when she said no more.

"I think she has learned how to be mistress of her own home," said Lady Blackburne in a very small voice. "When they married," she went on more firmly, "Eustacia asked that I teach her." She shrugged, pretending indifference. "It seems she has absorbed her lessons, Austin, and no longer needs a teacher."

Lord Hayworth went very still. Lady Blackburne had

used his first name! "There is much you could teach me," he said softly.

She glanced at him, away. "I doubt that."

"Nevertheless, it is true. I need you, Luce. I and my home need you for the wonderful things you do with plants. I need you for the music we make together. I need you—" His eyebrows waggled up and down. "—for another sort of music which the two of us might make, as well. And I know I will be more comfortable just knowing you are near, that I may see you, talk to you, whenever I wish. My dear, will you wed me? Please?"

Lady Blackburne looked to where the new gardener was explaining to one of the youngest gardeners on Renwick's large staff his method of digging in fertilizer around the base of old roses. It was not quite as she would have had him do it, but it wasn't *wrong*. She sighed.

"I am planning a conservatory off the back of the east wing," said Hayworth in idle tones. "It is a trifle larger than the one here. The builder and I have discussed the possibility of constructing it by the new method, using iron for the supports and for the frames for the windows."

Lady Blackburne's head came up, and she spoke sharply. "For a *conservatory*, Austin? Won't the metal make the room harder to heat?"

"I had not thought of that." He frowned. "Still, it will make for a larger glass surface. The framing will take less space, you know."

"Hmmm."

"Perhaps two closed stoves would solve the problem?"

"I would need to see it."

He cast her an insouciant look. "Perhaps we should wed at once and go home so that you could supervise the construction?"

She glanced at him. "You could teach a snake to suck eggs!"

"Luce! Such a thing to say to me." He pretended outrage. She giggled. He smiled. "I love it when you do that," he said softly.

She allowed her eyes to widen. "Say such things to you?"

"No, of course not. When you laugh that funny little laugh." He chuckled. "It makes me want to laugh."

"Laughter is important, is it not?" she said wistfully.

"Very." He spoke seriously, but his eyes smiled.

"Oh, don't pretend to be so solemn! It is important. I have always thought so. And—" A sadness settled around her eyes. "—I have no one with whom I may laugh."

"You have me."

She sighed. "I never thought to wed again. And to wed merely because we can laugh at the same things—that seems a trifle by the way!"

"But it is not merely that. Luce, I rarely allow myself to speak from the heart, but I want you to know that I love you, that I need you in many many ways and always will. But I don't wish to do anything that would make *you* unhappy. If marriage would make you gloomy, then of course we will not wed." She said nothing. "Would it?" he probed.

Lady Blackburne drew in a deep breath. Then, without speaking, she let it out again.

"You don't know," he suggested and drew in a breath of his own. "Well, we cannot know, can we? We can only judge by the times we have spent together and extrapolate that marriage would not change that, but only enhance it. Marry me, Luce. Today. Tomorrow. Next week. But, my love, not too long into the future. Please?"

The gardener moved away. Again Lady Blackburne drew in that breath. She held it for a moment. Then, on the exhale, she breathed, "Yes. I will."

Lord Hayworth closed his eyes for a moment. "Soon?" he asked softly.

"You forget the banns must be read. It cannot be so quickly done as you suggest."

"Can it not?" He unbuttoned his coat and put his hand inside. He withdrew it. Hooked to one finger was a small suede drawstring bag. He also held a stiff paper folded and folded again. "My dear, a license," he crowed.

Her ladyship huffed. "We are not children that we cannot wait for banns!"

"Not impetuous children, my dear, but it is our very age which suggests we should not waste a single moment remaining to us!" He handed her the license and reached for her other hand. He opened the bag and poured its contents onto her palm. "Do you like it? Will you wear it?"

Luce handed back the license and picked up the ring. It was a delicately contrived rose made of red gold with a tiny sparkling diamond in its heart. "Beautiful. Where did you ever find something so exquisite?"

"I ordered it made for you soon after I first decided to wed you."

One of Lady Blackburne's brows arced. "How soon?"

"Oh, immediately, I think. Or at least no more than within minutes of meeting you again after so many years." Two spots of color stained his cheeks. "Luce, I do not wish to wait. Tomorrow, Luce? And then we may go immediately home?"

"Home . . . day after tomorrow," she countered in her usual decisive manner. "Not everything can be accomplished even in that time, but I will keep you waiting no longer." She cast him a quick glance. "I do not believe we need tell anyone. I will write my nephew once we reach your home."

"Our home, Luce," he chided, but, since the wedding was to be weeks earlier than Lord Hayworth had expected, he added, "As you wish, my love." Feeling more than a trifle smug, he followed her into the conservatory and watched her reach for a flat of tiny seedlings. Feeling just a trifle light-headed that he had finally achieved her agreement to a wedding, he watched her prick them into a new flat, giving each seedling room to grow.

Lord Hayworth could not wait to transplant his new wife to his own home where he felt certain she would grow and bloom and become still more lovely. At least to his eyes.

Libby's new maid had pressed the gown requested for that evening and laid it across the bed. She had warm water waiting and fresh stockings, just in case Libby had snagged the pair she had put on that morning. The maid also had an air of suppressed excitement.

"What is it, Tibby? You are great with news, and had best speak out before you burst with it!"

The maid put her hands over her mouth, giggles slipping through her fingers and her eyes sparkling. "Oh, I am and I might and isn't it wonderful?"

Libby frowned. "Wonderful?"

"That Lady Blackburne is wedding Lord Hayworth day after tomorrow!"

Libby's frown deepened. "Nonsense!"

"But it isn't! The new gardener's lad—" Tibby's face burned red. "—well, he wasn't supposed to, of course. . . ." She looked up at Libby from under her brows, a querying look in her expression.

Libby sighed. "Come on. A round tale. And leave nothing out."

"But he's m'brother," said the maid, suddenly worried she would get him in trouble.

Libby smiled. "I'll not tell if he was a trifle naughty, but you'd better tell him he must do as he's told or he'll find himself without a position!"

"I will, my lady. I'll surely do that," said Tibby earnestly. "But—" The sparkle returned to her bright eyes. "—what he heard was Lord Hayworth asking Lady Blackburne to wed him and showing her a piece of paper that means they don't need banns and saying could it be soon, tomorrow even, and—" The words tumbled over each other. "—she said yes, but not tomorrow, but the next day and then—" She finished in a rush. "—they went away."

"I spoke to Lady Blackburne just before coming up to dress, and she said nothing of this."

"Oh, it is to be a secret. I think they mean to—" The chit's eyes grew very wide, and she lowered her voice. "—*elope.*"

"Hmm."

Tibby waited for more, but more was not forthcoming. Finally she sighed softly and asked if she should undo the fastenings on my lady's gown. Once Libby was nearly ready for the evening, she asked Tibby to take a message to Lord Wendover that she would like to speak with him before they went down. Tibby returned with the word that his lordship would await her pleasure in the sitting room.

Libby entered the sitting room just as Tony's door across the way opened. They smiled at the coincidence. Tony led his wife to one of the chairs set by the windows and, after he saw her seated, seated himself. "Now, my dear, what is it?"

"Did your valet offer you up a very strange story, Tony?"

"Gossip, you mean?"

Libby frowned slightly. "Well, yes, I suppose it might be considered gossip."

"He told me nothing new."

"I suppose Tibby might have had the news only because her brother could not keep it to himself and needed to speak to someone he felt he could trust. I wonder if one is duty bound to tell him he cannot trust his sister!"

Tony grinned. "If she is his sister, surely he knows by now if he can or cannot. If it were I, I'd leave well enough alone. Is that what you wished to know?"

Libby chuckled. "Not at all. Merely by way of an aside! Tony, she tells me Lady Blackburne and Lord Hayworth have a license and mean to wed day after tomorrow! Dare we believe her? And if we do, should we do anything?"

Tony tipped his head thoughtfully. "Perhaps they mean to announce it this evening."

"I saw Lady Blackburne just before coming up to dress, and she gave no hint at all that anything was in the wind."

"You believe they mean to elope?"

"Yes. But I cannot think it is what Lady Blackburne truly wishes. Tony, I think she will not ask, but I think she would appreciate it if we made an effort to make it more of an occasion."

"What do you have in mind."

"Flowers in the church, perhaps? She loves flowers so much I am sure she would like them there. And all of us to witness her marriage? And perhaps some sort of celebration by way of a wedding breakfast?"

Tony looked thoughtful. "Libby, I will have Abley discover if their servants are preparing to travel. If they are and no one has said anything, then I think we should talk with Lord and Lady Renwick and see whether they feel something should be done."

"Have Abley send a message to you as soon as he discovers the truth, please. There is so little time if anything is to be accomplished."

"Yes. If word is brought during dinner, I will nod to you. You may ask to speak with her ladyship as soon as you ladies leave the room, and I will ask to speak to Jase."

Lord and Lady Renwick, as soon as they were informed, also felt something should be arranged. "But I do not think it should be done behind their backs," said Lady Renwick.

"Lady Blackburne went upstairs immediately after dinner, did she not?" asked Libby. "Perhaps," she added, hesitating, "you might go up to her? If she is in the midst of packing, surely she must explain it to you, and that would lead into a discussion of what we might do."

"An excellent suggestion," said Lord Renwick.

"I agree and shall go at once. I'll not be long."

Once Lady Renwick left the room, Tony asked Jase about the book he and her ladyship were writing. "It is nearly finished," said Jase.

"I look forward to when it is in print and I may begin at the beginning and go on to the end!"

Lord Renwick laughed, but he sounded a trifle embarrassed to Libby. "I hope those who are *not* my friends will be so kind!"

"I wish you would write a book about Sahib," said Libby. "I am not entirely comfortable around him, but he fascinates me."

"He fascinates everyone," said Tony. "I think it an excellent notion. Perhaps you could write a story for children and someone could illustrate it."

"For children?" Renwick's hand dropped to Sahib's shoulder, and the great cat looked up at him. The animal made that odd sound that was akin to purring in a house cat. Renwick smiled. "It sounds to me as if Sahib approves the idea, so I guess I'll have to try. But not just yet. Eustacia and I must finish this book and we've started another volume about India. It won't be quite the same, although it will include observations from my journals to back up my thoughts. We have made notes for it and have written several essays which will be included." Renwick's head turned toward the hall. "Eustacia is coming."

Libby, who had heard nothing, wondered at the sensitivity of his lordship's ears. Not only had he heard footsteps before they had registered on her ears, but he had recognized them! She watched her husband go to the door and offer his arm to bring Lady Renwick back to her chair and thought, once again, what a perfect gentleman her husband was.

"What, my dear, did you discover?" asked Lord Renwick.

"That I am not wanted in her room and that I am not to be told what she needs with two rather large trunks brought down by the footmen only this morning!"

"You sound," said Lord Renwick with a chuckle, "as if you have been thoroughly insulted!"

Lady Renwick laughed. "I suppose I do feel that way. I had thought we were friends, but it is not the way of friends to exclude each other from something so important as marriage! Jase, I cannot allow her to be wed in such a scrambling fashion. We will, whether she wishes or no, give her a good send-off. I must instantly discover exactly when they mean to meet with the vicar and then must send invitations to all her nearby friends. And I must have a talk with Cook and the housekeeper and—" She shook her fists. "—there is no end of what must be done instantly!"

"Tell me what I am to do and I will begin," said Libby.

"We will all do what we can," said Tony.

"You, my lord, may ride to the vicarage with a note from Jase, who will threaten the man with loss of his position if he does not instantly reveal what we need to know." Lady Renwick grinned to take the sting from her words. "I will tend to the cook, and you, Libby, may have a little talk with my new head gardener and, since he is like most gardeners who hate cutting their blooms, remind him that this is Lady Blackburne's wedding which means she will be leaving Tiger's Lair. Since he has already, more than once, complained to me of her ladyship's tendency to interfere in his arrangements, I believe he will be so happy to hear she is leaving, he will provide a great number of bouquets in celebration!"

"That will not take long. I will be ready to help write out invitations as soon as you've word of exactly when the guests should arrive."

"Very good." Lady Renwick's thoughtful gaze settled on Libby. "My dear, just how did you learn of this situation?"

Libby blushed rosily, and her eyes flicked to meet Tony's. "My lady, I know better than to listen to servants' gossip, but my maid was so full of excitement she actually trembled. I thought it better to listen and get it out of her system. You can imagine how shocked I was by what she had to say."

"The servants! I swear they know what we do before we know!"

The men chuckled. "Of course they do," said Renwick. "Their lives are entirely woven into ours. It is important to them what we do. Tony, will you drive me over to the vicarage. I believe it might be better if I ask him to his face. That way I need not make threats unless absolutely necessary. One should never make threats one is unready to fulfill!"

"I will go beard the gardener in his den," said Libby.

"And I will send Cook into proper hysterics so that she may get over them and get busy." Lady Renwick sighed a lugubrious sigh and made a humorous face. "She is so predictable!"

Luckily Lady Blackburne was far too preoccupied to notice the suppressed excitement and the exceedingly busy people around her. Lord Hayworth was not so oblivious, but, a wise man, decided to ignore his suspicions, thinking it best if Lady Blackburne continued in ignorance. He kept her busy when she was not occupied with supervising her packing. Keeping her busy kept her from having time to have second thoughts about their marriage as well as noticing what the others were planning!

The day dawned with a sky dimmed by haze, but all the signs pointed to the fact it would soon improve. Libby, who rose far earlier than was normal to her, dressed quickly and went immediately to the workroom where the flowers were done each day. She looked around at the buckets filled with blooms. Most were roses just opening from buds. All colors. All sizes. There were also buckets of cut flowers. And of greens. She made a quick posture designating despair, but having done so, quite happily set to work.

Late the previous evening she and Lady Renwick had discussed which vases should go to the church, so she began with those. Lady Princeton, a cup of tea in her hand and a yawn distorting her face, joined her when she was finishing the third vase for the altar.

"How lovely," said Lady Princeton.

"It is easy to make lovely bouquets when you've such a wonderful choice of blooms. Are you good at making up posies? Mine always fall apart just when I am ready to tie them off. I think it would be nice to have one to hand her ladyship just before she goes down the aisle, do not you?"

"A very nice thought. I wonder if Mrs. Climpson could provide me with a well-starched doily with lots of lace that I might use for a collar. I will ask her." Her ladyship soon returned with the required piece of tatting. She held it up. "Large enough I will not have to cut the center for the stems but may simply wrap the bottom. I will take it and ribbon and scissors with us so that I can take the bouquet from water and dry it so it will not drip and then put the posy in the doily for carrying."

As Libby finished the last bouquet for the church, Lady Princeton began choosing particularly exquisite blooms for her posy. Forming the tight little bunch into a proper small bouquet was difficult. One had to balance size, color, and formation. Libby, doing up huge bouquets for the entry hall and salon, kept an eye on Lady Princeton's work and, when her ladyship reached for the wire, held her breath until the perfect little posy was tied off and set into water in a holder.

"Beautiful," breathed Libby.

"But, as you said, not at all difficult with so many blossoms from which one may choose!" Lady Princeton looked around. "What should I do next?"

"The low bouquets for the dinning room? I'll finish the blue salon with this vase and then do flowers for the other, and that should do it. The maids can use what is left for bedroom bouquets. There won't be enough, I fear. I suspect I've rather overdone the big arrangements, but it was such fun when I had only to reach out and have a lovely bloom in my hand!"

"I wonder how Eustacia convinced the gardener to allow so much to be cut."

Libby giggled. "That was my doing. I reminded him that it would be the very last time he'd have reason to deal with her ladyship and that he should show her just how well everything was doing under his management."

"Very devious. I wish one could use it as an excuse to pry blooms from a gardener more often, but, from now on, whenever I must entertain a famous gardener, I will be quite certain *my* gardener is informed."

A maid and a footman arrived just then. Libby gave orders that the church bouquets go off at once. The others, she warned the maid, must not be taken out until after Lady Blackburne left for the church.

She and Lady Princeton returned to the main part of the house and went directly to their rooms. They must change for the wedding at once or they would have to leave after Lady Blackburne and Lord Hayworth, which no one wished to do! Besides, Lady Princeton needed to be there early to finish off the posy for Lady Blackburne.

"Trixie, what if we are wrong and there is no wedding?" asked Lord Princeton of his wife, Patricia. He lounged back in the pew and cast a fond eye over his wife.

"Shush, Jack. The only thing worrying me is that they will see the church is occupied and will pass right on by, going elsewhere to do the foul deed."

"Foul deed, is it? Is that how you see *our* marriage?" he asked lazily, one finger idly curling a stray bit of hair which lay against Patricia's neck.

"You know it is not! It is merely an expression." She cast him a look, noted the teasing half grin which was his alone and sighed lugubriously. "I have done it again, have I not?"

"Done what, my love?"

"Played into your hands, dropped into the pit you dug for me, been done for a duck. . . ."

Jack grasped the wisp of hair and tugged. "Enough, woman! You'll come out with still worse and put me to the blush."

"Did you for a duck, too, did I not," she whispered into his ear.

The doors to the back of the church opened yet again, and a rustling indicated a number of people turning to see if, finally, the truant bride and groom had arrived. They had not. Lord and Lady Wendover moved down the aisle to the places held for them near the front.

Patricia leaned across Jack and forward. "Tony, have you any word?"

"Their carriage was nearly loaded as we left. Not that they knew we were off since we walked across by way of the path. The loading was done secretly out the back way rather than down the front as would be usual. I believe Lady Blackburne must mean to have most of her belongings sent along later, since there were only a few trunks and a number of bundles and one crate."

Patricia leaned the other way. "Jase, would you announce that it should not be long now?"

Jason Renwick rose to his feet and turned to face the waiting guests. "I am informed that the happy couple should arrive within the next quarter hour. Since they've no notion we are waiting their arrival, they've no reason to rush. Please be patient a while longer."

There were a few murmurs, and then the church fell silent again except for the occasional rustle. Patricia once more leaned forward. "Libby," she whispered. Libby turned. "Where is the posy?"

"I left it with a footman who is awaiting them just outside the church. He is to present it to Lady Blackburne with our compliments. At the last moment it occurred to me," said Libby, her cheeks scorching, "that perhaps she should have some warning that we know and that the church will not be empty."

"The carriages waiting outside will tell her that," said Jack.

"Yes," said Libby doubtfully, "except there were none. Someone had sent them away."

"I did," said Lord Renwick. "It occurred to *me* that Aunt Luce would turn tail at the least sign the church was occupied. It has taken her forever to come to the point, and I suspect she is shy about it now she's agreed. Why else would she have kept secret that she meant to elope?"

"One doesn't usually announce an elopement," said Jack softly, but with a laugh in his voice.

Others, overhearing, chuckled softly. But then the sound of voices reached them. Lady Blackburne's was a trifle shrill. "But, Austin, who can have known? Or did you tell?"

"Never, my love. It is a lovely posy. I wish I had thought of it. Will you not carry it?"

Lady Blackburne sniffed. Then huffed. Then sighed. "Oh, very well. But, Austin, I have the strangest feeling that beyond that door we'll find the whole household."

"Would it be so terrible? That your friends and relatives wish to see you wed?"

Lady Blackburne didn't answer, merely asking, "Is the reverend here?"

"He said he'd come at ten. It is nearer half past. Ready?"

"Hmm."

Patricia, catching Jack's eye, leaned to his ear once again. "She didn't need to sound quite so morose, do you think?"

"Morose? I thought it more a sound of resignation. Shush," he finished, glancing back as the doors opened. He nudged Patricia's elbow and rose, pushing himself up with his crutch. Others around them also rose to their feet, and soon the congregation was standing, half turned to watch the bride and groom come down the aisle to where the vicar awaited them. They passed the Renwicks' pew, and Lady Blackburne stopped. She patted Lord Hayworth's arm, released it, and leaned across Lord Renwick to Lady Renwick and, pulling Eustacia toward her, gave her nephew's wife a kiss on the cheek. They looked at each other and smiled through sudden tears.

"Be happy," whispered Eustacia.

"I will," murmured Lady Blackburne.

Ten minutes later she was no longer Lady Blackburne, but was a beaming Lady Hayworth. She and her new husband swept back up the aisle and were held back from leaving only by the friends and neighbors who surged from their pews and insisted on shaking hands and kissing cheeks. Lady Renwick managed to reach Lord Hayworth and tell him that they were expected to return to Tiger's Lair for their wedding breakfast. He glanced at his brand-new wife, who was certain to object, but nodded. One had obligations to family and friends, and he would have her to himself soon enough. Well, far sooner than he would have thought possible less than a week ago!

Later Patricia and Jack stood on the first landing of Tiger's Lair's front staircase and watched the small gathering in the entry hall below shift and shift again, forming new patterns constantly. "Once she accepted we really wished her well, she seemed quite content with all our plans, did she not?"

Jack frowned. "I have this odd feeling she feels guilty for deserting Jase and Eustacia."

"Eustacia needed her for a long time. When she and Jase were deeply involved in his writing, for instance. Eustacia had never dealt with a house this size or servants, so she needed all the help Lady Blackburne—"

"You mean Hayworth."

"—Lady Hayworth, could give her. But the book is about ready for the publishers and Eustacia has learned enough she'll have no trouble carrying on. Actually—" Patricia gave her husband a mischievous look and lowered her voice. "—she is anxious to try it on her own."

"Then, all worked out for the best."

"Oh, yes. Jack, did you watch Tony and his wife during the service?"

"Should I have done?"

"Hmm. While Lady Blackburne gave her vows, Libby kept staring from the sides of her eyes at Tony. Then, when Lord Hayworth gave his, Tony stared at Libby. And then, when the vicar pronounced them man and wife, the two looked at each other, noticed the other was also looking, and quickly turned away. And both faces flamed! What do you think of *that?*"

Jack frowned ever so slightly. "Trixie, when we attend weddings these days, I always think of ours. I—" He dropped a look her way. "—repeat my vows to you, if you know what I mean?" She nodded and grinned. "You do the same?" She nodded again. "Do you think, perhaps, those two . . . ?"

Patricia didn't nod for a third time. She sighed. "Gossip has it they don't sleep together. At all."

"Patricia!"

Jack never called her Patricia. She looked up at him, a

trifle worried. Then he grinned, and she breathed an exceedingly soft sigh of relief.

"You have listened to servants' gossip," he continued in a mock scolding tone. "Actually, I heard that myself some time ago, but could think of no way to interfere. So I didn't."

"I think we need to think."

Jack nodded to where Sahib lay. The big cat was watching Lord and Lady Wendover through slitted eyes. "I wonder if we need to. Sahib seems to be thinking for us!"

Patricia observed the scene for a moment and then grinned. "Oh, well! If Sahib is taking a hand!" She turned slightly. "Ah! Lord and Lady Hayworth are about ready to set off. *Again.*"

Jack took Patricia's arm and, with deft use of his crutch, moved toward the massing group of people waiting just outside the open door, with small baskets of rose petals, ready to waft the newly wedded couple off on a rose-scented breeze.

An hour later the last of the neighbors went home as well, and the house party and their hosts adjourned to Lord Renwick's study. It was the first time Libby had entered the room, and she looked around, surprised by how workmanlike it was. The furnishings were there to be *used.* And, although everything was ordered neatly, there were piles of manuscript and notes and drawings and notebooks and the other necessities of a working writer such as pens and inks and fresh paper. Libby had known Lord Renwick was writing a book about India, but it had not, previously to seeing this room, occurred to her how much of a project that would be.

"Well. That's over. I hope Lady Black—er—Lady Hayworth did not object to our making it such a public affair," said Tony.

Libby felt a pang. Although their wedding had been public and Lady Princeton had arranged things ever so nicely, she could not recall it without pangs of guilt. Tony had not wished to wed her, had married her only for his honor's sake and had regretted it ever since. She sighed. Softly. *She* no longer regretted it, but so long as Tony continued doing so, there was nothing she could do.

Libby looked up and found Lady Princeton's eyes on her, her gaze affectionate, and warming. Libby forced a gay smile and turned to listen to Lady Renwick, who was describing some of the breakfast's happenings to her husband. He smiled at his wife's tale of a local widow's coy behavior when discussing an upcoming fete with the vicar, who listened politely but noncommittally and, vocally, breathed a sigh of relief when their tête-à-tête was interrupted by a gentleman who wished to compliment the reverend on last Sunday's sermon and ask a question concerning the text. The widow had wandered off disconsolate—until she managed to corner a recent widower only a few years younger than herself!

"Widow Harkness," Eustacia explained when she realized Libby was listening, "has been doing all she can to gain herself a second husband and has been ever since the first was buried. Since the neighborhood is well aware that Mr. Harkness lived under the cat's paw, she has had no luck in her endeavor!"

Libby laughed, but felt a trifle sorry for the widow. Perhaps she was lonely. Perhaps the right man could teach her to be a loving wife rather than a shrew. Libby, wanting love herself, tended to wish for it for everyone. But then the realist that lived within her offered another thought: *Or perhaps the woman is a shrew to the bone and would only make any man miserable!* Libby glanced to where Tony talked to Lord Princeton and hoped, once again, that she would never do anything beyond what she had already done to make him unhappy.

"What are you thinking?" asked Lady Princeton, sitting rather abruptly in the chair beside Libby.

"Thinking?" For half a moment she considered confiding in Lady Princeton. If only the lady were not so much older than herself, not so secure in her own marriage, perhaps she might have felt able to do so. Libby glanced across the room. She wondered if she could talk to Beth—but Beth was unmarried and would be no help with the dilemma presently disturbing Libby. "Nothing, my lady. Nothing at all."

Patricia grinned. "Pretty deep nothings, I'd guess. If you change your mind and wish to discuss whatever is troubling you, then I will try to help in any way I can."

"Thank you."

"We are your friends, Libby. You are one of us now. Don't forget that."

Libby blushed. "If I could forget that I'd no business being one of you, then perhaps I could believe you are my friends!"

"Lady Serena—" Patricia cast Libby a querying look. "—Ian McMurrey's wife?"

Libby nodded.

"She married under protest to save her mother from threatened beatings. She didn't wish to be any man's wife. Ian wed her in place of his brother who was affianced to her but died. Now there was a difficult beginning! It has nevertheless become something very special despite it. Serena actually held a knife against Ian on their wedding night!"

Libby's eyes widened. "How did she dare?"

"Serena is an unexpected woman in many ways. When the two finally admitted they loved each other, they went through a second marriage ceremony and reaffirmed vows neither felt had held much value the first time they'd been said!"

Libby stilled. "I didn't know it was possible to . . . to reaffirm?—"

Patricia nodded.

"—one's vows."

"Jase and Eustacia did so on their first anniversary."

"And you and Lord Princeton?"

Patricia grinned. "I mean to suggest it to him when our first anniversary rolls around! We've only been married a few months, you know. Well, more than half a year now, but it will be after Christmas before I ask him if he's willing!"

"Hmm."

Patricia eyed Libby, decided she had inserted quite a number of hints into what she believed to be fertile soil, and moved on to where Beth talked to Ian McMurrey's brother, who tutored Prince Ravi. "Aaron," said Lady Princeton when the two looked up at her, "why did Prince Ravi refuse to attend the wedding?"

Aaron shrugged. "He complained that it was not worth seeing, but mostly, I think, he was pouting because no one would allow him to arrange the sort of pageantry he loves so much."

"Pageantry, Mr. McMurrey?" asked Beth.

He grinned a quick flashing grin. "My prince believes all such occasions must be surrounded by all the pomp and ceremony one can manage. The richer and more brilliant the display, the happier he is. He loves silks and satins and plumes and swords and jewels and—" He raised one brow. "—have I perhaps said enough?"

"Indeed, you have. When we had to do what we did in such secrecy, it would have been impossible to lay on the sort of frills of which you speak."

Aaron laughed. "Actually, with his highness organizing things, it would have been quite possible. Even if he had ordered his men to put themselves into place in the middle of the night, they would have done so with no complaints and would not have lounged around, as would most English soldiers. They would fear to crease their best uniforms. They enjoy display as well and get little enough of it here."

"It must be very interesting teaching the prince."

Aaron looked around, leaned nearer the two women, and whispered, "I'd have said frustrating rather than interesting. The prince is a very bright boy, but he is stubborn to the point of idiocy, and, if he cannot see the point of something he is asked to study, he will refuse to do so. Lord Renwick has become adept at coming up with reasons why one should study thus and so." He leaned back. "On the other hand, I have learned a great deal about the East from the lad, their way of thinking, which is quite different from English ways and quite fascinating. I mean to travel with the lad when he returns home and remain in India for a time."

"And, perhaps, make your fortune, Mr. McMurrey?" asked Beth.

Aaron blushed. "I would not object to such an outcome," he said, looking her squarely in the eyes.

But then the look changed. Some very private communication passed between the pair. Neither noticed when Lady Princeton quietly withdrew and moved to her husband's side. "Ah, me," she sighed. "Alas."

"Alas?"

"I am getting old, Jack," she moaned, but her eyes twinkled.

"Nonsense."

"Young love wears me out these days."

"Are you still worrying about Tony and his wife?"

"Well, yes, that too."

Jack eyed her. *"Now* what are you going on about?"

"Miss Browne. And Aaron McMurrey. I just watched them fall in love."

Jack instantly sobered. "Oh."

Patricia's brow arched. "Oh?"

"What of her father, Trixie?"

"Oh."

They eyed each other. "Oh, no you don't!"

"Don't what, Jack?"

"Don't interfere!"

"Me?"

"Miss Innocence!"

"But of course I am innocent."

"This instant, perhaps," he said ruefully and sighed. "I don't suppose there is anything one can say to dissuade you?"

"I haven't a notion what you are going on about," she said in an airy manner, which fooled Jack not at all.

For a long moment he was silent. "You will do as you think best."

"Yes."

Jack chuckled. "What is more, it very likely will be for the best. I see Tony is talking to Jase. Excuse me."

"Don't forget that particular problem while moaning that I've involved myself in another!"

Jack grimaced. "I've not forgot. Finding the proper opportunity to say anything is the problem."

Thirteen

The next day Tony wandered the gardens. His hands clasped behind him, he looked neither left nor right, and was startled when Sahib suddenly appeared, blocking his path. "Sahib?" He glanced around. "Ah. Jase. Taking the sun, are you?"

"I come here fairly often," said Lord Renwick. "I hope the gardeners manage to keep things as they are, now my aunt has left and won't be here to order things to her will."

"I have seen the new gardener, and he appears to know his business."

"New gardener? Ah. Yes, I believe Eustacia did tell me our old head gardener asked to retire, insisting he was too old to manage all the changes her ladyship demanded."

"Did he mean the new water garden and the enlarged rhododendron plantation?"

"Those and her plans for a Gothic ruin and a wild area to go with it!"

"Are you having one of those?"

"Well, I don't suppose I'd have interfered, but—" Jase cast a grin in Tony's direction. "—now she is gone I believe I'll cancel that last project!"

Tony chuckled and then fell silent.

"What is it, friend?"

Tony drew in a deep breath, held it for a moment, and then released it. "I can't talk about it."

"Has to do with your marriage, then," suggested Jase. He felt Sahib rise and move around in front of the men, who sat on a bench under a rose-covered arbor.

"Yes."

"The first year or so is the hardest, you know."

"If the year ever begins!"

Jase bit his lip. "If that means what I think it means," he began carefully—After all, he, too, had heard the servants' gossip that the couple kept to separate beds. He went on when no comment was forthcoming, "—then you need to woo her, Tony."

"Woo her?"

"Hmm. Little gifts. Touch her whenever there is an opportunity. You know the sort of thing I mean."

"Woo my own wife?"

Jase chuckled. Sahib moved a step forward and nudged Tony's knee, staring up at him.

Embarrassed, Tony shifted uneasily. "Yes, but what if she doesn't want to be wooed."

"I think," said Jase carefully, keeping in mind something his wife had recently said about Lady Wendover's feelings for Tony, "that it would be worth the attempt. You cannot go on the way you are. If you do, you'll find it even harder, perhaps impossible, to change the way the two of you have arranged things."

Tony felt his face flame. "Does the whole world know how we have—arranged things?"

Jase repressed a smile. "Tony," he said patiently, "that was an exceedingly stupid question."

Tony sighed. "Yes, of course. Where there are servants, of course the world knows." He sighed again.

"Think about wooing her," urged Jase, and Sahib nudged Tony again.

"It is so embarrassing, the notion of wooing one's own wife!"

"There speaks the society maven," said Jase, a wry touch to his tone.

Tony shook his head, realized Jason could not see him, and cleared his throat. "No, it isn't that, Jase, but think how very awful failure would be."

"You are a man of great address, Tony. If you put your mind to it, I am sure there is not a woman in England who would not succumb to your wiles!"

"A great compliment, indeed, Jase, but I don't believe it. I've never been a ladies' man and have no practice in how one goes about making a woman fall in love with one."

"Do you love her?"

Tony was silent for a long long moment. "I . . . am unsure," he said. "I . . . don't know."

Jase thought carefully before he spoke again. "Tony, I hope you do, because love should be reciprocal. If you want her love, then you must give love."

"I want the sort of love my parents have," said Tony more than a trifle mournfully.

"As I said," reiterated Lord Renwick more than a trifle dryly, "one must give love to receive love." His tone lightened. "The most difficult thing in the world, I think, is admitting to another that one loves them deeply and forever. One has this need to protect oneself, does one not? On the other hand, until the other knows you love them, they are having the same difficulty, are they not?"

"You aren't suggesting Lily is in love with me?"

"Lily?"

"Did I say Lily? Meant Libby, of course." Tony wondered if his face would ever stop flaming and, for this once, was glad his friend was blind. Sahib nudged him again and stared up at him, seemed to be searching him to his very depths with those hot tiger eyes. He sighed.

"Is Lily your pet name for her?"

"It was," admitted Tony reluctantly.

"Before you married?"

"Hmm."

"And then you grew angry with her and refused to use it?"

Tony sighed. "Childish of me, isn't it?"

"Yes."

Tony turned his head to glare at Jase, discovered his friend smiled, and grinned ruefully. "Well, yes, but that's another thing, isn't it?"

"Another hard thing?"

"Hmm. But maybe something I can do if I try. . . ."

"Very good."

"What?"

"A step in the right direction, I'd say. I believe Lady Wendover spends an hour or so in the music room about now," he added.

"The music room? Ah. Wonder if she's mastered those runs." Tony stood.

"Perhaps you should go see."

Sahib was already pushing Tony toward the house— not that much effort was required to get Tony headed the way he should go. Sahib watched him for a moment and then returned to Lord Renwick. He put his great head on Renwick's knee.

"Things going all right, Sahib?" asked Renwick softly. "Have we set them on the right course?"

The tiger pressed his chin into Renwick's thigh.

"Does that mean yes or does that mean you hope so?"

The tiger growled softly.

"Hmm. Just hope so, is that it?"

Sahib lifted his head and opened his mouth in that silent roar of acknowledgement that intrigued everyone who knew him. No one was exactly certain just how much the beast understood. Nor, assuming he understood, could one know what he thought of human antics!

* * *

Tony opened the door to the music room cautiously. Through the panels, he had heard his wife uttering words he was surprised to discover she knew! He slipped in and looked across the room toward the pianoforte—and smiled. Libby had one fist raised to the music and was shaking it vigorously.

"You . . . you . . ." It seemed she could think of no words bad enough to suit her.

"Impossible notes?" asked Tony.

Libby jumped. Her neck turned bright red, and she turned slowly. "Oh. It is only you. I feared perhaps someone had come in who would tease me about my anger at this awful music."

"Perhaps *I* shall tease you," he said, once again flirting with her a trifle.

"I won't *mind* that," she said. "It is all right when you do it. But your friend, Lord Princeton—why, I might never return to my properly pearllike countenance."

Tony chuckled. "I think you would. In fact, I think you would very likely turn the tables on him, and Jack would be the one who must worry about his complexion! What is the difficulty? Another problem with the fingering?"

Libby slid near to one end of the bench, and Tony took his place. Libby pointed, and Tony put his right hand on the keys, tried several different fingering styles. One attempt very nearly worked. He tried it again. Then again. Libby put her hand on an octave farther down the keyboard and tried a minor change in his version and, laughing, did it again.

"There. You see? It wasn't so difficult after all," said Tony.

"Ha! I've been working on that for over half an hour, and it would not come right whatever I did."

"Let me hear how you are coming," suggested Tony.

He stood up and prepared to turn the pages while Libby moved back into position and set her fingers to the keys. For a while, as Libby played, Tony felt a contentment he had not known for a long time. In fact—tension returned—not since his marriage. Then he told himself he was being more than a trifle silly, that if he had found contentment alone with Libby, then it was nonsensical to allow old resentment to interfere.

In fact, looking at his wife as she concentrated on her music, he wondered why he had felt so resentful for so long. She wasn't the most beautiful woman in the Ton, but she had countenance and she had style and she had a kind heart that saw into other people's hearts. Not only did she see into them, but also she did something for them once she noticed there was a problem. That she claimed not to know what she did or why—well, that didn't change anything.

"Libby," he said softly—too softly. He didn't catch her attention, and then he forgot what he wanted to say when—she had reached the part they had just mastered—she smiled so glowingly it seemed to brighten up the whole room.

It certainly set a blaze in Tony's heart. For a moment he felt half choked by the odd antics of that organ which seemed to rise right up his throat. His voice was gruff when he murmured, "You are so very lovely, Lily."

This she heard. She blushed and glanced at him, then quickly back to her music. But her fingers stumbled, and the discord made her wince. She raised her fingers from the keys and put her hands in her lap.

"It is coming along very well," said Tony, unsure what else he might say. He was embarrassed by the emotion he must have revealed when he told her how lovely he found her, was incapable of telling her he wanted her as a husband wants his wife, and certainly he dared not tell her he had fallen in love with her! The dressing gong was rung just then, and Libby slid off the bench to the far side of where Tony stood.

"I must go up," she said. "Until Finch returns, dressing is something of a problem."

"Can you not ask Eustacia for a maid to help you?"

Libby smiled a quick mischievous grin that erased the rather worried expression she had worn. "Well, that is part of the problem. Finch arranged for a young maid to help, and, mostly, it means taking twice as long to do everything as if I did it myself alone!"

"You might try another one."

Libby's smile faded. "I might, of course. This poor girl is so determined. She tries so hard. And it is true she never makes the same mistake twice, but, Tony, she knows nothing of style or what is proper to an occasion and has no sense of how to put bits and pieces together to make it all go together. I find I am constantly giving her lessons as we go along." Libby brightened. "The thing is, I think I rather enjoy teaching her. She learns quickly, you see, and is so appreciative it is almost embarrassing."

Tony smiled in return. "Then, we'd best go up, had we not? So you may begin her newest lesson?"

Libby flushed delightfully. "Yes, please," she said demurely.

The next few days passed quietly. Tony, determined to make things right between himself and Libby but exceedingly embarrassed by the thought of actually wooing his wife, was so erratic in his behavior toward her the poor girl became confused.

Lady Princeton noticed. "Libby, why do we not take a walk and see how the new garden is coming along."

Libby made a face but then smiled. "Yes, do let's. Not that it will look like anything but chaos, of course. Such things never do until they are actually finished. Or very near to being finished. But perhaps the gardener will be the sort who likes explaining things and will like the opportunity to give us a lecture on all we see."

Patricia laughed. "You will listen to the lecture only because it will make the gardener feel good?"

"It sounds strange, but perhaps that is what I do mean."

"Libby, no matter what you do," said Patricia just a trifle urgently, "you cannot make the whole world love you."

Libby's face flamed. "Is that how it seems? That I want everyone to love me?"

"I am out of line. I apologize."

"No. I will think about it."

Their rambles had taken them in the general direction of the new gardens designed by Lady Blackburne before she became Lady Hayworth. Somehow, though, they veered away from the new work and went toward a glade in the woods one kept catching tempting glimpses of as one walked.

"Ah!" said Patricia when they entered it.

"Lovely," agreed Libby. "A fairy glade."

"Shall we sit?"

A rustic bench was placed near a small burbling spring that formed a rill that traced a rocky path off and into the woods. Overhanging limbs provided shade but were not so dense that a spattering of light did not find a way through to sparkle off the water. And the water itself gave the tiny glade an unexpected coolness.

For a long moment they sat in silence. Then Libby sighed.

"A confusing world, is it not?" asked Patricia softly.

"I am certainly confused," said Libby.

Patricia chuckled at the rueful note. "Want to talk about it?"

"I can't think what there is to talk about."

"Because you do not wish to talk or because you don't know how?"

Libby blushed softly. She glanced at Patricia. "Why do you wish to help me?"

Patricia's smile blossomed, and her eyes sparkled. "Libby, you will think me mad if I explain."

"Try."

A huge, overly done, soulful sigh drew Libby's gaze, and she could not help but laugh at Patricia's expression.

"Is it so difficult?" asked Libby.

"If I tell you, you will laugh at me."

"I doubt that."

"Then, I will explain. You see, I had a great deal to do with the two of you actually getting yourselves wed. All that planning and seeing everything done properly even though there was no time. I've a proprietary interest in your marriage, Libby, and will do anything to see it come right."

"But," said a suddenly sober Libby, "nothing can be done. Tony resents what I did so much he will never wish to make ours a marriage such as you enjoy."

"Will he not? Are you certain?"

"I thought, there for a day or so, that perhaps he was coming around. He seems to enjoy helping me with my music, for instance. And listening to me play. And there have been compliments which I am almost certain were sincere, but then, just when I think all is well, he reverts to being a bear!"

"Perhaps he is even more confused than you are, Libby."

"Well, maybe, but if so, then what can I do?"

"Under normal circumstances I would suggest patience."

"The circumstances are not normal?" asked Libby, alarmed.

"I misspoke. The thing is, Eustacia is more and more preoccupied, waiting for her baby to be born. I think we should all take ourselves off by the end of the week so she need not concern herself for anyone but herself, and I want you and Tony to come to your senses before we must leave!"

"Come to our senses?"

"Libby, it is so very obvious that the two of you are made for each other that I believe the only ones who do not yet know it are you two yourselves! Even Sahib is aware you belong together!"

"Is that why he corners us in a room and will not allow us to leave it?"

"Does he do that?"

"Oh, yes. It has happened often since we arrived. Once he even—well—*herded* Tony into the music room where I had just finished practicing."

Patricia laughed. "Yes, I can see it. Sahib is magnificent. Oh, very well, if Sahib has everything in hand, then I may stop worrying."

Libby's smile, which had grown in response to Patricia's laughter, faded. "What do you mean, Sahib has things in hand?"

"Did you not know? Sahib has put a paw into each of our marriages. So far he has not been wrong, and I doubt he has begun making mistakes with you. You, too, should stop worrying yourself about Tony. Sahib will sort you out."

"Surely you are jesting."

Patricia turned a sober eye on Libby. "Do you think so? Well, you just listen. . . ."

And she told Libby exactly how Sahib had had a role in perfecting each of the first three marriages among the Six.

". . . So I've no doubts he'll put yours to rights as well," finished her ladyship.

The next time Libby saw Sahib she eyed him curiously. Everyone who spoke of the big cat attributed special powers to the beast, but, lying sprawled in a sunny spot near where Lord Renwick sat talking to Lord Princeton and Tony, he was, so far as Libby could see, simply a huge and rather frightening carnivore!

Prince Ravi approached her just then. "You are looking at Sahib," he said.

"He is very beautiful," said Libby.

Prince Ravi laughed. "You are not, however, certain you like him?"

"I cannot help but fear him. He is so big. Even if he did not mean to harm one, might he not do so, merely because he does not understand his own strength?"

The prince's eyes narrowed. "It might happen as you say. It *might,* I suppose. But I think not. Sahib might be rough if he felt it warranted, but he is very intelligent, you know."

Libby nodded, thinking about what the boy implied. "Then, you do not think he has magical powers?"

The prince stared at her and then swallowed. "I did not think you English believed in such things."

"I don't think we do. And yet, when faced with a phenomenon like Sahib, one begins thinking all sorts of nonsense!"

Ravi's countenance fell. "Nonsense. I see. I had hoped . . ." He shook his head and wandered off.

Libby stared after him. What had she said? Done? She sighed.

"What is it, my dear?" asked Tony, who had approached in time to hear her expression of discontent.

"In some manner I upset Prince Ravi and I do not know how. I am sorry for it."

"Should I discover it for you?"

"Would you? I should like to apologize but cannot if I do not know how I erred."

Tony nodded and followed the prince from the room.

Later that evening Tony waited for Libby to come down for dinner. He wanted to explain to her that she had done nothing but imply she did not believe Sahib magical. The prince *did* believe it and had hoped he had found another believer. The white tiger was a very rare and special creature in his father's kingdom. The prince, however, only reluctantly admitted to such beliefs, having discovered the Renwicks' friends did not.

Libby, when she came down, was with Lady Princeton and immediately joined the other ladies. Tony didn't like to interrupt their conversation for such nonsense so did not approach her with his discovery.

Instead, he became involved in a discussion of the morality of the waltz and forgot he had a mission to fulfill for Libby, so he took her in to dinner without mentioning it. He recalled it during the half-hour he and the other men spent with brandy and cigars, but a discussion of the war once again sent it right out of his head.

Lady Renwick had had a card table set up, and Jack commandeered him as a partner, so there was no occasion for explaining Prince Ravi's disappointment during the evening. And then Libby went upstairs rather earlier than he expected. So, too, did the other women right after Lady Renwick quietly took herself off to the Renwicks' quarters. It occurred to him that her ladyship had looked just a trifle out of sorts, but then the men began drinking, and the card game grew a little more than a trifle wild and the betting more than a trifle hilarious—the Six never wagered *money* with each other—and once again Tony forgot he had meant to tell Libby what he had discovered.

In fact, he had pulled off his clothes and put on the long white nightgown Abley had set out for him when, suddenly, he recalled it. Tony said a few words he perhaps should not have said, stared at the door to the sitting room from which another opened into his wife's room, and shook his head. Even though he was a trifle up in his altitudes from the wine he had consumed, he could not bring himself to do it. He could not go to her in her bedroom. Not when the both of them would be in night attire.

He couldn't.

On the other hand, given his mind was in a rather bemused state thanks to his drinking, would he, in the morning, remember to explain to her?

Tony feared he would not. Hesitantly he opened the door and looked into the dim sitting room. Across it, against the far wall, was a desk. Tony nodded. He would write it all out and slip it under her door. Her maid would find it in the morning and would give it to her. Tony didn't bother with a robe, but tiptoed across the room just as he was, his white gown rather ghostly in the dimness.

Then he decided he needed more light and went to the banked fire where he lit a spill—and discovered his wife, a book fallen to the floor, asleep on the sofa. And then the spill grew so short it singed his fingers, and he tossed it into the fire. But the glimpse he had had of her had been intriguing to a very great degree. Had she been wearing a very solid robe? Plaid wool, of all things? The sort he had seen his *father* wear?

Tony lit another spill and set it to the wick of the candles on the mantel. He turned. And smiled. Yes, his bride wore a nice warm, but hardly feminine robe which muffled her pretty well from neck to toe—except where it had fallen away and showed one very neat ankle and the lower part of a calf below a night shift devoid of lace or ruffles!

Tony found it rather endearing that his exceedingly feminine wife should wear such exceedingly unfeminine nightclothes. He took another look and frowned. The poor dear would wake with a crick in her neck, sleeping there on that couch which was too short for her. Should he wake her? Tony's frown deepened. Could he carry her to her room and to her own bed *without* waking her?

He blushed at the thought of waking her under such circumstances. What would she think? Oh, dear, what *could* she think! No, he didn't dare try to carry her, still asleep, to her bed. But he should wake her and suggest she take herself there, should he not? Tony reached for her shoulder—

The door opened, and Sahib put his head and shoulders into the room.

—and shook her lightly.

Libby woke. She blinked up at Tony. "What . . . ?"

"You are on the sofa. You'll not be comfortable here." Sahib oozed on into the room.

"Did I fall asleep? Oh. My book!" She leaned over the edge of the sofa to pick it up—and saw Sahib. She froze, staring.

Tony turned. "Sahib! What are you doing here?"

The big cat stared from one to the other, his eyes seeming to burn into them. He opened his mouth in a silent snarl.

Tony backed a step. He could not help himself. His legs hit the edge of the sofa, and, abruptly, he sat. Libby, squashed against the back of the sofa and unable to move, reached for Tony's arm.

Sahib snarled again.

"What is the matter with him?" whispered Libby.

"I don't know. I've never seen him like this," answered Tony.

"I'm afraid of him."

"I don't think he'll hurt us," said Tony, but he spoke a trifle doubtfully.

"What can we do?"

Tony glanced around and, quickly, back to Sahib. He put his hand on the back of the couch, his foot on the seat, and rose to hop over the back. He reached for Libby and, with a grunt of effort, lifted her over the back as well.

Sahib snarled still again.

Backing carefully, Tony reached Libby's door. "You go in and shut it. Lock it. Sahib seems to have discovered how to open doors, but he can't if it is locked."

Libby remembered Lady Princeton's tales. Was Sahib trying to help?

"Don't leave me!" she said.

"Lily . . ."

"Don't leave me here alone, Tony." She felt warmed when his arms tightened. "I'll not sleep a wink. I'll spend the whole night afraid." She pulled her arm more tightly around his neck. "I'll not be afraid if you are here," she finished so softly he almost didn't hear it.

Sahib took a step toward them, and, although he would not have admitted it, Tony didn't really wish to be alone either. And then he recalled stories of Sahib interfering in his friend's marriages. He opened Libby's door and slipped inside, setting her to her feet, although she would not release her grip on him, and, just as Sahib moved toward them, he closed and locked the door.

Her heart beating faster, Libby blinked back sudden tears. "You saved us."

"Did I?" Tony, now he was safe, was remembering more details of the stories told about Sahib's penchant for matchmaking.

"Of course you did."

Libby showed no sign of moving away from him, and Tony cleared his throat. "Lily . . ."

She looked up. The moon was full and shone straight into her window, allowing her to see the wistful, wanting look on his face. She felt herself blush. But it was what she wanted, too, was it not? Proof they were not estranged? Proof they might have a real marriage? Children?

"Tony?"

He cleared his throat, unable to think what to say. From the other side of the door came a muffled roar, and Libby, half frightened and half ready to use the fear to push Tony into properly husbandly behavior, jumped and pressed against him, muffling her face against his chest. His arms went around her. Tightened.

"Lily," he said into her hair, "I think we . . . *you* . . . should go to bed. Sahib cannot get through that door, so we . . . you . . . are safe." His hands, all by themselves, wandered over her back, up into her hair, found her head and tipped her face up to his. They stared at each other. Then he kissed her.

And kissed her again. And, shyly at first, and then more enthusiastically, she kissed him back.

And later—much later—he found himself in her bed looking down at her wide eyes. "Lily?"

"Tony," she breathed . . . and reached for him. Again.

Out in the sitting room, Sahib nodded his head, turned it to look at the hall door and, as silently as he had come, removed himself from the room. Sahib might include Renwick's circle of friends within his aura, but at the center was Renwick himself. And Lord Renwick's needs came first.

Dear Friends,

Tony had never really considered how or when he'd marry. He had merely assumed that, when it happened, it would be a love-match. Much to his surprise, his and Libbys' scandalous beginning turned into something wonderful!

The next in the White Tiger series is THE PERFECT MATCH, Alex, Lord Merwin's story. Alex met the woman he wished to wed before any of the others met their future wives. That he didn't marry first is due to his prospective bride's father. Sir Vincent, a rabid Whig and an admirer of Napoleon, is determined there will never by a Tory in his family. Artemisia is torn between her love for Alex and her love for her mother who believes Artemisia is duty bound to obey her father. Napoleon himself gives this ill-starred affair a push in the right direction. Sahib takes it from there, of course. THE PERFECT MATCH will be out in October, 2001.

The final book in the series, Miles Seward's story, won't appear until March of 2002. Miles has assumed he will never wed. His style of life is not one befitting a pampered tonnish miss. Waterloo is over, but there is one French smuggler who continues the trade, a wily devil who has evaded Miles again and again. Miles is determined to capture the ship and bring its crew to justice—and he does. Except how can he bear to see stretched the pretty neck of the loveliest captain in the world! And why, in any case, has a gently bred Frenchwoman taken to smuggling? And, after discovering the answer to that, how can Miles save her? Miles has always been a man of action. In this case action is not the answer!

I love to hear from my readers. Snail mail reaches me

at: P.O. Box 833, Greenacres WA 99016. My email address is JeanneSavery@yahoo.com.

Wishing you all the very best reading,

Cheerfully,
Jeanne Savery

<u>BOOK YOUR PLACE ON OUR WEBSITE</u>
<u>AND MAKE THE</u>
<u>READING CONNECTION!</u>

We've created a customized website just for our very special readers, where you can get the inside scoop on everything that's going on with Zebra, Pinnacle and Kensington books.

When you come online, you'll have the exciting opportunity to:

- View covers of upcoming books
- Read sample chapters
- Learn about our future publishing schedule (listed by publication month *and author*)
- Find out when your favorite authors will be visiting a city near you
- Search for and order backlist books from our online catalog
- Check out author bios and background information
- Send e-mail to your favorite authors
- Meet the Kensington staff online
- Join us in weekly chats with authors, readers and other guests
- Get writing guidelines
- AND MUCH MORE!

Visit our website at
http://www.zebrabooks.com

More Zebra Regency Romances

Discover the Romances of
Hannah Howell

Merlin's Legacy

A Series From
Quinn Taylor Evans